FROM PARADISE TO HELL

Michigan Tales of Terror

Tom Sawyer

A Black Bed Sheet/Diverse Media Book
March 2016

Library of Congress Control Number: 2016935378

ISBN-10: 0-69265801-7
ISBN-13: 978-0-6926580-1-7

From Paradise to Hell

A Black Bed Sheet/Diverse Media Book
Antelope, CA

Paradise
HELL

Dedicated to My Cousins

Cheryl & John Hornung, Randy & Leigh Ann Langdon, Jim & Annette Dennis, Patrick & Vicki Alber, Tom & Janet Pulliam, Richard & Kimberly Skalneck, Bob Langdon Jr., Richard & Jeanine Langdon, Cindy & Joe Hyaduck, Jodie & Bob Michalak, Bob & Rhonda Starick, John Starick, Stephanie & Mark Karrick, Tom & Rita Boucher, Jim and Tennie Boucher, Penne & Todd Caswell, Curt & Vigul Langdon, Teri & Mike Rich, Pam & Scott Sprague, as well as all of the second and third cousins too numerous to mention here.

I have been very blessed to have you in my life. For no one has had better cousins and friends than you.

Acknowledgements

First and foremost I must once again thank God. He gave me some ability and talent that enabled me to write this as well as a wonderful life. I may be a lot of things, tend to screw up more than I care to admit and be nowhere near perfect, but I still feel blessed, especially with so many great people in my life. I will keep acknowledging him here first as long as I am writing.

Next, my wife Colleen whose continued support, love and honest opinions on my writing have been the best thing to ever happen to me. She lets me know when I have written a good story. I can tell by her reaction whether I have written a good story or not.

My children, Jonathon, Kathleen and Elizabeth for their love and support as well. I am proud of all three of you. Jonathon I cannot thank you enough for your editing work before I submit my stuff to a publisher. Keep writing, son, you have talent. Kathleen, thanks for the love and support. Keep doing your art work. Elizabeth, you are the reporter and writer I could never be. Aim high kid! Write for no other reasons than yourself and for the love of writing.

My brother Tim, who may no longer be with us, but his influence and spirit are still there. I still think about you daily. I still go to Kennedy's Irish Pub to feel and listen to your spirit when I hit a dry spell writing. It usually works. You are still truly missed.

My mother for warping my young mind enough to love horror movies and stories.

Sherryl, Jack and Brent Green and their continued love, support and critiques of my stories have also been a big help. It's great having you as such big fans.

Jerry and Nancy Wern I appreciate your love, support and help more than you could ever know. All I know is that I could not have asked for better In-laws. Thanks.

My dad, and step-mother Gene and Joan Sawyer for their encouragement.

Next my writing mentors, Richard Lech, Al Nahajewski who taught me to grab the readers early when it came to journalism. I hope I have learned those lessons well and made you both proud. Rich, you are still greatly missed after all of these years, but your influence lives on.

Al thanks for your advice, help and introducing me at the Troubadad's performances as a Michigan author.

Mrs. Catherine Lobb, who was able to get me started in writing and introduce me to Richard Lech and Al Nahajewski. You were truly a teacher in every sense of the word and even though you are no longer with us, the lessons you have instilled in me are still there. I hope I have made you proud as one of your students.

Next my friends Mike Cavin, Tim Hudson, Pat Mueller, Mary Makrias and others for their years of friendship, love, support and help. You are like family to me and I cannot express strongly enough how I feel about you all. I love you all. For you are my brothers and sisters from other parents.

All my cousins, aunts and uncles. You are too numerous to name here, but I am truly indebted and appreciative of all you love, support, help, generosity and so much more. It is an honor and privilege to know as well as have you all as family.

My former boss and co-worker, Ken Davis and Dave Brush, though I no longer work with you, your friendship, influence, help and support are still greatly appreciated.

I also need to thank Mary Fronczak and Kay Ouwerkerk for being a kind of test market for my stories. Thanks ladies, I appreciate your help and input. I hope that I have kept you entertained.

I would like to thank Adam and Jennifer Gifford for their help in attempting to come up with the title for the book. The real story of how the title came to be is worthy of a story or possible book itself. I would also like to thank my friend Donna Jerry for her winning cover artwork. Much appreciated.

If I have left out anybody, I sincerely apologize for the oversight and meant no offense.

Again, thank you one and all for your love and support. You have my love and deep appreciation.

Like I have said before, I am still truly blessed.

From Paradise to Hell

Tom Sawyer

Contents:

Once In a Blue Moon

AUGUST - 1968

After several hours of driving, the small group of travelers finally arrived in their VW van and began the task of setting up camp their camp.

Having pitched their tents and built a roaring campfire, the small group settled down and relaxed. Loud music blared from the transistor radio on the nearby picnic table.

"*Who cares what games we choose? Nothing to live for, and nothing to choose…*" the chorus from Strawberry Alarm Clock's hit *Incense and Peppermints* echoed at dusk.

Selecting the spot had been very easy. It was located in a nice place with decent campground amenities nearby and a spectacular view of Lake Superior. A nearby backdrop of some limestone ledges, along a scenic trail surrounded by majestic pines, oaks, elms and spruces, led the way to the lake. It was a setting that would have made a picture postcard jealous.

In spite of the warnings and pleadings the locals had of not camping in this area, at this particular time, the visiting flower children thought the area was just too good to pass up. They wanted to be one with Mother Nature.

The four campers huddled together, roasted hot dogs over the fire, and listened to their music. After dinner the small group shared a joint, passing it back and forth until there was nothing left.

It was perfect. The Age of Aquarius was in full swing, while peace, love and flower power were almost everywhere. They were part of it, just enjoying life, nature and each other's friendship. For now, they enjoyed the relative peace and quiet, and their music in the northern Upper Peninsula outdoors.

At midnight the full moon shone brightly overhead as the small party had grown weary. The two men of the group stood up as "*It's the Time of the Season*" by the Zombies played on the radio.

It was then, that they first heard it. A faint, but unmistakable sound of motorcycles. Not one, but many, and they were getting closer.

"*It's the time of the season when the love runs high…*"

The motorcycles were getting louder. Soon, all four campers were on their feet wondering who was approaching.

As the motorcycles headlights bore down on them and their roar became deafening, wonderment gave way to sheer terror as they realized what was upon them. Soon, their screams of horror, pain and anguish were drowned out by the deafening roar of the motorcycles screaming off into the night.

The once tranquil campground had become a graveyard.

Both tents that had once been pitched were destroyed, the sleeping bags shredded, and debris strewn across the blood covered ground, as the campfire continued to burn.

"*Tell you what? I really want to know. It's the time of the season for loving...*"

AUGUST 2008

For Debbie Wilkins, it was a chance to get away from the monotony of watching her kid brother Bobby, at home. He wasn't the typical annoying little brother, but it still wasn't that easy. Their parents had to go out of town on a business trip and she, home from college, was a convenient sitter.

This trip let her get away with her boyfriend Steve and yet still watch Bobby without any trouble.

She would have plenty of help with her babysitting. Her friends, Gary, Ron, Wayne and their girlfriends Jenny, Lori and Terry.

Debbie's friends didn't mind Bobby coming along and treated him like one of the gang. He was glad to be hanging with the bigger kids and felt like one of them.

So, after their parents had to go out of town they loaded up Steve's van and ended up outside the town of Pauguk.

"Man, this is really beautiful," Debbie commented, as she scanned the nearby woods that overlooked the lake.

Steve came up from behind and put his arms around her. "It sure is." he said as he squeezed her tight.

"Do you think the others will want to stay here for a few days?" Debbie asked

"We may never want to leave," he replied.

"Cool," she said as she turned around and kissed him.

Ron and Gary took a break from gathering fire wood.

"Hey, Gary what did you think about those people in town?" he asked. "Do you think they were being honest or just trying to scare us about this place?"

"Naw," Gary responded. "They probably don't care for tourists or out-of-towners and were trying to scare us. Probably afraid we'd vandalize the place.

"You think?" Ron asked.

"Yeah, I do."

"But, they seemed so adamant about not camping here." Ron continued. "They seemed pretty sincere."

"They were trying to frighten us," Gary replied.

Ron started to get visibly angry. Rotten bastards!" he exclaimed. "And to think we still bought some supplies from them."

"Forget about it already,"

Wayne walked by dragging a large dried out tree limb. "Hey guys, I found this. It should burn real good broken up."

"Cool," Ron responded.

Meanwhile, Debbie, Lori, Jenny and Terry had finished setting up the inside of their tents and arranging their food and supplies in the automobiles.

"Are we really keeping it boys in one tent and girls in another? Jenny asked, obviously disappointed.

"Yes," Debbie answered.

"Shit."

"Bobby's here and I don't need him telling my parents about my sex life," Debbie replied. "Or any of us for that matter."

"You got a point," Jenny agreed.

"Don't worry once Bobby's asleep, we can get with the guys," Debbie explained. "That's why I had the guys play with him so much and take him swimming once we got here. I want them to wear him out."

"Cool," Jenny said.

"You are a devious, Deb," Lori said.

"With Bobby around, I have to be," Debbie replied. "He can't keep his own secrets let alone mine."

"Does this mean we can late-night skinny-dip?" Terry asked.

"Yeah, but only a few at a time" Debbie replied. "Somebody has to stay in the camp. Besides who wants to be around the others when they're getting it on. It kind of kills the intimacy."

The girls all nodded in agreement.

"Shouldn't we be starting dinner?" Lori asked. "It's getting late."

"Yep, hot dogs, chips and beans," Debbie said.

"Just be sure to keep the beans away from Wayne," Terry said. "If he eats them he'll be farting all night."

"That will kill the mood," Debbie commented. "And any nearby wildlife."

The women looked at each other and broke into laughter at the comment.

The guys heard the girls' sudden laughter and wondered what was so funny.

"It must be a good joke," Gary muttered to Steve.

"I guess so," he replied. "At least they're having fun."

While his sister and her friends were working around their campsite, Bobby set about to explore a little bit until he was needed again. He was free to play and explore. Like any other kid his age he was curious and energetic. He climbed on large rocks and trees with low-lying limbs and even on the nearby wooden picnic tables.

"I think we're cool on the wood," he replied. "We can always grab another piece or two on our way to and from the outhouse or wherever."

"I don't know about you, but I ain't staying too long in that friggin' outhouse," Ron said. "It really stinks in there."

The others nodded in agreement.

"Hey, Bobby," Steve called out.

"Yeah?"

"Come here a minute,"

Bobby jumped off the picnic table and bounded over to Steve and the guys. "What?" he asked.

"Would you go over to those pine trees near the outhouses and gather up some pine needles?" Steve asked.

"Sure,"

"Just in case the fire goes out, we can use them as kindling to help start another one," he explained.

Bobby headed off to do his assignment.

"We could have done that Steve," Ron commented softly.

"I know, but I'm trying to keep him involved and wear him out," Steve replied. "I want to get laid tonight, too."

Bobby began to gather up the pine needles. He slid his foot sideways and pushed them into a small pile. He continued to push them into a pile with his foot. As the pile began to get a little higher he began to rake them with his hands.

"Ow, shit!" he exclaimed as a few of the sharp needles stabbed his hands and fingers. He quickly caught himself and then looked around to see if anybody heard him. When he realized the others hadn't he giggled softly. If his parents heard it, he would have been punished. He went back to sweeping the needles into a pile.

It was then that he made a gruesome discovery. In the dirt, that had once been covered by the pine needles was a tooth. He knew upon sight that it was a human molar.

Unsure of what to do, he decided to pull it out of the ground. He found it tough at first. Finally with all of his might, he yanked it out of the ground. He found there were three other teeth were attached to part of a jawbone.

Bobby screamed in terrified surprise, quickly dropped the jawbone and ran towards the others.

"I found a dead body!" he shouted, running over to the others. "I found a dead body!"

Everyone stopped what they were doing and looked over at Bobby. The guys, having finished what they were doing walked over to Bobby and the girls.

"What?" Debbie asked.

"I found a dead body," he repeated, almost hyperventilating. "I found some bones!"

Debbie had a skeptical look on her face, but knew Bobby well enough to know when he was telling the truth. "Are you sure?" she finally asked.

"Uh huh," he grunted.

Debbie looked at Steve with uncertainty.

"Come on Bobby, let's go take a look," Steve said.

"Okay," Bobby said, nodding. "I'll show you."

Bobby led the way, with the others following close behind.

Returning to the exact spot, Bobby pointed. "There," he said.

"I guess you were telling the truth," Steve said, immediately seeing the jawbone.

"Holy shit!" said Wayne.

It's gross," said Lori, grimacing at the thought of a dead body nearby, while the other girls echoed her statement.

"I wonder who it was?" Terry asked out loud.

"Could be Jimmy Hoffa for all we know," Wayne joked.

"That's not funny, Wayne," Jenny said.

"I thought it was," Wayne replied, off-the cuff. "Besides, it's too late to get worked up over it anyways."

The guys moved in closer.

"You see anything else?" asked Terry.

Steve moved some of the pine needles to see if there was anything else sticking out of the ground. "Nope." he responded.

"Who or what do you think it's from?" Debbie asked.

"Hard telling," Steve said. "It could be a year old or a hundred years old."

Ron reached down to touch it. "We can tell by looking closer at it," he said.

"No! Don't touch it," Steve said. "This could be a crime scene. We should alert the authorities."

"Yeah," agreed Lori. "We need to leave it for them just like on CSI."

"She's right," Wayne agreed. "We had better stay away from here, except to use the outhouse."

"Let's just leave it for now," Steve said. "I'll go into town and get the police. Let them handle it."

The group started back to their small camp area and sat down at the tables.

"We're almost done with dinner when Bobby made his discovery," Debbie announced

"What about the body?" Bobby asked. "Shouldn't we guard it or something?"

"Bobby," Steve said, "If it's a dead body or even part of one, I don't think it's going anywhere. It's not likely to wander off."

The others laughed.

"Oh, okay," Bobby muttered, realizing that Steve was right.

"Okay, let's eat," Jenny said.

The group sat down at the picnic table and dug into the food. There was some small talk early on about the jawbone, but other conversational topics soon took over.

"Can I have some more beans?" Wayne asked.

"No," the other said in unison.

"Why?"

"They make you fart!" everybody said at once.

"Well excuse me," he said.

As night approached, the guys built up the fire to help light the star-filled night.

"Well, I had better run into town to tell the authorities," Steve announced. "I want to get back in time for the fun."

Steve kissed Debbie before hopping into his van and heading down the road.

Once Steve arrived back in Pauguk, it looked almost deserted. Only a few buildings still had their lights on and showed any signs of life inside. His eyes soon settled on the small police station.

Steve walked into the police station and was greeted by a tall gray-haired man in a police uniform. "Can I help you?" the officer asked.

"Yes, you can," Steve said. "My name is Steve Chambers and my friends and I are camping just outside of town. My girlfriend's little brother dug up something that looks like part of a body."

"Do tell."

"Yes," Steve continued. "I decided to come in and report it to you guys so you could check it out."

The policeman just nodded. "Okay," he finally replied. "Charlie, Roger, get in here," he called out. "Sorry, but as you can see, we're a little short-handed."

"I was saying that we think we might have found a body, or at least part of one, near a large pine tree at the campground just outside of town," Steve repeated.

Charlie and Roger, the other officers that were summoned entered the room. "What is it, Chief?" asked the one, with the nametag Roger on his shirt.

"This man claims his group found a body out at the campgrounds," the chief announced.

Both officers' faces became ghostly, ashen pale as they looked at each other.

"Tonight?" the officer known as Charlie gulped. "Dear God."

Steve wasn't sure what was going on, but figured he had done his part and was ready to get back to his friends. "Look, officer, we'll all be glad to answer any questions you have," he said. "We'll even show you where we found it. I just thought…*we* just thought we had better report it."

"You did the right thing," the chief said, as he put his arm around Steve. "I'm Chief Kelly. Mac Kelly. You did good."

"Thanks," Steve replied, feeling more at ease. "But, that's really all I know. Do you want to come out tonight or do you want to wait 'til morning?"

"I think we're gonna wait," Kelly answered.

"Well, I have to get going now," Steve announced, as he pulled away from the chief.

The police officers looked at each other and then the chief.

"I'm sorry, but you're not going anywhere, not yet," Kelly announced.

"What?"

"You're not leaving yet," Kelly said.

"Why? I didn't do anything!"

"That may be so," Kelly answered. "But you have to look at it from my side. You said your name was Steve Chambers and that you found a dead body. A person I have not seen or met before announcing the finding of a dead body. I don't have any positive I.D. or information on you. Now, please calm down and sit in that chair."

Steve didn't like where this was headed, but did as he was told.

Charlie moved over towards the chief and leaned close to him. "It's almost time," he whispered.

Roger looked out the window, turned back to Kelly and Charlie. "It's another blue moon." he announced.

Steve listened to this and was confused. "What is going on, officer?" he asked.

"Nothing, yet," Kelly responded. "You just take it easy.

"I'm tired of this shit" Steve shouted. "Either let me go or I'll call a lawyer!"

"Sit down and shut up!" Kelly shouted back. "You ain't going anywhere except into a cell."

"What?"

"Detain him," Kelly ordered.

In an instant, both Roger and Charlie were on Steve and wrestled him into a jail cell, while Steve resisted and spat all kinds of profanities.

"You rotten mutherfuckers!" Steve yelled as the cell door slammed shut in his face. "I didn't do anything! You hear me! I didn't do anything. I just tried to report something! I'm innocent!"

The three police officers turned and walked away. After a few minutes, Steve stopped yelling, sat down and resigned himself to the fact he was not going back to camp any time soon.

"What now, Chief?" Roger asked, as they looked out the large front window at the night sky.

"We wait."

"We can't hold him legally," Charlie opined. "So how long do we keep him?"

"I'm hoping his friends will come in before too long," Kelly explained.

"Oh, I see," said Charlie.

"Yep," Kelly replied. "That's what I'm hoping for. They will be safe here. As it is, there is nothing we can do for them."

"The moon's up," Roger announced. "It's beginning."

Back at the camp, the group sat around the campfire waiting for Steve's return. The radio was on and it was tuned to an oldies station. The song "*Blue Moon*" played.

"Do you think something happened?" Debbie asked.

"He's fine," Ron said, trying to alleviate Debbie's fears. "He's probably just giving a statement. Sometimes they take awhile."

"I'm sure he's okay," Jenny said.

"It's almost midnight," Debbie answered. "You'd think he'd be back by now."

As the campfire continued to burn, the moon had risen steadily in the sky. Jenny and Gary huddled together, occasionally kissing, as the others sat nearby.

Sometime later, Bobby began to get fidgety. "Deb, can you go with me to the bathroom?" he soon asked.

"Oh, all right," Debbie said. "We'll be right back."

Debbie and Bobby headed off towards the outhouse with flashlights in hand. They could tell they were getting closer by the foul odor.

"Please hurry up in there," Debbie said.

"Don't worry, I will," Bobby hollered after shutting himself inside.

There was a faint but distinct rumble in the distance as the Zombies' song "*Time of the Season*" began to play.

"You hear that?" Ron asked.

"Yeah," some of the others responded.

The rumble started getting louder.

"*It's the time of the season when love runs high…*"

"Motorcycles?" Ron said standing up, somewhat confused.

Wayne and Gary stood up wondering what could be heading in their direction. Their girlfriends joined them.

The noise was grew louder and closer. Finally, before anything could be said the group saw what was coming at them. Riding on the motorcycles were what looked like a cross section of corpses in various states of decay. Their mouths were wide open, as if to anticipate their long overdue next meal.

The lead cyclists were skeletons wearing tattered and rotted leather biker clothes with leather vests, pants and caps. Behind them in differing states of skeletal remains and decay were others wearing everything from old and faded jeans, swim suits, pajamas and orange hunting outfits. There were a dozen child sized dead riding along with the adults. One was a little girl on the front handlebars of one cycle with a doll that appeared to be undead as well.

The women screamed, as the motorcyclists crashed into their peaceful campfire and started to attack them.

Hearing this, Debbie rushed forward. "Bobby, whatever you do, stay there," she said. "I mean it. There's something bad happening. You stay in the outhouse and hide. No matter what. Stay in there."

Debbie rushed back to her friends and came upon what was like a cross between scenes from *Night of the Living Dead* and the *Wild One.* The first motorcyclist's had driven through the campfire and pounced upon Ron and Gary. Gary was screaming as he was being ripped apart. Immediately they began to devour him, before he was even dead. Ron fought off a couple, only to be overwhelmed and tackled by six of them who began to eat him.

Lori was run down by a dozen motorcycles and pounced on by several of the riders. Her screams were drowned out by the sickening blood orgy of flesh eaters.

Terry was grabbed by a motorcyclist and whisked off with little effort, her death screams echoing down the road and into the night. Jenny made a run into her tent, followed by the undead invaders. Soon blood splattered across the insides of the tent as grunts and groans of the dead gorging themselves emanated from inside.

Wayne had taken off and was headed towards the road. Some of the cyclist took off after him. Before he could get fifty yards, the bike with the undead child on it caught up to him. She threw her doll at him, knocking him down and then jumped onto him. Soon, she was joined by the other undead youths who began to feast on him. The last thing Debbie saw was Wayne's head being stuck on the front of one of the motorcycles.

Before Debbie could turn and run to the outhouse, one of the cyclists spotted her. She took off towards the outhouse, then stumbled and fell, just a few feet away. Soon, a horde of these dead motorcyclists were upon her. She was disemboweled on the grass and feasted on. Her screams, that would have normally echoed through the night, were drowned out by the deafening roar of the motorcycles.

Meanwhile, Bobby was looking out through one of the small slots in the outhouse. He could only see a little and that would be enough to give him nightmares forever.

He saw corpses and other dead things tearing apart his sister and her friends. The corpses closest to the outhouse were only partially covered with flesh and had much of their skeletal frames and skulls exposed. On top of that, they smelled like badly-rotten meat. He was almost ready to puke, but managed to refrain from doing so.

Bobby gasped in horror. Upon hearing the noise, one of the motorcyclists moved closer to the outhouse, like an animal sensing some nearby prey. As it moved closer to the outhouse, Bobby was too scared to move. His sister told him to stay here and for once he was going to do what she said.

The corpse-like horror was greeted by the foul smell that emanated from the outhouse. It grunted a few times in disgust, made a bad face and then returned to its motorcycle. Even as bad as the corpse smelled it could not stand the smell of the outhouse.

Soon, the screams were all gone and the sound of the motorcycles was headed off into the distance to parts unknown. Once they were gone, there was only dead silence.

Bobby didn't like the bad smell of the outhouse either, but knew he was safer in there. He knew the others would come and get him when this was over. That is if any of the others were alive.

"It happened again, you know that," Charlie said.

Chief Kelly just nodded his head in acknowledgement. "I know," he muttered. "I know. How is our prisoner?"

"He's fine," Roger answered. "He's lying on his bunk. We'll let him out in the morning."

When morning arrived, Roger and Charlie escorted Steve out of his cell. "What's going on now?" he asked.

"You're being let go," Kelly announced.

"What?" Steve asked, angrily.

"We'll go take a look at that body now," Kelly announced.

"Great, just frickin' great," Steve complained. "You keep me here all goddamn night and now you want to go!"

"You may not believe this son, but there was a reason," Kelly said. "Come on Charlie, let's you and me go for a ride. Roger hold down the fort until Glen, Dave and Millie get in."

"Right, Chief."

"Two shotguns?" Charlie asked.

"Yep, with extra ammo too," Kelly replied. "Let's go for a ride, Mr. Chambers.

Once the two police officers and Steve arrived at the campgrounds, the place looked like it had been vandalized. Large parts of the ground were covered with blood and debris, the tents were all collapsed, ripped open and covered in blood.

"What in the hell?" Steve said as he got out of the police car. "What in God's name happened?"

The officers patrolled the destroyed campground, shotguns in hand, with cool slow deliberate moves like two soldiers on patrol. All three men moved carefully across the campground. Chief Kelly and Charlie looked over at each other and shook their heads.

"Mr. Chambers, are you all right?" Kelly asked.

"Where in the hell is everybody?" Steve asked.

"Are you all right, son," Kelly asked.

Steve looked over at Kelly. "You knew," he said accusingly. "You knew something was going to happen."

Kelly took a deep breath and then exhaled. "Yes, I did," he confessed. "I held you, hoping that your friends would come in for you and then you would have all been safe."

"What? Why?"

"I didn't think you'd believe me if I told you," Kelly admitted. "But believe me when I say it's something terrible. I know some of the townspeople tried to get you to not come here. I know some pleaded with you. You didn't listen."

"What? What is it?"

"It happens every blue moon," Kelly started. "Charlie, go and check over near the outhouse and make a complete sweep of the area."

"Right, Chief."

"So, tell me what is it?" Steve insisted.

Before Kelly could reply, Charlie interrupted. "Hey, Chief, I found somebody!" he shouted. "And he's alive!"

Kelly and Steve went over to Charlie at the outhouse. There asleep on the floor was Bobby.

"It's a kid," Charlie announced.

"Bobby," Steve said, both excited and upset. Bobby didn't answer or even acknowledged them right away. "Bobby. Bobby, it's me. Steve. Steve Chambers."

Slowly, Bobby raised his head. He was still groggy. Even half asleep, his eyes looked dazed, just staring vacantly.

"He's in shock," Kelly said as he moved past Steve and into the outhouse. He then leaned over and Bobby instinctively raised his arms to lift him up. "It's okay, son."

"Them," Bobby muttered softly, after Kelly had picked him up and carried him from the outhouse.

"Them?" Steve wondered aloud.

Kelly finally set Bobby down and walked him over to the picnic tables. Bobby sat down at the picnic table, with Kelly next to him still in a stupor.

"Them," Bobby repeated softly. "Them."

"Who in the hell is *Them*?" Steve asked, now frightened.

"Them motorcycles," Bobby blurted out. "They came out of nowhere. They came out of nowhere on motorcycles. It was awful."

Bobby began to sob and leaned into the Police Chief for comfort and reassurance. "It's okay, son, you're safe now." he said, patting Bobby on the back.

"What is he talking about?" Steve demanded.

"You want me to tell, him, Chief?" Charlie asked.

"Yeah, go ahead," Kelly replied as he held the sobbing boy.

"Yeah, clue me in, huh," Steve growled angrily.

"Like the chief said earlier, you ain't going to believe this one," Charlie said. "But, here it goes."

"I'm listening."

"Back in 1958. Right after the bridge was built. A motorcycle gang on some cross county trek stopped and camped out."

"The story goes they desecrated some nearby Ojibway Indian grounds. I guess and elder or maybe a holy man of their tribe warned them about it, but they messed with it anyways. Supposedly he cursed them."

"You're telling me this place is cursed?" Steve asked.

"Not, exactly," Charlie replied. "But, our town is named after one of these Ojibway Manitous, Pauguk. It was said that this being was somebody who did what Cain did to his own brother, Abel and was destined to exist between the underworld and the heavens. This was supposed to have been a place he favored when he was mortal. "

"Anyways. They were warned and they vandalized the place anyways. It was during a blue moon. We don't know what happened, but some swore they could hear screams, some gunshots and revving motorcycles. The next day, some other campers found the place a mess. There were some body parts found and blood all over the place."

"And, you're trying to tell me this happens every blue moon or something?" Steve commented, matter-of-factly.

Charlie took a deep breath and then sighed. "Kinda," he admitted. "A blue moon happens every twenty-seven months. In the winter we don't really have to worry too much because there's hardly anybody up here, except for the rare snowmobiler. In summer…"

"In summer it's different," Steve interrupted. "You get people like us. People who don't listen. No matter what."

Charlie just quietly nodded.

Steve looked down on the ground. "What in the hell is that?" he asked, as he bent over to pick it up.

Kelly moved towards Steve and also crouched down.

"It's a campaign button," Kelly announced.

"Bobby For President?" Steve asked.

"Bobby Kennedy," Kelly said. "He ran for president back in 1968."

Steve's jaw hung open as his face turned pale, momentarily shocked. He came to the realization this had been going on a long time. "Then we're not the first ones," he finally said.

"No," Charlie said, sheepishly. "You are just the latest."

"How many?" Steve asked.

"No one knows exactly, kid," Chief Kelly answered. "I've been here for thirty years and I don't know for certain."

Bobby finally stopped sobbing enough to ask. "Can we go home now? I want to go home. I hate this place and I'm hungry."

"Let's get back to town and get him some food," Kelly said. "Then we'll call the county sheriff and others."

"What was the name of this motorcycle gang that started all this stuff?" Steve asked as the men climbed into the police car.

"Do you really want to know?" Charlie asked, as he stopped climbing.

Steve nodded. “Yes.”
“The Undead.”

Living like a Pig

Stacy Thurmond was tired. She had just worked twelve hours at the Big Boy restaurant as a waitress. While the lunch time business had been busy, the dinner time crowd had been almost overwhelming. So much so, she felt like she was going to collapse at one point from exhaustion.

Thank God, her car ride home was straight down M-59 towards Highland Township. She was basically on automatic pilot as she drove home, having consumed large quantities of caffeine.

As she pulled into her driveway, there were three other vehicles there. Once parked in her driveway, she slowly got out of the car. Stacy knew right away that her husband, Todd, had somehow managed to invite his friends to play cards, drink beer, watch the game or some stupid movies. This infuriated her. Since being laid-off from the shop, he had basically collected unemployment and did nothing all day.

Except now, the unemployment checks had run out, and he still did nothing. He occasionally worked on cars for a little money and beer, but that was about it. For the most part, he sat on his dead ass all day or shot the bull with some of his friends. He hardly ever looked for any kind of work.

Somewhere along the way, Stacy had become the bread winner. The adult between the two of them. Todd was unemployed and had no interest in doing anything other than something like the job he had. That was not happening, so Stacy had the role of bread winner. While this added burden did not physically age her, it made her feel older than her twenty-five years. She did not think marriage was supposed to end up this way. She had not signed up for this.

She had hoped that he would rise to the occasion and do what it took to keep them afloat until something better came along. Unfortunately, for her, that didn't happen.

As she walked towards the house, exhaustion made her legs feel like they were going to give out from under her. She only had a little further to go. Once inside, she was welcomed by the stench of beer, cigars and cigarette smoke, pizza, body odor and flatulence.

She looked around and instantly began to seethe. The dishes from this morning had not been done, and had, in fact, doubled. Opened bags of potato chips littered the kitchen table as well.

As Stacy entered the dining room and living room area, she saw Todd and his buddies playing cards. All over the table and the floor were beer cans, crumbs of food and cigar and cigarette ashes.

"Hi, Honey, Yuh wanna beer?" Todd asked, not thinking anything was wrong.

Stacy just shook her head no. She was too angry to think, let alone speak.

"We got pizza and pop, too, if you wannit," Todd announced proudly as if he had spent long hours cooking it himself.

Tears welled up in her eyes. "Todd, I'm going to bed," she said. "I'm tired. Goodnight."

Todd's friends did not to say anything. They could tell Stacy was mad and did not want to get her any angrier.

Stacy quietly headed off to their bedroom.

Five minutes after changing into her nightgown and climbing into bed, Todd came in and sat down beside her.

"Don't you think you were a little rude to the guys?" he asked.

"Rude?" Stacy asked as she sat up in bed. "Rude?! How in the hell was I rude? Todd, I did not say a word."

"That's what I mean," he responded. "You didn't say hi, or even bother to acknowledge them."

"Todd, under the circumstances, I was quite polite," she said angrily. "My house is a pigsty. You don't clean up. You drink beer all day with your buddies when I work twelve hours. No, Todd under the circumstances I would say I'm pretty goddamn restrained!"

"Shhh, keep it down," Todd said as he gestured with his hand to talk softer. "The guys don't need to hear us fight."

"I don't care!" she responded. "Tell me Todd, what did you do all day? I mean besides drink beer, watch TV and fart? How can we afford beer and pizza when we can't afford to do repairs around the house? Tell me, Todd. I'm tired of taking orders. Tired of being on my feet all day. Tired of you not doing anything.

"I'm tired of doing all the work. Go play cards with your friends. Now, I'm going to bed because I have to get up for work tomorrow."

"I made two hundred dollars today working on a guy's Ferrari," he snapped, defensively. "That's what I have done."

"How much is left?" Stacy asked

"A little more than a hundred and forty-four dollars," Todd said a little sheepishly. "I owed the guys. They came over and helped out. Plus I kept ten for myself."

Stacy shook her head. "Dammit, Todd!" she said. "Everything I make goes for bills, food or gas. I don't blow any of my money. You need to find a job. I can't keep doing this. I can't keep living like…like….a pig."

"Hey, at least I brought in something," he shot back. "Jesus, I figured you'd be happy about that. I ain't takin' no burger flippin' job. That's for losers. Shit! I hate it when you're PMS-ing."

"Anything is better than nothing," she replied. "It's a paycheck. It will help pay the bills. Most of all it will help us keep the house."

"Yeah, well I ain't doing just anything," he snapped. "I'm better than that."

Todd got up and left to rejoin his friends.

Stacy let out a wounded sigh and cried herself to sleep.

When Stacy woke up, she found the house was an even bigger mess than before. It was littered with more food and beer cans throughout the house.

Todd and one or more of his buddies must have drunk more beer while watching TV after playing cards. This was easy to figure out. Todd was sprawled out on the couch with empty beer cans on the floor next to him. She knew he would sleep until noon.

She knew he had not been the same since he lost his job. While, not the most motivated person, he at least did some things around the house when he worked. But, she also knew other people who lost jobs and took other work that wasn't quite up to what they had wanted or expected either.

She had found out the hard way that Todd wasn't that way. He wasn't about to take something he considered beneath him.

She was too tired to be angry about this. She quickly washed the dishes and then took a shower. She got dressed and headed to work, as Todd snored loudly, dead to the world.

Stacy's workday was hectic. The Big Boy had been busy almost right away. Worse yet, there was no let up. By noon, they were swamped. She filled up on diet coke, hoping the caffeine would keep her going.

At home, Todd woke up around noon and picked up all the empty cans. Not so much because of the mess, but because they would give him extra money.

When the lunch time crowd finally subsided, Stacy looked exhausted. Her co-workers made mention of it, and asked if she was okay. She thanked them for their concern and told them she was just tired.

About two o'clock, Stacy's best friend Leslie Velsey stopped in and sat down for lunch. Leslie was a brunette and twenty-five just like Stacy. They had been friends since middle school. Where Stacy was more practical, Leslie had been a kind of a free spirit who wasn't afraid to try new things.

"Hey, how are you doing?" Leslie asked as Stacy walked over to wait on her. "Man, you look exhausted. Are you all right?"

"Yeah, I'm all right," Stacy responded. "I'm just tired. I've been working a lot lately. So what can I getcha?"

"The usual," Leslie answered. "Todd, the clod still hasn't found work yet, has he?" already knowing the answer.

Stacy shook her head.

"That lazy bastard," Leslie said strongly, yet softly so she would not be overheard. "You're killing yourself, making things go and he's not lifting a finger to help. All because he lost a job. You deserve better. You deserve somebody like Jim Crawford over there. Now, there's a man. Todd couldn't hold his jock, and I mean literally."

"I know," Stacy said. "I've been after Todd. I'll bring your iced tea."

A couple of minutes later, she returned with Leslie's iced tea.

"I've been after Todd," said Stacy. "The work wouldn't be so bad, if he just helped out at home."

"In other words he's as useless as tits on a boar hog," Leslie said. "Rolling around all day not doing a damn thing except eating, drinking and taking a dump. He's worthless."

Stacy could not say a word since it was all true. A few minutes later, she returned with Leslie's Caesar salad.

"Are we still on for next Wednesday?" Leslie asked, trying to change the subject.

"Wednesday? "Stacy asked, momentarily forgetting what Leslie meant.

"Oh, yeah, our lunch date. I dunno. Money is a little tight right now."

"It's my treat, Stace," Leslie said.

"I can't do that," Stacy said sadly. "That isn't right."

"Hey it's my birthday present to you," said Stacy. "I bet you almost forgot it was your birthday, didn't you?"

"Yes, I did," Stacy admitted.

"That doesn't surprise me with Mr. Underworked at home, sapping all of your energy," Leslie said bitterly. "I bet he doesn't even remember it himself."

Stacy knew that Leslie never really cared for Todd, but was willing to give him a chance when they'd first married three years ago. Leslie never stopped by when Todd was around, but would attend parties and get-togethers. They were polite and got along, but there was always that underlying tension. She knew that Leslie especially despised him since he was unemployed. She wanted to say that Leslie was not being fair. But, Leslie had said everything that she, herself had been thinking lately.

"Oh, he will," Stacy said, a little defensively of Todd

"I'll be there at nine sharp," Leslie said. "It's a girl's day out and I have got some big plans for us."

"Thanks, Leslie," Stacy said. "I love you."

"I love you too, Stace," said Leslie. "You're my best friend and I just want to see that you're happy. You deserve the best."

Stacy reached down and touched Leslie's hand, squeezed it and smiled. She then went to wait on some other customers. Leslie finished her salad and left a ten dollar tip. On her way out she hugged her best friend and quietly left.

"Stacy, order up!" called out one of the cooks.

She picked up the order and delivered it to the table of one of her favorite regular customers and friend, Jim Crawford.

Crawford was a builder and had been one of Stacy's customers since she started at eighteen. He knew her before she had gotten married. He had also been the antithesis of Todd. Todd was twenty-five, while Jim was twenty-seven.

Where Todd had been laid off and just sat around collecting unemployment, Jim had gone to work for himself and did whatever it took to keep a steady income.

He did everything from mowing lawns and pouring cement, to carpentry, and bricklaying to earn money. Where Todd drank a lot of beer, sat around and shaved every couple of days, Jim had stayed clean-shaven, in shape and always seemed to stay active. While Todd was not ambitious and waited for things to happen, Jim took charge and made his own opportunities and luck. He had always liked Stacy and was probably one of her most loyal customers. She liked Jim a lot more than she cared to admit as a married woman.

Especially since he had always been so kind to her.

"Uh, Stacy, I ordered the sandwich on rye not dry," he said, almost apologetically

"I'm so sorry," she said, visibly upset. "I am just tired. I've been working a lot of hours. I'm so sorry, Jim."

"Hey, Stace, it's alright," Jim said with an understanding smile. "I just didn't want you to get it mixed up with somebody else. I'd hate to see you lose a tip from somebody."

"Thanks, Jim," she said, rubbing her eyes. "It's on me."

"No way, Stace," Jim replied. "I'm not just one of your regulars, you know. We're friends. I know you're hurting right now. It's no problem. Just take care of yourself. Is there anything I can do to help?"

"No," she answered. "I wish there were."

"Well, pardon me for saying so," Jim said, with some resignation in his voice. "But I don't think you're being very appreciated. You are a fine woman who needs be treated right and appreciated. By God, I know I would. You wouldn't have to work again if you didn't want to, if you were with me."

Stacy reached out and touched his hand. "Thanks, Jim, you're such a dear friend." she said. "Thanks a lot. You are really a dear and I appreciate you. Thanks for caring so much."

"I'm sorry Stace, I was out of line," Jim admitted. "I just care about you, that's all. You look bad….I mean, tired. Please take care of yourself."

"Thank you," she replied, knowing what he meant Stacy went to check on some other customers.

She came back and refilled Jim's coke and continued her rounds. Jim finished his sandwich, paid his bill and left. He left behind a twenty dollar tip. She remembered how he had asked her out several times, but she had some ridiculous rule about dating friends. She now regretted that one. It had possibly been one of her worse decisions ever. Both she and Leslie knew he was a great catch, and they had talked about it numerous times together both before Stacy's marriage and after.

When she returned to pick up her tip, tears welled up in her eyes at the sight of the twenty dollar bill.

Once she arrived home, the house was a little better, but still a mess. At least Todd had picked up all of the cans, pizza boxes and other food containers.

"Small wonder," she thought.

"Hey, honey what's for dinner?" Todd asked from the living room couch.

That question hit Stacy like a ton of bricks. "You tell me," she snapped.

"What?" Todd asked, dumbfounded.

"You tell me," she repeated. "I worked all day. What did you do?"

He didn't answer at first. "Well, I'm hungry," he protested. "I'm so hungry I could eat the butt outta a skunk."

"Then make yourself a Goddamn sandwich!" she yelled. "I worked all day! You didn't!"

"Hey, I don't cook," he yelled back. "Besides, you do a better job of it! Whatever happened to love, honor and obey?"

"Goddammit, Todd!" she yelled. "I cook, clean, work and do laundry and you don't do shit! And whatever happened to take care of in sickness and in health? I thought you were supposed to be the man of the house!"

"Hey, I was out looking for work today," Todd said defensively. "I put in applications at a place on Dixie Highway."

"Wonders never cease," she said, sarcastically. "How many places did you go to before you called it a day? Two? Shit, for as much as you do, you could put in for a security guard job. Those morons get paid for doing nothing."

"What's your Goddamn problem?" he yelled. "I went out looking for work, like you wanted. I even picked up a little and took the cans in! And that still ain't good enough for you!"

Stacy kicked off her shoes. "I'm happy you went job hunting," she said. "I wish you would have started about six months ago. We could have used the money a lot sooner, instead of waiting forever for you to be hired back. The only reason you took the cans in was to give yourself some money."

"Man, nothing's good enough for you!" he shouted. "All you do is bitch, bitch, bitch. You don't even put out anymore! We ain't had sex in weeks."

"Todd! That isn't fair!" she shouted back. "You don't do shit around here. Name one thing you fixed recently. You won't get off your dead ass to do anything! Maybe if you helped out, I wouldn't be so damned tired. I am just too damn tired! What happened to the man I married?"

"Yeah, right," he said sarcastically. "I'm going out! See you later!"

He left, slamming the door behind him.

Stacy just shook her head. She made herself some dinner, washed some clothes, did the dishes and cleaned up a little. She sat down and watched a little television and then went to bed, depressed about the way her life was going.

She had to do something or her life would deteriorate even more and she knew it had to do with Todd. But, what that something was, she did not exactly know.

Leslie arrived at nine a.m. to pick up Stacy for "their day out." Todd was still asleep in bed when they left.

"Sit back and enjoy the day," Leslie said as Stacy climbed in her new red Ford Mustang.

Leslie first treated Stacy out to breakfast. After breakfast it was shopping. Then it was lunch followed by more shopping.

"Boy, I'm beat," Stacy said as they climbed into Leslie's car.

"We've got one more stop," Leslie announced.

"Oh, Leslie, you did too much already," Stacy protested.

"Well, this is actually for both of us," Leslie replied.

"Where are we going?" Stacy asked.

"To the spa," Leslie announced. "Be prepared to be treated like royalty."

The two women spent the next few hours getting facials, massages, manicures, pedicures, mud baths, showers, saunas and whirlpool baths. Just relaxing in grand comfort exchanging small talk on everything from fashion and new shows to their mutual friend Jim Crawford.

As they sat there soaking in the whirlpool, Stacy leaned over to Leslie.

"Leslie, I can't thank you enough," she said. You're my best friend and I love you."

"You're the sister I never had, Stace," Leslie replied. "Here." She handed Stacy a small decorative plastic bag with another present in it.

"You shouldn't have," Stacy said.

"Yes, I should have," Leslie responded. "It could be helpful, if not useful."

Stacy opened the present. It was a book titled, *"Witchcraft For Dummies: A Beginners Guide to the Black Arts."*

Stacy looked a little surprised and skeptical. "Thanks, I think," she said, with a strange look on her face. "So, what does this do? Cast spells? Are you really into this and have you used it?"

"A little," admitted Leslie. "Trust me, it could come in handy. You could use it on Todd. Maybe put a spell on his sorry ass to help out and find a new job. Or turn him back from being a toad and into Prince Charming."

"You're terrible," Stacy laughed.

"No, seriously, Stacy, I know this Wiccan lady, and we were talking about relationships one day," Leslie explained. "We went from ourselves to our friends and I mentioned you and your situation. The lady explained to me that although a true Wiccan wouldn't harm anybody with a spell, there are spells that exist that can bring about some kind of justice. She said there are spells that those who are not committed to the arts can do."

Stacy was not thrilled that Leslie mentioned her to a Wiccan, but knew how she meant it. "So, how have you used it?" she finally asked.

"I had a real problem with a little trouble-making assistant at work," Leslie explained. "I tried being fair and had to spell everything out to the letter or it would not get done. She was a real sabotaging little bitch. I was getting chewed out for her backstabbing antics and I had had enough. I tried to rise above it, but she was trying to do anything to basically take my position…screw me over."

"So what did you do?"

"I read the book and practiced a little," Leslie continued. "Then I cast a little spell. I won't go into detail, but she ended up being fired."

When Stacy got home, Todd was gone. She figured that he must have gone to out with his buddies again.

Then one of his buddies called, saying they were looking for him to see if he wanted to meet them at the bar. As soon as she hung up the phone, she became suspicious. Instinctively, she knew that Todd was up to something.

What, she did not know. When he wasn't home, he had usually hung out with his friends. Something did not sit right with her.

When Todd came home, he had a bag from the White Lake Wal-Mart. "Here," he said.

"Happy birthday. I hope you like it."

She pulled out a gaudy nightgown with a large gold butterfly on it that was much too large for her body, and not anything she would normally wear. It looked like it belonged on an old lady who was trying to look years younger.

"Thanks," she said trying to mask her hurt feelings and suspicions, while she was steaming.

"Do you like it?" he asked. "I wasn't sure what to get."

"Oh, it's more than I ever expected," she replied, sounding falsely enthusiastic.

"Well, Stace, I'm going to bed," he announced. "I'm tired. I been hitting it hard all day."

"Oh, I bet you have," she thought to herself.

The next day at work, Stacy approached a regular customer, Tom Cowley, who was a retired policeman.

"Would you do some detective work for me?" she asked.

"Depends," he responded. "What is it?"

"I need surveillance on somebody," she replied.

"Your husband?" he asked, already knowing the answer from years of police experience.

"Yes," she answered. "I think he's cheating on me and I want you to find out for me."

"Okay."

"How much, do you charge?" she asked.

"Tell you what Stacy," he said. "You buy me lunch every day for a month and we'll call it even. Oh, yeah, plus dessert."

"You got a deal, Tom," she said. "And thanks a bunch."

"No problem, kid," he said. "You're too good a kid to have to put up with that bullshit."

Stacy gave him all of the information that he needed to conduct the surveillance.

Five days later, he returned with his report and some pictures.

Tom looked sad. "Well kid, how are yuh doin'?" he asked.

"Just give it to me straight, Tom," she said. "I can take it."

"Yeah, he's cheatin' on you," he said, hesitantly. "I'm sorry Stace, I truly am."

Tears welled up in her eyes. She was angry rather than sad. "Give me the details."

"Well, he's been seeing a woman named Brittany Seavers," he continued. "She's a twenty-two-year-old college student who works part-time at the Overtime Sports Bar on Dixie Highway in Waterford. She's a real party-girl. She has a history nailing married men. She needed her car repaired and he's a regular there. That's how they met. She also doesn't care that he's married. I got that from some of her co-workers. She's done this before. Seems they've been together for a couple of months. She has a regular routine around their afternoon interlude. She usually hits the gym or the racketball court and the sauna at the Raquetball Club on Waterford

Hill everyday from 9:00 a.m. to11:30 every day prior to their meeting."

"So, she's equally at fault," Stacy said as she shook her head.

"Apparently so," he replied. "They meet up at her place between her classes from noon to two almost everyday."

"Thanks, Tom," she said. "I'll take it from here."

"Just don't kill him or cut his nuts off like that Bobbit fella," Tom warned. "Take him the friggin' cleaners."

"I will," she responded. "Lunch is on me, for an extra month, Tom, thanks."

That night Stacy read the book that Leslie had given her. She studied it intently. A couple of nights later, after she finished the book, she decided that she would practice on this Brittany Seavers. Stacy then paid a visit to The Overtime Sports Bar. She sat down at the bar and quietly observed the woman who was servicing her husband while she worked to keep them afloat.

Brittany Seavers, from what she observed, treated the male customers especially well.

The only thing missing was a lap dance. She would openly flirt with men, even if a girlfriend was there. She made almost no pretense of who and what she was. It was like a game to her.

Finally, Stacy watched her head to the bathroom and followed. As she entered the stall next to her, Stacy heard her on her cell phone. "Hello, Todd…?"

Brittney said from the other stall. "Are we still on for tomorrow? Yeah, I'm free after 12:15. Good, I'll see you then," she said and then hung up.

As Stacy fumed with anger, she waited for her to leave, before leaving herself. She decided that she would get Miss Brittany Seavers in a less crowded place. The sauna would be perfect. She would just feign illness at work and leave early.

The next morning, about 11 a.m., Stacy told her manager that she felt ill and asked to leave. Stacy then headed to the racket club, paid and went into the sauna along with her new book and waited.

Just like clockwork, Brittany Seavers entered the sauna in her towel and swimsuit. From what Stacy could see, Todd's mistress had nothing on her in the looks department. Nonetheless, Stacy smiled at her when she entered the sauna like most people do.

"Boy, it's warm," Brittney said. "You new here?"

"Yeah, I was just checking things out to see how I like it," Stacy replied.

"Really," Brittany said, mocking a kind of interest as she closed her eyes and leaned her head back. "It's pretty nice here."

Stacy began to softly recite the spell she had decided on.

"At this time with spirits close. Within the grasps of souls and ghosts. Abandon all and heed my call. Upon which that you may broach and cast this soul upon a roach."

"What are you reading, poetry?" Brittany asked, looking at Stacy warily.

"A spell," Stacy replied, as the steam built up, engulfing Miss Seavers.

After a few minutes the steam dissipated and Brittany Seavers was gone. In her place was a cockroach. "Damn! That's not what I wanted, exactly."

Before she could recite another incantation, two other women entered the sauna and sat down nearby.

Almost immediately, one of them noticed the cockroach in the corner and shrieked loudly.

"Aaaahhh, a cockroach!!!" said one of the women. "Yuch!"

The other woman took the sandal off of her foot and smashed it down on the helpless cockroach causing a loud crunch. The woman continued to smash the roach until it was more like mush.

"Management should know about this," said the woman who killed the cockroach.

Stacy started laughing and both women looked at her. "I'm sorry, but you should've seen your face. You looked like you were going to throw-up."

"Yeah, you really did make a funny face," said the roach killer's friend. "It was funny."

The woman who had screamed started to laugh, herself.

All three women in the sauna enjoyed a laugh about the incident. For Stacy, even though the spell wasn't quite what she wanted, the results were. She soon left.

The next night, she picked up Todd's favorite take-out meal, Kentucky Fried Chicken.

"What's the occasion?" Todd asked.

"Oh, I just thought that it would be nice to do," she answered. "I know how much you love this, so I thought I would treat you."

"Cool," he said as he grabbed a paper plate and started serving himself some food.

By the time he finished, Todd had packed away eight pieces of chicken, a container of mashed potatoes and gravy, and four biscuits.

"Oh," he moaned after gorging himself. "I am full." He then belched. "Damn, that was good. I can barely move."

"Glad you liked it, honey," she said.

"It was," said Todd, before he interrupted himself by another belch.

"Great." he undid the top button of his jeans. "I need to go lay down. I ate like a pig."

On his way to their bedroom, he continued to belch and moan.

"Serves you right, you rotten pig," she said under her breath.

In a matter of minutes, Todd was sleeping like an overfed glutton.

Stacy cleaned up after dinner. She got out her *Witchcraft for Dummies* book and turned to the casting of spells section. She then lit some candles and placed them in the bedroom with Todd as he lay dead to the world, in a deep sleep.

She soon began to read and chant an incantation.

"On this night with spirits close. Within our grasps our souls and ghosts. For those that wander aimlessly. Heed the call and abandon thee. Remove yourself from your strife for promise of a better life. For those of you that still have trust. Relinquish your spirit unto us."

A wind seemed to blow through the house, making the candles flicker.

Stacy continued the chant.

"On this night of nights where spirits reign divine. I summon thee to bring forth the power. To change this man into a swine."

The wind began to grow stronger. A vortex began to build in the bedroom where Todd now slept. It built into a swirling mass that descended downward towards him. Soon he was engulfed in the swirling mass until he disappeared.

The vortex continued to feverishly spin around for another minute. Then it just disappeared. As it disappeared the candles blew out.

The spell was done.

Stacy got up from her place on the floor in the living room and entered the bedroom. Todd was totally covered by the blankets. She pulled back the covers and lying there on the bed was a rat, sleeping.

"Shit!" she muttered softly and tried the incantation again.

Once again, the wind grew stronger and swirled as before, filling the house and then disappearing. The rat was gone and this time, Todd had changed into an ugly toad.

"Damn," she thought. "Both fitting, but still not right."

Once again, she started reciting the incantation and for the third time the wind built up and the swirling vortex reformed. Finally after the vortex died down and there in bed was a large sleeping pig.

She jumped back, startled. "Oh, my God, it worked." she said, hardly containing her glee. "I don't believe it. It really worked." She started jumping for joy. "Yessss."

The pig that had once been Todd Thurmond continued its deep sleep.

Stacy then went to her purse and pulled out a business card of butcher who worked out of his garage, and called him.

"Hello, Mr. Taylor," she said, while on the phone. "This is Stacy Thurmond. Do you still process animals? You do….good. You see, somebody delivered us a pig when we thought it was supposed to be already cut up. I was wondering if you could come and get it and process it for me. Yes, a standard cut would be fine. When can you come over? Thirty minutes. Okay that's fine. You have my address right? Good, I will see you then. Thanks. Goodbye."

Roughly thirty minutes later, Mr. Taylor and his two sons arrived to take the pig away in the livestock truck. Once they put the snare around it, the pig struggled and squealed loudly for all it was worth, as the men wrestled it into the truck.

"Get in there, you oversized ham hock," said one of Mr. Taylor's sons as he kicked the pig in the ass, hard.

"Sometimes the goddamn things seem to know where they're going," Mr. Taylor commented. "He's sure one big pig. You'll get a lot of meat out of him."

"Should I pay you now?" Stacy asked.

"Naw," Mr. Taylor replied. "When I git him done, I'll just bring it to your work and you can git me then. It should only be fifty dollars at the most. You should get some decent hams and sausage. Not to mention bacon."

"Please," Stacy replied.

The pig continued to squeal loudly and struggle, as if in protest. It struggled against the ropes and snares that secured it inside the livestock truck.

"Boy, he's pretty upset, ain't he," commented Mr. Taylor about the pig's squealing. "Take it easy big boy, you ain't going to a pig roast, only the slaughterhouse. I'll see you in three days, Stacy."

Stacy nodded as the men got in the truck and drove away with the pig squealing all the way.

A sense of great satisfaction filled her, as she took a deep breath. Stacy turned around and headed back in the house. It looked like things were going to work out just fine, after all. Once inside, she picked up the phone and dialed, confessing everything she did to Leslie.

"See, I told you the book would come in handy," Leslie laughed. "Now, you better cover your bases. I would burn his clothes and other things."

Stacy then said, "I'm already on it," as she headed out to burn his clothes in the fire pit that they had in the back yard that was surrounded by large gray concrete blocks. Stacy made sure that she left some older and smaller personal items behind so as not to draw suspicion. She then made another phone call. "Hello… Jim, this is Stacy… Todd left me tonight…"

The next couple of months went fast for Stacy. She filed for annulment only a couple of days after Todd had been taken to be processed. A couple of days after that, she had a freezer full of pork.

The police came by asking some questions, since both Todd and his mistress had both virtually disappeared under mysterious circumstances. She had an alibi and witnesses to her whereabouts and there was no incriminating evidence, so she was not a suspect. Stacy told the authorities that she found out he was having an affair and decided to confront him. When she finally got home, he was gone, suggesting that maybe they ran off somewhere together. Stacy was adamant that she did not care where he was and did not want him back.

With no evidence and the testimony of ex-policeman Tom Cowley, the police let the matter go. They had more important business than finding deserting husbands. For their kindness and courtesy, Stacy donated some of her now-processed pork to the police when she went by the station. She even gave some to Todd's friends who had stopped by out of concern for her as well, plus destroying the bulk of the evidence.

She then took control of her life. Since she called Jim the night that Todd had been taken away, and he came over, they had been an item; dating regularly.

When her annulment was finalized, Stacy and Leslie had a weekend long celebration of her new freedom. After their evening out, Stacy was up early cooking breakfast. Leslie woke up to the smell of bacon being cooked and eggs being fried. She walked into the kitchen and hugged Stacy. "Mmmmm. That smells good," she said. "But you didn't have to do that for me."

"I don't mind," Stacy said. "Besides, Jim's here and he's starting on fixing my garage."

"So, how does it feel to be officially independent and single?" Leslie asked.

"It's better than I remember it," Stacy replied. "It's like I woke up from a three-year nightmare."

The two women carried the food into the dining room, sat down and enjoyed breakfast while still in their night gowns.

"You've done a lot with the house," Leslie commented. "It must be expensive. How are you affording it?"

Before Stacy could answer, Jim walked in. "Hi Leslie." he said. "Stace, you're going to need some new garage door metal working. Not much. It should be easy enough. Other than that it's fine."

"Good, I was hoping the door was still fine," Stacy said.

"It's going to cost you," he said with an all-knowing smile. "Maybe even double."

"I know, it always does," Stacy said as she stood up and kissed him. "I think I can handle the payment plan."

Jim gently patted Stacy's left rear cheek and headed back outside to work on the door.

"I see how you're paying for this now," Stacy said smiling. "You little tramp."

"He's a good man," Stacy said. "I was lucky. I got a second chance."

"By the way, what did you do with the book?" Leslie asked.

"I burned it with Todd's clothes," Stacy said. "You know Leslie, I was right about one thing."

"What's that?"

"That Todd was good for something after all," Stacy said. "I mean he did provide us with the best part of this delicious meal."

"You got me there."

"More bacon?" Stacy asked as she passed the plate of bacon.

"Please," Leslie said with a large smile

Something in the Wind

During the night the wind had screamed and howled, as if it were alive as the snow blanketed the Northern Michigan countryside. The storm that had crossed Lake Superior from Wisconsin left at least a foot of fresh snow on the ground.

The cold, steel-gray cloud-filled sky revealing the dim and distant yellow-white winter sun. Even so, the newly-driven snow glistened brightly like millions of diamonds. The tall green pines, spruce and naked birch stood erect with thick layers of snow covering their branches like icing on a cake.

The Northern Michigan countryside looked like a winter landscape painting.

Wendell Chapman looked out the cabin window, surveying the sparkling landscape to see just what last night's snowstorm had brought in. It was beautiful, he thought, but, very deceiving. Its beauty hid the fact that it was also dangerous. Dangerous even for an experienced woodsmen and trapper like himself. After a few minutes, he started to cut up and fry some bacon and potatoes.

The sound and smell of bacon crackling in the metal skillet woke up Chapman's friend and partner 'Chink' McCullers.

McCullers groggily got up out of his bunk and started to put on his clothes. "Been up long?" he asked.

"Nah, not tuh long," Wendell answered. "It stormed like hell lass night. Mus be a foota snow or so out there."

Chink rose and walked over to the window and grunted an acknowledgement about Wendell's statement. He turned around and walked over to the table and plopped himself down at the table in the center of the cabin. "Smells good," he muttered.

After a few minutes, Wendell was served breakfast for the two hungry men.

"Think we better check the traps?" Wendell asked.

"Mmmm," grunted Chink, as he rubbed his unshaven face. "I'll check 'em after breakfast."

"You goin' alone?" Wendell asked, a little surprised.

"Yeah," Chink responded. "I kin handle it. Ain't nuthin, I ain't bin through before. Besides, the cole weather bothers yer leg since you broke it a couple years ago."

"Thanks, Chink," Wendell replied. "Much appreciated. I might go out and scout around after I do some of the chores around here."

Chink nodded and started to get ready to go check the traps near the swamp. He dressed warmly, in layers and grabbed some of the large leather pouches to haul back any pelts and carcasses in. Last, he put on his snow shoes.

Wendell handed Chink his Spencer Rifle.

"If I git a mind to, I'll bag us something, so we doan hafta use our stored supplies." Chink said.

"I kin use it fer stew," Wendell commented.

Chink nodded, picked up his pouches, draped them over his shoulders and grunted a "Later" and was out the door.

Wendell watched him head north through the snow towards the swamp, through the partially frost covered window.

Concern filled him as he watched his friend head towards the swamp. He turned away and started with the daily chores of the cabin.

Wendell had met Chink, whose real name was Charles, about ten years earlier in 1879. They met at a trading post near the Straits of Mackinaw. They became fast friends and decided to head up beyond Copper Harbor for better fur trapping.

At the time, Wendell was easily pushing forty, and Chink was in his late twenties. Wendell had been the son of a farmer, and Chink had been the son of a carpenter.

After a couple of years of trapping, the men decided to build their present cabin to live in. They had lived in a glorified shack the previous years.

Both worked and hunted well together. They made decent money from trapping and fur. When Chink caught influenza late one fall, Wendell took care of him and nursed him back to health. He managed to receive some help from a nearby Ojibway medicine man named Nawautin who they had known for over five years. Wendell handled the work load of cooking, cleaning, hunting and trapping until Chink recovered.

Later, when Wendell broke his leg after falling down a ridge and it was Chink who splinted his leg and helped him back to the cabin and to health. Chink did most of the outdoor work until Wendell's leg healed.

Chores were pretty much split down the middle. They both knew it had to be done or they would not make money and worse yet, they could die. Both knew what to do and when to do it.

Wendell's leg hadn't been the same since the fracture. While it wasn't weak, it did ache. The pain seemed to sharpen when temperatures dropped. Aches and pains or not, he was still able to pull his share of the work, even in the winter.

He went over to the window and looked outside. His friend was now out of sight.

A sudden, brisk wind blew from across the lake, howling loudly against the cabin. This caused him to jump a little. It had come out of nowhere and interrupted the quiet and stillness of the woods in winter.

In spite of the growing numbers of miners, lumberjacks and other trappers in the region, the outdoors was still dangerous. The elements were as deadly as any wild animal.

Bear were still plentiful and a bull elk, if threatened could be pretty nasty. He knew of one guy who had shot an elk and was field dressing it, when a larger bull elk attacked and nearly stomped the man to death. As far as Wendell knew, the man still never had recovered from that attack. That didn't even count the weather and the other things.

Other things.

The stories and legends some of the Ojibway Indians told. Some folks thought of them as mere myths, but Wendell had been doing this long enough to know there was some truth to them and they were not to be taken so lightly. Just because the white man didn't see or was ignorant of the culture, didn't mean that these things didn't exist. While he didn't necessarily believe them, he wasn't going to close his mind to them either. Something, Wendell knew, just couldn't be explained.

He started peeling potatoes, carrots and onions in preparation for stew that he would make later.

Their fur trading had helped them stock up with vegetables from a couple of nearby farmers. They always had managed to trade for potatoes, onions, carrots and a little corn at harvest time.

As he began cutting the vegetables for stew, Wendell heard the wind howl again as it came off of the lake.

A slight chill ran through him. The wind was more than howling.

He couldn't be sure but, it sounded as if it were shrieking.

Wendell shook his head and went about finishing his work. He had to have been imagining it, so he thought.

He knew that Chink would be gone for at least half of the day, because, there was a pretty good amount of area to cover, not to mention the snow would slow him down some.

He finished cutting the vegetables and threw them into the pot with water. He then tidied up the cabin and went outside to retrieve some fresh water from a nearby stream, and split some fire wood just in case of another storm.

As he chopped the wood, he sensed another storm approaching in the distance. Just from the looks of things, he could tell it was going to be as bad, if not worse, than the previous one. He decided that he had better bring in a good load of firewood to carry them through for a couple days if necessary.

After about an hour, he carried some kindling and split logs in, a little at a time and placed it next to the fireplace. The last load he placed in the fireplace and stoked the embers. Soon a roaring fire blazed and Chink took a break to warm himself up.

Sitting next to the fireplace, warming up, he heard the wind howling again. Then, he heard it again -the shrieking.

By God, he thought, the wind was *shrieking*. It had actually been *shrieking*. Something outside was alive or something in the wind was alive. Yes, there was *something* in the wind.

He knew it.

Immediately, he thought about his partner. He hoped Chink was all right on his trek to the swamp. Now even warmed up and dry, Wendell felt a chill go up his spine.

Sitting down at the table, Wendell started working on one of their many tanned deer hides. As he worked on the hide, the wind continued to howl and scream.

He focused more intently on his work. There was no way he was going to look outside to see what it might be that he thought he heard. After about a half an hour of working on the hide, he noticed the wind, while blowing harder, was no longer screaming and shrieking. He got up to look. Snow was steadily falling. He knew the weather was going to get worse.

He pulled out his pocket watch, it was almost noon. He had a couple of hardtack biscuits and a cup of coffee. It was now snowing harder.

He knew that Chink should have reached the traps by now and be heading back. He knew it would take him longer to return because of the snow. Wendell wondered where exactly Chink was at as he drank some coffee.

Chink had just finished checking the last of the traps when the snow hit. He was very surprised to find all of the traps empty. He figured that a few would be empty because of the weather, but not all of them. That was just strange. They had never found all of their traps empty. Even stranger, was the fact that he saw no signs whatsoever of animal tracks. Anywhere. Some of that could be attributed to the snowfall, but near the water, where the snow wasn't as deep, there was nothing.

Chink didn't even see or hear any birds. Just dead quiet stillness.

Chink knew damn well, there were plenty of animals nearby. Be it, bear, deer, elk, beaver, badger, bobcat, it was around. And plentiful. Very plentiful.

But, today, nothing.

Absolutely nothing.

Then the sheer quietness of the woods was uncanny and eerie.

Like Wendell, Chink had heard stories of the Indians legends. Some he believed, while others he took with a grain of salt.

He saw the snowstorm was growing worse, and he realized that he might have to find a place to wait out the weather. He had done it before. He could wait it out at their old shack that he and Wendell stayed in before the cabin was built.

The quietness of the snowfall engulfed him. He did not like that feeling. He shrugged it off and started towards the shelter. As the snowfall came down more heavily, he decided, he should hurry. He was just under a half – a –mile from the old shelter.

Halfway to the shelter, near the clearing, Chink stopped. Frozen in his tracks. It were as if he forgot how to breathe.

Directly in front of him were footprints. Large, bare footprints. Much larger than any man. They were gigantic. He had never seen anything like it.

He had heard tales of some kind of wild men out west by other hunters and trappers, that the Indians called Sasquatch, but these were much larger. Far more larger than the tale he's been told, as if made by a giant.

He knelt down and felt the footprint. "Godalmighty," he muttered, hardly believing his eyes.

Then in the distance he heard the wind coming off of the lake howl. At least he thought it was the wind. It sounded like an animal shrieking in the distance.

Chink stood up, grabbed his rifle and decided to hurry towards the shelter that was just inside the woods. Carrying his rifle, he huffed and puffed as he sprinted his way through the snow towards the shelter. His breath filled the cold air as he labored through the deep snow. His lungs felt like they were burning as he ran for shelter.

As he neared the shelter, he heard the wind howl again. This time it sounded exactly like something shrieking. When he reached the shack, he heard what he thought was a loud "poof" sound, as if something large had just stepped down on fresh snow. Then he heard another sound like it, as if something just took another step. Quickly, he opened the door and entered, keeping his rifle at the ready.

He took one last look before closing the door, seeing nothing and only hearing the wind howl and shriek. He knew there was something nearby.

Something big.

And horrible.

Chink, knew it was something he did not want to see. With something that big, and, that shriek, it, had to be horrible. He knew it.

He wasn't a coward. But, he was smart enough to know that whatever it was had to be dangerous. Dangerous and probably hungry. Chink crouched there and waited, peering through the small peep hole in the shack, trying to get a glimpse of it.

Meanwhile, the storm worsened and the shrieking wind grew louder.

Back in the cabin, Wendell heard the distant shrieks. It sounded as if they were coming from where the two men trapped. He wanted to sure Chink was alright, but knew it would be foolhardy to venture out in this weather now. He also knew Chink had enough sense to find shelter and food in his pack, so he could ride out the storm somewhere. The only question in Wendell's mind was, if he were even able to even get any shelter at all.

He went back to working on the hides.

All he could do was wait and worry.

Intently working, he jumped with a pounding on the cabin door and a shout "Is there anybody in there? Let us in." Then more pounding.

The pounding on the door startled Wendell.

He then, headed towards the door and cautiously opened it, uncertain who it was.

Standing there, covered with snow, were three men. Wendell recognized the first one; it was the constable, Axel Jacobson. He wasn't sure who the other two men were, even if they did look familiar.

"Axel, come on in," Wendell said as he waved his hand for them. "Before, yuz freeze yer arses off."

"Thanks, Wendell," uttered Axel as he entered and stomped his snow-covered boots on the hard dirt floor.

The other two men followed him in and did the same. All three men brushed the heavy wet snow off themselves, lowered their rifles, and removed their coats, setting them near the fireplace to dry. As Wendell was closing the door he heard the wind howl and scream. They seemed relieved to be inside.

"Hava seat," Wendell instructed. "I got some coffee if yuh wannit."

"Thanks," answered Axel as he sat down. "Wendell, this is Pastor Paul Radler and this is our guide Pawaugun. He's Ojibway. From the local tribe.

The men quietly nodded.

Pastor Radler and Pawaugun sat down at the table as well, while Wendell brought over three steel cups and the coffee pot.

"So, what in the hell are you doin out in this goddamn snowstorm?" Wendell asked, as he poured the coffee and realized what he just said. "Sorry Pastor. I mean yer a ways from home and in bad weather."

"We got word that something happened to the miners just west of here," Axel explained, between sips of hot coffee. "Apparently the Kovack boy went to deliver them some mail yesterday and he found their camp in ruins. There was blood all over on the snow and no bodies. We just checked on 'em."

"Claim jumpers?" Wendell asked.

Axel shook his head. "Don't think so," he responded. "The kid said he saw some large footprints in the snow. But, by the time we got there they were filled in with snow. We did see blood. Pawaugun's people don't think so either. Turn's out a coupla them are missin' too. They went out yesterday an' didn't come back."

"If not claim jumpers, then who?" Wendell asked.

"I dunno," Axel answered. "I'm just a guy they hired for the job 'cause I know the region, can shoot fairly well and can read an write. I doan know what to think. That's why we stopped here. Tuh see if you an' Chink might know anything."

"Nope, nothin' here," Wendell said. "We bin here all day. Well, at least I have. Chink went out after breakfast to check on traps."

"Bass Eckhardt thinks it was the niggers at the rail line, where the timber is taken, who did it," said Pastor Radler. "Their boss said, they couldn't have done it since he was with them whole time workin' until long after dark."

"Yeah, an' besides, they never come out here anyways," said Axel. "Besides, Eckhardt blames niggers for everything. My God, there's only four up here and probably only a dozen in the whole upper penninsula. If they weren't up here he'd blame the Indians. That's jus Eckhardt."

"So, what do yuh think it is?" Wendell asked a little apprehensive.

Axel gave Wendell a look that he would not forget. It was as if, he knew, but couldn't explain. Or, even begin to try. There was a long uncomfortable silence.

"Pawaugun says it ain't humans who done it," said Pastor Radler, breaking the long silence. "He says it's some kind of … some mannytoo er something….it's some kind of Indian legend called..uh…"

"Wendigo," said Pawaugun, breaking Pastor Radler's temporary memory lapse.

The men just looked at each other in silence.

"Apparently, Pawaugun and his people believe this Windaga is the cause," said Pastor Radler.

"I heard tell of it," said Wendell. "But, I doan know much about it. I juss heard the name."

"From what Pawaugun told me it's some kind of manitou," said Axel. "It eats people or something."

"Wendigo," uttered Pawaugun, once again. "Bad. Very bad manitou. Very bad. It eat man. Never stop. Always hungry. More it eat, more it have too. It smell bad, like death. Long death."

Pastor Radler drank his coffee and a look of disbelief on his face. "I don't mean to sound rude, but I can't believe our heathen friend here and his people's legends." he snapped. "There's no such thing. A Windigo? What next? Elves and fairies?"

Axel gave the Pastor a look that bordered on contempt. "Pastor, you yourself heard something out there on our way here." he said. "We all heard something out there. It was like some God-awful netherworld scream in the distance. Then, down wind, that rotten smell. Why d'ya think Pawaugun started to run the last half mile? Somethin' out there scared him."

"It was probably just the wind," Pastor Radler responded sharply. "Our friend got scared from all his people's legends. Nothing more. We probably got down wind of a dead animal. As for the wind howling. It only sounded like a…like a…"

"A shriek," Wendell interrupted.

The men looked at Wendell.

"Yeah, I heard it too," he continued. "I heard it durin' the night and it came back agin' shortly after Chink left. It gave me the willies, I gotta admit."

"Could I have some more coffee?" Pastor Radler asked.

"Yeah," Wendell answered. "Anybody else wanna refill?"

Axel and Pawaugun handed him their cups for him to refill. Wendell poured them and himself another cup of coffee.

"Thanks," said Axel, as he got up and walked over to the fireplace. "We can't overlook what the kid said he seen."

"Constable, for all we know the kid could have done it," said Pastor Radler.

"Pastor, I think that's a buncha manure," said Axel. "One of the miners was Black Mike Mulligan. An' he was one of the toughest sonofabitches I ever met. Ain't no kid gonna kill him."

"I gotta agree," Wendell said. "Black Mike was one of the toughest. His whole damn crew was."

"It was just a thought," said Pastor Radler. "The kid coulda snuck up on 'em when they was sleepin'."

"The kid was fourteen," Axel responded. "Besides, it was Brent Kovack. He's a good kid. Honest and trustworthy. Black Mike trusted him to bring supplies and run an occasional errand fer him."

"I can't see Black Mike letting someonc sneak up on him either," agreed Wendell. "It jus' don't sound right. He slept with his knife and always hadda gun nearby."

"That's why we're here," said Axel, as he turned away from the fireplace and walked back over to the table. "Tuh see if you and Chink know anything at all."

"I doan know a goddamn thing," Wendell said. "Sorry, Pastor." He looked embarrassed for speaking the Lord's name in vain again. "We doan know nothin'. Except that wind's bin sounding pretty creepy lately. Thass all we know."

Axel and Pawaugun just looked at Wendell, knowing exactly what he meant.

There was another long pause with no conversation as the men gave fleeting looks and stared into space for what seemed like minutes, but was only seconds.

"Yuh worried about Chink?" Axel asked.

"Mm mmm," grunted Wendell. "I felt funny as soon as he left. I know Chink's as good as anyone else out there. But, I just hadda feelin' somethin' weren't right. The day felt funny."

"Didja hear anythin' during the night?" Axel asked.

"Nope," Wendell responded. "Me an' Chink sleep like dead men. The only thing I heard durin' the night was the wind. But, I was too tired tuh pay it any mind."

"How do yuh know Chink was asleep?" Pastor Radler asked. "I mean, he coulda got up and ventured out into the night. You, yourself was asleep. How wouldja know if he was there or not?"

Wendell glared at the Pastor. "Yer outta line there, Pastor," he finally said. "Yeah, I was asleep. But if Chink had went out into the night I woulda heard him leave 'cause the door squeaks when it gits cold and I woulda felt a cold draft from the door bein' open. I bin partnered with Chink long enough tuh know he ain't that kinda fella. He justa soon leave everybody alone. I think yer supposing too much, Pastor."

Pastor Radler was speechless. He knew that he had misspoken.

"I didn't mean to git that way, Pastor," Wendell said. "But, it sounded like yuh weren't showin' Chink the proper respectability. We might not be book learned like you, but we doan go supposin' and we treat everybody with the same respectability."

"I apologize, if I offended you an' yer friend," said Pastor Radler. "Do yuh know where about Chink is?"

"He wint out this morning to check our traps," said Wendell.

"Do yuh know where he's at?" asked Pastor Radler.

"If I had tuh figure," Wendell responded. "I figure he's holed up at our old shack. We built it to stay in. It's small but, it's big enough tuh stay in with a small fire. It's juss pass the swamp an on the edge of a clearing just inside the woods."

"Maybe we should go ask him," Pastor Radler said. "To see if he knows anything."

Axel and Wendell shot Pastor Radler a look.

"We ain't goin anywhere in this," Axel stated. "It's snowin' like hell out there. Only a goddamn fool would go out there."

Pawaugun got up and walked over to the fireplace. He then turned to the other men. "Pawaugun not go out," he said. "Very bad. Don't go out there, Jesus man. This Wendigo time. Wendigo snow. Go… Wendigo get you. Very bad manitou."

The men looked at Pawaugun, stunned. He had said little up to that point. But, what he did say carried great weight with Axel and Wendell.

"We wait then," Axel said, with authority. "I hope you doan mind the extra company, Wendell."

"Naw, that's fine," he said. "I got some playin' cards and some whiskey, if it lasts a while. I also got some stew cooking."

Wendell got up and the wind outside howled and screamed.

This caused the others to pause and look towards the windows. Wendell picked up a bottle of whiskey, uncorked it and took a slug. He grimaced a little and then resealed the bottle. He thought of Chink.

Chink was getting colder. Colder and tired. His last hurried trek in the cold weather had worn him out. He had been sitting there for hours as the wind continued to howl and shriek.

He knew there was something nearby. The wind sounded like some kind of large animal than it did anything else. He also heard the sound of something large stepping in the snow. He knew he did. He might have been cold, but he was not deaf. The worst part was the terrible smell. It smelled like death and decay, rot and corruption. It was rancid, like that of a dead animal baking in the hot sun.

Chink sat there chilled by more than just the cold.

Chink kept checking through the small peep holes. He knew something was out there, but he could not see it. He couldn't figure it out. How could something that sounded that large, not be seen? It didn't make sense. He was dumfounded and frightened.

Chink leaned his head back against the shelter's wall. He closed his eyes for a few seconds to just listen. As he listened, he thought he heard a throaty, hoarse-like growl. But, he could not be sure. For all he knew it could be a black bear since they were plentiful in the area. But, he doubted it.

While, Chink could not see he, he definitely could smell it. The putrid, sickeningly sweet smell of death and decay had grown stronger. Whatever was nearby, its stench made him feel sick and want to vomit. He had never smelt anything so bad.

He had started shaking again. Not just from the cold, but from fear.

Chink lowered his head and placed his hand over his face. He felt safe for now.

Just then, a large wailing, ear-piercing shriek rang out through the howling wind. The shelter started to rattle and shake. Before he could move the shelter collapsed on him. A large piece of wood fell and hit him on the head, severely dazing him. The rest of the shelter fell on top of him.

As he regained his senses, he managed to open his eyes, and he noticed that rotting overpowering stench that made him feel sick and looked up to see those blood-red eyes glaring down at him. It was then that he noticed he was looking into the face of a creature that truly was the worst of man's nightmares. Chink tried to let out a scream, but nothing came out.

The creature's large freezing-cold hand grabbed Chink around the waist and began ripping him to pieces. Chink's screams of agony could be heard for miles. Some time, just after the first scream, Chink died. As the creature feasted on the man, it let out even louder shrieks than it had earlier. As the creature feasted, its hunger grew. It knew there were more men in the area. And it wanted them.

Badly.

After drinking six cups of coffee and a few sips of whiskey, Pastor Radler had to use the outhouse. Just as he was heading out the door, carrying a lantern, he thought he heard a scream somewhere out in the snowstorm.

"Did you hear that?" he asked to the others.

The others all jumped up and headed towards the door. Pastor Radler and Wendell stood just inside the door watching and listening in the snowstorm. A few moments later they heard a loud ear-piercing inhuman shriek in the distance. They stood there a few more seconds more, and they heard the shriek again. This time it sounded as if it was closer.

The first shriek had almost caused Pastor Radler to wet his pants. So he hurried up and urinated not far from where the others were. The others continued to listen.

An even closer ear-piercing shriek erupted again.

"What is that?" Pastor Radler asked. "What kinda animal is it?"

Axel just shook his head, not knowing.

"No animal," Pawaugun said. "Wendigo."

Pawaugun, turned and quickly headed back in the cabin.

"I think we better join 'im," Axel said, as he followed Pawaugun.

Wendell and Pastor Radler just stood there, oblivious to what both, Pawaugun and Axel had just said and done. They now heard a new sound. The sound of large footsteps in the newly driven snow. They listened as the footsteps came closer. They did not move. Wanting badly to see what it was that they had heard.

"Pastor, Wendell!" Axel yelled from the door. "Get in here, now!"

Both men ignored Axel's pleading and kept listening.

"What is that?" Pastor Radler asked Wendell softly.

"I doan know," Wendell responded. "Maybe it's, Chink."

"Chink?!" Pastor Radler called out. "Chink?! Is that you?!"

"Chink?!" Wendell joined in the calling of his friend's name. "Chink?!"

"Pastor, Wendell!" Axel Yelled again. "Dammit! Get in here. Pawaugun says there's something bad out there. Come in, now!"

"Hold on," said Pastor Radler, as he turned and waved away Axel, annoyed. He then turned to Wendell. "I think I see something near the woods? I think I see two red eyes. What is that God-awful smell?"

Wendell squinted and looked hard through the falling snow. "I dunno," he answered and then sniffed. "But, it smells like it died."

"Maybe it's Chink," Pastor Radler suggested. "Maybe he fell in something."

"I dunno, Pastor," Wendell replied. "Somptin' ain't right. I ain't ever smelled nothin' like that."

"Get your asses in here!" Axel implored as he yelled from the doorway.

Pawaugun stood next to him. "Wendigo come. Very bad. Come inside. Be safe. Wendigo come now."

"Poppycock," said Pastor Radler, disgusted with Pawaugun's stories of manitous and other legends. "Wendell, I'm goin' out there to see if that's Chink. You wanna come with me?"

"Maybe we better wait here, Pastor," Wendell suggested. "I never heard tell or saw a person with red eyes before. Even deer eyes shine yellow in duh night with a light."

"Your friend could be hurt," Pastor Radler suggested as he picked up the lantern and held it as high as he could.

Wendell eyed the Pastor and shook his head. He knew something was out there but he didn't know exactly what. He was filled with doubt. What if it was Chink? He couldn't just leave him out there.

"Don't go out there!" yelled Axel. "Wait till after the storm. We'll all go then."

Just then another loud ear-piercing shriek rang out. The two men froze in their tracks. The footsteps they heard earlier were even closer than minutes before.

"Runnnn!!!!" yelled Axel and Pawaugun. "Run!"

Pastor Radler looked upward and saw that the two red objects that he had seen were eyes to a very large creature. "Dear, God," he gasped in horror. The words barely escaping his mouth.

Wendell saw it too. The creature was the thing of many a bad dreams, a legend come alive. A story the Ojibway had told him that was now, all too real. Pastor Radler was looking at something so horrible, he felt as if his heart skipped a beat. The stench of death and decay filled the air, causing Pastor Radler to fall to his knees. He looked up at the creature and let out a blood curdling scream. He tried to scurry away on his hands and knees, but could barely move. The scream seemed to hang in the air even after the creatures sharp fingernails tore through him and ripped him apart. After being disemboweled, the creature picked him up and devoured him.

Wendell had started for the cabin door, where Axel and Pawaugun waited. He had almost reached the door when the creature finished devouring the last of Pastor Radler. The creature let out another ear-piercing shriek. As Wendell hit the door, the beast's icy hand reached out to grab him. Wendell screamed out in pain, as the creatures fingernails tore through his clothes and skin.

Wendell stood there momentarily in shock, grimaced and grabbed his back. Pawaugun and Axel grabbed a hold of Wendell's arms and pulled him into the cabin. As they did so, the three men stumbled to the floor. Outside the creature howled in anger and disappointment about being denied its next meal.

Axel and Pawaugun covered their ears as the creature howled, as if in some pain. The men sat there momentarily breathing hard and terrified as the creature continued its temper tantrum outside.

They could not see the creature through the open door, but they knew it was just outside, lurking and waiting. Just as they were about to relax, a large bluish, off-white hand with large sharp fingernails reached into the door, trying to grab its prey. The stench of death and decay filled the small cabin.

The men frantically scrambled away as they tried to escape the creature's clutches. Axel headed over near where the food supplies were kept, while Pawaugun crawled over near the fireplace. Wendell grimaced in pain as he crawled away. He kicked at the creature's hand as he headed towards the far side of the table. Pawaugun grabbed one end of a log that had not yet started to burn from the fireplace and jabbed the burning end into the creature's hand.

The creature screamed out in great agony as the burning log touched its flesh. The smell of the burned rotting hide filled the cabin as the skin of the creature burned. The creature's gigantic hand disappeared out of the cabin and it disappeared into the snowy night. Shrieks of great pain and anger could be heard growing fainter, as it moved further and further away. Soon they could be barely heard.

Axel got up and closed the front door to the cabin. In shock, he just looked blankly at Pawaugun and Wendell without saying a word. His expression of disbelief spoke volumes. Wendell seethed in pain as he pulled himself up to the chairs at the table.

Pawaugun instinctively went over and helped Wendell up to the chair. Wendell nodded in appreciation, mouthing a "thank you" for the help. Just like the other Ojibway he had encountered, he found Pawaugun's kindness and character most honorable.

Axel walked over to Wendell and started checking on his back.

"Damn," Axel said as he checked Wendell's ripped, blood-soaked shirt. "That's pretty damn nasty. We can treat it. But yer goona be hurting. Can you take yer shirt off?"

Wendell started to, but winced in terrible pain. Tears filled his eyes with agonizing pain. "No," he finally said as he shook his head. "Yer juss gonna halfta cut it off."

"Okay," said Axel.

Pawaugun had already stuck his own knife into the fire to cauterize it. Axel took out his knife and after a couple of minutes cut off all of Wendell's shirts. On his back were three two foot wounds, scrapes from three middle fingers from a very large hand. While not fatally deep, they were wide and gaping, like someone had gouged their fingernails and deeply dug into another person.

Pawaugun grabbed the bottle of whiskey that they had been drinking from earlier, looked at Wendell's back and took big slug of whiskey first and handed it to Axel. Axel gave Wendell a swig and then poured some on Wendell's back.

"Holy goddamn, sonofabitch tuh Jesus Christ all to hell!" Wendell shouted as the whiskey hit the wounds as he tried to stay sat down in the chair. "Goddammit, that stings!"

Pawaugun handed Axel the knife as he started to work on the wound. Wendell seethed and grimaced with pain. Tears rolled out of his squinting eyes, as if pushed out. Axel pried out a piece fingernail that had broken off from the creature. He checked over the wound for more and did not find anything else. He poured more whiskey on the wound. Pawaugun threw the fingernail part into the fire, where a small explosion happened after it caught fire. Axel and Pawaugun then found some white cloth and bandages and bandaged Wendell up.

"That should do," Axel said. "I wouldn't move around tuh much for a day er two. When we git back tuh town I'll sent Doc Adams out here tuh see how yer doin'."

"I hope yuh fellas doan mind but I needa big drink o' whiskey," Wendell said still wincing from the pain. "Juss, tell Doc Adams tuh bring some drinkin' whiskey with him, alright?"

Axel went over to the supplies and found another bottle of whiskey and handed it to Pawaugun. "Here," said Pawaugun, handing the bottle to Wendell.

Wendell took the bottle and took a very large swallow from the bottle.

"Well, Pawauguh, what do you think?" Axel asked. "Do we stay the night?"

Pawaugun shook his head and replied. "Wendigo time. Still out there. Still hungry. Still angry. Very angry."

"Will it be okay tuh leave in the morning?" Axel asked.

"Wait and see," Pawaugun replied. "Will know when sun come up. Wendigo not out when weather clear."

"Wendell, it looks like we're spending the night," Axel announced.

Wendell just nodded. He had polished off almost half of the bottle and was starting to feel no pain. He also started to eat some of the dried venison and left over biscuits as if he were famished and starving. He soon had polished off the whole bottle of whiskey. Axel and Pawaugun sat there, somewhat amazed at Wendell's capacity to suddenly eat and drink.

Within an hour Pawaugun and Axel helped Wendell to his bed where he crashed in a drunken stupor. In the distance the creatures' shrieks could occasionally be heard in the howling and screaching wind that had kicked up once again. After a few hours, both men grew tired. They tried to keep sleep away as long as possible, until it finally overcame them. Pawaugun grabbed what had been Chink's bunk and crashed while Axel grabbed some animals' skins and slept on the floor near the fireplace.

Somewhere in the night the creature outside continued to shriek in great anger and pain as it tried to quench its insatiable appetite. Meanwhile, the men slept hard, recovering from the day's events.

When morning arrived the Pawaugun and Axel woke up when a cold gust of wind blew the cabin's door open.

"What the hell…?" Axel said, as soon as he felt the frozen air.

Pawaugun looked over at Axel. "Him gone," he said.

"What?" Axel said as he stood up and walked over to Wendell's bunk.

Axel started searching the bed. He looked down and there were Wendell's clothes. They looked as if they had been shredded. As if he grew out of them and they ripped apart as he grew. Axel held the clothes up confused and shaking his head.

Pawaugun looked at the clothes and then headed over to the door. He looked outside where he saw a set of bare human footprints in the snow.

"Here," Pawaugun said, waving to Axel. "Look."

Axel walked over to the door. He looked at the bare footprints. He noticed that they grew in size as they got further from the cabin. They were of enormous proportions as they headed out of sight.

"What in God's name happened?" Axel asked.

"He now Wendigo," Pawaugun said.

"But, why?" Axel asked. "Why?"

Pawaugun just shook his head, not knowing the answer. "I not know." he said.

"There has to be a reason," Axel insisted. "But, I'll be damned if I kin think of any. You think it's safe to leave?"

"We leave now," Pawaugun said. "Weather clear. It safe. Wendigo gone now. Another storm come soon."

Axel and Pawaugun got on their outdoor clothes, grabbed their rifles and headed outside.

"First, let's check the supply hut in back," Axel said, as he nodded his head. "We might be able tuh grab some jerky er something."

Pawaugun nodded his head in agreement and followed silently.

The two men went around the back of the cabin to the storage hut. On the way there they found a set of bare human footprints leading to the hut. Once at the storage hut, they noticed the hut's door was open and flapping in the breeze. They approached the hut cautiously. Axel entered first. Pawaugun was right behind him.

Pawaugun was frightened, but, was more afraid not to follow.

Once in the storage hut, Axel noticed right away the place was a mess. It looked as if somebody had gone berserk and ransacked the place. All of the food supplies that Wendell and Chink had stored up for the winter were all eaten. Broken or open mason jars, smashed open boxes, torn open food tins, smashed crates, dented buckets and ripped open flour and grain bags all littered the floor.

Axel and Pawaugun stood there in stunned silence. It was as if a wild animal broke in looking for food. Both scanned the darkness of the supply hut. Finally, their eyes fixed on some movement in the corner. They focused their eyes in the dark end hut, trying to make out what they were seeing. Finally, they were able to make out the silhouette of a large man in the corner. It looked like Wendell. Or something that passed as Wendell.

Both men automatically readied their rifles to fire, as if they were confronting some kind of wild animal.

"Wendell, is that you?" Axel asked, apprehensively.

There was no immediate response. Both Axel, and Pawaugun listened intently. There was a noise that was like a groan or a wheezing kind of a deep breath. It was followed by a haggard, rough kind of breathing. Then there was a slight groan.

"Wendell," Axel called again. "Is that you? Are you hurt?"

Axel could see the silhouette of the person's head look up. What little light that did get through, made whoever it was in the hut, eyes shine like something non-human.

Axel pulled back the lever to his rifle. "Wendell?" He called once again and then took a very cautious step forward. "Pawaugun, go get a lantern from inside so we kin see."

Pawaugun quickly turned and ran back to the cabin. Meanwhile, Axel stared intently in the dark supply hut. His eyes had almost become acclimated to the darkness. He was almost positive that he was looking at Wendell, but there was something else to Wendell. It was as if he had changed or was not completely Wendell. Hell, for all he knew it wasn't Wendell at all.

Finally, Pawaugun returned with the lit lantern and handed it to Axel. Axel took the lantern and held it up to light the hut. Pawaugun covered Axel with his rifle as they crept slowly further into the hut.

As the light grew, both men could finally see Wendell inside. He was naked and covered with flour, syrup, and other foods. They knew he made the mess had also eaten everything in the supply hut. Both men stood back in silence and shock. They noticed that his stomach wasn't even bloated and his skin grayish and pale. He was almost sepulchral. His eyes blazed like that of a crazed animal in the darkness, and yet something about them was empty and lifeless. A certain madness or sickness filled them, and yet a familiarity there was once Wendell's. His fingers and hands were ripped and bloodied from tearing open and smashing the containers that held the food. His mouth was the same way, from biting through the packaging and containers. He smiled, revealing a sharp, jagged set of animal-like teeth that made both men freeze in their tracks.

When they approached Wendell, they noticed a putrid stench permeating the shed. They noticed Wendell stunk. It wasn't an odor from not bathing recently. It was different. It was an odor of death and decay. As if, Wendell had died and was decomposing. It wasn't as bad as the night before, but it was like the smell that came from the Wendigo.

They also noticed his fingernails and toenails had grown longer and more jagged. He also had the beginnings of hair growth on his hands and feet. It looked like Wendell was changing into something other than a human being.

Pawaugun wanted to leave, badly. Pawaugun did not want to be there another day and neither did he. He knew that Wendell was becoming whatever it was that they had faced last night. Axel didn't want to end up like Pastor Radler.

"Wendigo," uttered Pawaugun.

Axel turned to him and yet still kept an eye on Wendell. "We're leaving," he said softly. "Let's get outta here."

"We go now?" Pawaugun asked. "Good weather not last long. Another storm come."

Wendell just sat there, staring and madly grinning. Too tired to really move, just yet.

He was hungry again, and the men smelled like meat to him.

Both men quickly exited the shed, with Axel backing out of the door last. "Him Wendigo, now," Pawaugun said to Axel, as they got further away from the cabin. "He eat us if we stay. We not stay. Not safe here."

Axel, not knowledgeable on Native American legends, shook his head and agreed.

He knew they had to leave or they were in grave danger. He figured that they had about a good hour or so, if they were lucky, before Wendell might try to follow them. That was if, he went through the food in the cabin.

Once they were a few miles away and up on a distant ridge that overlooked the cabin, the two men turned and took one last glance at the cabin. Then they saw it, the naked figure of what was once Wendell, leave the cabin in the snow and head towards the woods, shrieking like the creature they heard the night before.

"Him go away from us," Pawaugun said.

"I think he's headed towards Jack Beauchamp's camp," Axel said, matter-of-factly. "Let's get outta here. Maybe, we can come back with some help later."

Both men knew there was little they could do now, by themselves, as they headed back to town. Their main concern was getting back to town and to safety.

The shrieks they heard in the distance were from someone they once knew. Someone who had become a creature with an endless appetite.

As the snow returned, Wendell found himself just inside the woods near Jack Beauchamp's camp that night. He watched, naked and in seclusion as the men were moving about in the camp, doing chores and fixing supper.

He did not feel the cold. Wendell was famished like he had never been before. His eyes filled with tears, of an endless hunger as he smelled food cooking. Real cooked food.

That, and the smell of man. Both would do nicely, he thought, to try and satisfy his hunger. Both were the same to him.

Slowly, Wendell moved closer to the camp.

His ravenous, eternal hunger possessing him.

The Ghost of Tom

Have you seen the ghost of Tom?
Long white bones with the rest all gone (Have you seen the ghost of Tom?)
Ooo-oo-oo-oo-oo-oo-ooh (Long white bones with the rest all gone)
Wouldn't it be chilly with no skin on? (Ooo-oo-oo-oo-oo-oo-ooh)

-Children's song

It all started when our cousin Tom passed away. After getting what he called a pretty good buzz at a party and carrying on with his wife, he died in his sleep. He had been a good guy, even if he did occasionally do things in excess. He had been a party animal in his younger days. He always offered to help when we needed it, fun to be around, told a lot of bad jokes, played numerous practical jokes and pretty much spoke his mind, so you always know where he stood on things. He lived a good and full life, not to mention a happy one.

It is still hard to believe he is gone; we were all pretty close. In fact, I shared the same first name. Our mothers had us about the same time, shared the same hospital room after delivery, so that was partly it. So, in a sense we had always been a little closer than the others were.

Story goes, the lucky bastard died in his sleep after having sex with his wife. He always said that was the way he wanted to go. He said it sure beat getting hit by a Mack truck or dying of cancer. And he did have cancer once. He always joked he would have come and gone in the same night. And well…luckily for him, he did.

The day of the showing was nice. The type of summer day that he always enjoyed. A nice, sunny, warm day. Then again, he always said God shined on him throughout his whole life. Why should today be any different?

Like all funerals, the whole family turned out. That included his immediate family, wife, kids, grandkids, brother, in-laws, cousins, second, third, and fourth cousins, friends, old co-workers, acquaintances and others who knew and loved him. We had grandparents who had ten kids and they all averaged three kids each and we all averaged three and so on and so on.

Putting it bluntly, there was a hell of a crowd there. The funeral home had broken out all the extra chairs that it had on hand and it still wasn't enough. There was standing room only.

Wall to wall people.

Different groups of teary-eyed people offering their condolences to his wife and kids, laughing, shaking their heads and talking about Tom. Many were just reminiscing about him with the more memorable and funny stories. Believe me there were plenty. Like his streaking down Dequindre and 13 Mile on the night of his bachelor party, driving through a McDonald's naked and asking for Big Macs with extra sauce, farting next to a local politician and blaming him for it, mooning a cop on New Year's Eve of 1979, getting drunk in a bar, pouring mustard on himself and yelling "I'm the goddamn mustard man" and so on. You get the idea, the man had fun. And, a lot of it. Sometimes too much.

You could basically catch parts of sentences people were saying like "That crazy…" or "I can't believe it…" or "He was a good guy…" and "He always said what he thought…didn't stab anybody in the back…always helped out…he had a lot of fun in life…"

Sentiments we all shared about the man.

When somebody first approached the casket they were greeted with a pretty unusual sight. He was dressed in his favorite blue jeans, an ugly blue Hawaiian shirt, tennis shoes, with a loosened three stooges tie. He seemed to have a bit of a grin or smirk on his face, like he had heard or knew of a joke and he was the only one in on it. Beside him was his Detroit Tiger baseball cap that he had gotten signed many years ago by Hall of Famer Al Kaline. He also had two sports cards of Kaline and Gordie Howe his two favorite athletes of all time. He also had an old t-shirt with Rod Serling on it draped in the casket.

"That sonofabitch…" my brother, Jim said. "He's got that same expression he had when he let a bad fart near us and nobody realized it was him."

"He died a happy man," said Tom's brother Tim. "I hope I'm that lucky."

Jim went on to comment how he had some of his favorite items in the casket with him, which basically was old Detroit Tiger and Red Wing stuff. It was a tradition we did since our grandmother passed away back in 1986. Little things that we knew were part of what the person liked and was proud of.

"I see, the Tigers and Red Wings are represented," said another cousin, Bob, as he walked up next to us. "I see he hasn't got any Lions stuff in there with him."

"Shit, you know he wouldn't be caught dead with Lions stuff in there," Tim said. "He hated the Lions. He enjoyed heckling them when they lost. They still haven't won a Super Bowl. He was right about them."

"Hell, I remember that game that he gave up on them," I said. "It was 1970 and the day after Christmas and most of us came back over grandma's to help do something in the basement with the uncles. They finished working on it by game time and we sat and ate leftovers. A few of you weren't around. Anyways, Tommy bet Uncle Bunky that the Lions would win. He had just earned $45. Bill Munson came in and threw an interception late when they were driving on the Cowboys and they lost 5-0, on a field goal and a safety. There was a bonfire outside and he took all of his Lions wear and even his football cards and hats and burned it all. He never cheered them on again. In fact, he hated the Lions ever since. If he watched them it was to make fun of them and their ineptness."

"That's right," Tim said. "He said that if they ever won anything it would be the end of the world."

"We oughtta put a Lions jersey or pennant in there with him, as a last joke," said Jim.

"I don't know, man." Tim said. "He'll probably haunt yer ass. And I don't believe in that shit. But he would haunt yer ass."

"That would be great!" laughed Bob. "I owe him big time for the inflatable doll prank he pulled on me, twenty years ago."

"Yeah, and I owe him for sending that fat, ugly stripper to my 50th birthday. I swear to God, she looked like Grosie O'Connell, or whatever that bitch's name was."

Just then two more cousins, Bob and John, who were brothers walked up. Jim filled them in on what he was thinking about doing. John passed; he had been a marine and just didn't like the idea of pulling jokes on the dear departed as he called it. He said it didn't seem right. Besides, he said Tom hadn't pulled any worse jokes on him than he pulled back. He didn't feel the time was right.

Bob was neither here nor there on it. He thought it would be great if Jim and our other cousin Bob did it, but he didn't want to really be involved.

"What about you?" Bob asked.

"I don't think so," I responded. "I was asked to speak on behalf of the cousins, so I better not."

"Do you have a Lions pennant or Jersey? Jim asked Bob.

"Nope."

"There's a sporting good store just down the road, I'll go in half with you on some Lions stuff, if you want to do it," Jim said.

"Deal."

So Jim and Bob discreetly left the funeral home to put their plans in motion, while the rest of us mingled and visited with each other.

Within fifteen minutes they were back with some generic Lions jersey with a number twenty-four on it.

"You guys don't think it will bother the family do you?" I asked.

Tim spoke up for the first time. "Hard to tell, just be careful when doing it," he cautioned. "I don't want his wife and kids upset."

"We will just shove it down under him or something," Jim said. "Besides, we're all pallbearers and we're the only ones who know about it."

Jim took the jersey and placed it just under Tom's leg in the casket, without anybody hardly noticing. He stood there nonchalant still talking to Bob, Tim and myself. A few seconds later a real bad smell permeated the air near us. It was as if somebody had cracked one off.

"Godamn, Tim, did you have to shit your pants?!" Bob said, with a look of disgust.

"Hey, I didn't," Tim said, "I thought it was one of you."

We all looked at each other, figuring somebody wasn't telling the truth about which one of us farted.

"It was probably Tom," said Jim. "Cracking one off for old times' sake for us to remember him by. Man, next to some of the uncles he was one of the worst."

I looked back at Tom, and could have almost sworn that his grin was a little more like a smirk.

We then walked away and started talking to other friends and family members for the next few minutes about our cousin and how everybody was doing.

I really don't know who noticed it first, but I was talking to one of Tom's oldest and best friends, Mike, when I happened to look over and saw a female friend of Tom's picking up something off of the floor. It was the Lions jersey.

I walked over and explained what it was and why it was there. She laughed and handed me the jersey.

"Hey, what's going on? Jim came back up and asked.

"Somebody found it on the floor," I replied.

"Somebody must have removed it," Jim said.

"I don't know," I said. "I didn't see anything or anybody."

Jim took the jersey and refolded it and put it back in the casket underneath the pillow underneath Tom's head. It was out of sight and mind.

"There,' he said. "It's in a different spot and nobody will be the wiser."

Just then Bob came up. "What are you doing?" he asked.

"It was on the floor and I'm just putting it back," Jim answered.

"How's it get out in the first place?" Bob asked

"Beats the hell outta me," Jim said.

Jim and Bob walked away, but continued to keep an eye on the casket, to make sure they could see who really removed the Lions jersey.

I knew it wasn't me, because I was trying to figure out what I was going to say and I wasn't much of a speaker. I also knew it wasn't Tim, because he was busy with family members and helping do things for Tom's family at the funeral.

Jim soon went out to have a cigarette and Bob had to take a leak. When they got back in, they found the Lions jersey back on the floor next to the casket. There was also that bad fart smell nearby.

"Seriously," Jim said to me, about the jersey, "are you fucking with us?"

"No, Jim, I don't have time," I said.

Bob looked skeptical about my reply, but did not say anything. "If you're not, then somebody is," he finally mumbled.

"Yeah, but, who?" Jim asked.

"I couldn't tell you," I responded. "I don't have a clue."

We continued to visit with family and friends. During that time we all kept our eye on the casket to make sure that nobody was taking anything out of the casket. A few people put mementos in it, and kissed Tom's forehead, but that was it. They walked away without any clue as to there being a Lions jersey in the casket.

By nine p.m. the showing was winding down for the evening and people were slowing shuffling out. Jim went back to check on the Lions jersey to see if it was still there.

"What the fu…" he said as he lifted up the pillow to see, the jersey was gone. "Where in the hell is it?"

Bob, Tim and myself walked back over to the casket.

"It's gone again?" Bob asked.

"It's probably Tom's ghost, throwing the jersey out," laughed Tim. "You know he hated the Lions."

Jim finally looked behind the casket and found the jersey between the casket and the wall on the floor.

"Here it is," Jim announced. "I will put it down near his feet this time and I will stay right here until just about everybody is gone."

Jim complained later, that the fart odor he smelled earlier was back again as well.

We had all been to enough of these things to know that most of us never really left on time. It was as if everyone felt compelled to stay. By five after nine we were finally winding our way to the doors. Jim hung back near the casket to make sure nobody removed the jersey. Finally, the funeral home attendants came and closed up the casket, with the jersey still inside with Tom. The last of us left at ten after nine, into a nice warm peaceful night.

Fitting, yet sad.

Tomorrow would be tough. We all knew it well. We had come to regard it as the big send-off or the big show. The actual funeral itself.

The next day came and like clockwork we were all there early. As soon as we were let into the parlor, the first thing we saw was that damned Detroit Lions jersey on the floor next to the casket.

"So what are you going to do now?" Bob asked.

"I'm going to put the fucker back in there, just before it gets closed for the last time," Jim answered.

The funeral service was beautiful. It brought tears of both sadness and laughter to just about everybody's eyes. A few of us got up and told our stories and shared our memories of the deceased. It was one of the best, and sad to say, funniest funerals I had ever been to. Four of us as speakers and we all pretty much nailed the eulogy to a 'T". We knew the family loved it.

Everyone paid their final respects with the immediate family being last.

Just afterwards, Jim placed the jersey back into the casket, down near Tom's feet, before the funeral home staff closed the casket. "It's now his jersey forever," he announced.

Bob laughed. "Remind me not to tell you what I don't like," he said.

"I think we're getting a little old for this shit, anyway," I said.

So, we loaded the casket into the hearse, got in our vehicles and headed towards the cemetery in our long funeral procession. Once there, we carried the casket to the grave site and lowered it onto the straps that would lower it into its final resting place.

"Okay, everybody please take your places so we can start the last of the service,' the Funeral Director said.

The minister told us to bow our heads in prayer and recited the Lord's prayer. The service was concluded and we were on our way back to our vehicles that were parked nearby, so we could head to the luncheon afterward. As we stood there talking for a moment one of the funeral home people approached us.

"I found this on the ground next to the casket," the Funeral Home Attendant said. "It's a Lions jersey. Somebody must have dropped it."

Jim's eyes were as big as saucers. His mouth was open and he was in shock. I don't think I had ever seen him in his seventy-odd years this shocked.

I took the jersey. "Thanks," I said as the attendant left and I handed Jim the jersey. "You want to give it back again?"

"Yeah, do it, Jim," Bob interjected. "Throw it in on top."

Jim just nodded. The casket was being lowered and he threw the jersey in. He told the cemetery attendants it was alright, his cousin told him to do it. The problem was the cousin who told him wasn't Tom.

Tim walked over to us. "I told you he hated the Lions," he said.

"Well, I didn't see anybody remove it," said Bob, trying to figure it out. "We were the only sonsofbitches who knew it was in there. I didn't see anything, and now I'm damn glad I didn't. This is unbelievable."

We all agreed.

We then left for the luncheon where we spent much of the day talking and fondly reminiscing about him.

None of us still know what to think or believe.

I just think back to what Tom said. "He wouldn't be caught dead in a Lions jersey, or with any Lions stuff."

True to his word, he wasn't.

One day later, I got a call from Jim who had to tell me that he and his wife went home, after staying at our place after the funeral. It turns out that once they got home, they found a dirt-covered Lions jersey hanging over their dining room chair. It still had the price tag, from where Jim and Bob had bought it before the funeral. Jim's wife was cussing him out for leaving his dirty outdoor work clothes on the chair and not in the hamper. He also said that there was a really bad smell, like a really bad fart in his house. They had to open the windows to clear it out.

Jim threw the jersey away and never played another joke on anybody, especially a dead man.

I don't know if any of us believe in ghosts or not, but I know none of us are ruling anything out. I just know that when I watched another potential Lions quarterback throw another interception on what appeared to be a fluke, during their first pre-season game, I could not help but wonder if that was Tom heckling his least favorite football team from the great beyond.

Sometimes when we still get together, we try to rationalize what really happened. We wonder whether maybe somebody was playing a joke on all of us, or if it really was the ghost of Tom. Hard telling, but one thing's for sure the Lions still suck and according to Tom, doomsday is still some time away because of that fact.

I think one day we will all find out…

P.E.T.Z.

TO: CENTRAL COMMAND
FROM: MIDWEST SECTOR; ALPENA, MICHIGAN
CAPTAIN CORBIN HEARNS, 2nd AIRBORNE RANGERS
SUBJECT: COMBAT MISSION REPORT AND ASSESSMENT

Immediately upon our arrival at Alpena County Regional Airport, we came in contact with the hostiles. In spite of air support from Cobra helicopters, twenty-three managed to breech the perimeter.

Due to our superior firepower, coupled with the targets' slow movements, they were easily dispatched. Lt. Thomas and 1st platoon finished off the remnants and the partially mutilated undead with shotguns and machetes.

Once the perimeter was re-secured and we completely unloaded with all of our necessary equipment, General Simmons briefed us on Operation Hammer & Anvil. This operation involved securing of Alpena and the surrounding region.

Our unit brigade was split into six companies and they in turn were split into six platoons. The Army had great foresight in attaching civilians and locals residents with us as guides. This helped immensely. We made our sweep from the east on Highway 32, while others made theirs from north and south on US 23.

No sooner had we began our sweep, that we made contact with the hostiles. We quickly dispatched them with 50-caliber fire from our armored vehicles and air support. We counted twenty more. Half of the bodies were elderly men and women and the rest were young children. I sent senior NCOs with full squads to make sure they were completely dispatched

*A personal note: The men took no pleasure in this. Even after all the combat with the undead we had encountered, the termination of elderly, women and the young still bothered a lot of the men in the unit, though it was necessary. The men will need some major R & R and possibly even some counseling, to deal with all of this. To quote Lieutenant Randal. "One of those reminded me of my third grade teacher, and for all I know it could have been."

We continued our trek down Highway 32 and encountered fewer targets. The first group would prove to be the largest all day. The fact that this is a popular hunting region did not hurt. We ran into residents and other civilians who helped us complete the sweep.

Some were posing for photos with the dispatched undead by standing on them. We tried to dissuade them from doing so out of tastefulness and for safety reasons. Our efforts were only mildly successful.

By 12:00 hours of July 31 Alpena was considered secure and free of the undead and infected. Overall, the brigade suffered four casualties. Three from infection by bites, resulting in termination, and one accidentally shot by a terrified civilian.

August 1, 2012. 06:15. Alpena County Regional Airport

We received orders to proceed to Hillman, a town thirty minutes to the west to complete Operation

Hammer & Anvil. Once again, we had locals and residents to act as guides and assistants to us.

On Highway 32 we encountered twenty more targets and promptly took them out with 50-caliber fire from our vehicles. SOP called for the deployment of full squads to make sure they were completely eradicated.

As we arrived to the outskirts of town, we were approached by locals and asked to stop at the VFW hall. The convoy stopped there and formed a defensive grouping at the intersection of Highway 32 and State Street.

We were informed by the local VFW post commander, Jim Hadley that some of the more enterprising youth of the town led a large group of the infected individuals into a nearby ballpark. Once the undead were secured inside, they sealed off the entrances, thus transforming the park into a large holding pen.

At 07:50, the commander informed us of a problem. While the ball field held some one hundred plus dead individuals, a radical group similar to P.E.T.A. had come in and taken control of the site. They had beaten several locals, thus hospitalizing them. At last count there were approximately twenty of these activists. The radical group is called P.E.T.Z. or the People for the Ethical Treatment of Zombies.

According to the post commander they had come in via a small airport just northwest of the town near Road 451. One of the biggest causes of the controversy was that one forth of the people in this group were citizens of Hillman and known by most of the civilian population. He pondered whether any of them were completely sane

At 08:30 we proceeded forward, after deploying our vehicles around the ball field with the heavy machine guns trained on its occupants and their protectors.

Once in position, the VFW post commander, myself, and my two senior lieutenants, Christie and Gifford, approached P.E.T.Z.'s leader. I introduced myself and my men and she introduced herself as Pat Shelley, Midwest leader of P.E.T.Z.

I asked Ms. Shelley about her purpose and motivations for her actions.

Her response to us was that the undead were people too and deserved to have the same rights as the living. She believed, we had graduated from killing animals to people and just because they were infected did not give us an excuse to do so.

I replied it was because of the infected that there had been a holocaust that had taken years to eradicate. Many innocent people died and suffered during this time. I explained, we had nearly completed our objective when she and her group had gotten in the way.

Her response irritated the VFW post commander who had been a combat veteran. Commander Hadley said this was outrageous and that if he could, he would kill them (the radicals) right now.

Ms. Shelley reached for her revolver, to which I reminded her that our 50-caliber machine guns were trained on her and the undead and I stated I had no qualms about mopping up her remains. She then stopped.

I calmed down the post commander and told Ms. Shelley that she and her group had until 13:00 hours to cease and desist or I would be forced to open fire with no regards to their safety.

She replied that we had three hours to leave or she would release another holocaust upon "us goddamned people." She announced her plans to the residents that were present as well.

The post commander had to be escorted away by Lieutenants Gifford and Christie before he did something rash or drastic. He told her that if given the chance he would love an excuse to "shoot her in her ugly goddamned face and sleep peacefully having done so." The rest of the residents and locals were not thrilled with her plans either.

I then asked how many of the undead the commander had penned up in the ballpark. He replied about a hundred give or take.

August 1, 2012. 11:30. Hillman, Michigan.

The VFW post commander organized a town meeting between the gas station and Jaques Family Restaurant. We were not invited, but knew they were making their own plans. We witnessed the locals participate in some kind of oath ceremony with their hands raised led by a Montmorency Sheriff's Department officer.

I called my officers and NCOs together to prepare for the ultimatum deadline. Before we could finish, the post commander returned and explained his situation. He wanted us to let the ultimatum pass and then do whatever was necessary. Despite our hesitancy to shoot civilians, he knew we were given emergency discretion to do so through Federal action.

Commander Hadley also explained that townspeople would handle the radical group and its members if we would take care of the infected. That was agreeable to us, since they had all been deputized by their earlier oath and were allowed to dispatch the P.E.T.Z. group any way they saw fit.

While we waited in position, the townspeople brought us food and water from the local restaurants. Some of the local ladies struck up conversations and flirted with younger members of our unit when they were relieved during the wait. The officers and NCOs felt it was safe to let a third of the men take a break every hour, since we had the support of the locals nearby.

I did not chastise them for this breach.

August 1, 2012. 13:45 Hillman, Michigan.

Fifteen minutes before the deadline, most of the townspeople, armed with shotguns and hunting rifles, took position near our vehicles, fixing on individual P.E.T.Z. member targets. At 13:50 two of the radicals deserted the group and ran to our position, where they were escorted away and then arrested by the sheriff's department.

This appeared to have irritated Ms. Shelley since she ordered her people to unseal the entrances. The townspeople opened fire on the group, immediately killing half. The other half were wounded and fell victim to the undead. After a few minutes they too became the undead.

I gave the order to open fire with the 50-caliber machine guns, thus decimating the undead.

Almost as soon as she had fallen victim to the infected, Ms. Shelley became one of them as well. The post commanded dispatched her with a shotgun to the head.

He then commented "I told you I'd shoot you in the head you goddamn ugly bitch, and I'll sleep goddamn good too."

Our firepower had been so overwhelming that no shotguns or machetes were needed to complete the mission. We then disposed of the corpses by burning them.

August 3, 2012. 09:00. Hillman, Michigan.

The next two days were mop-up operations in the area. The town invited us to a celebration to take place on August 4.

Upon hearing the announcement from Central Command that the war was over and all of the undead had been eradicated, I gave permission to the men to take part in the town festivities. With your permission, I will participate as well.

On a personal note: I'm pleased with the outcome of events and the demise of Ms. Shelley.

Respectfully,
Captain Corbin Hearns
Easy Co.US 2nd Rangers

TO: CAPTAIN CORBIN HEARNS, 2ND AIRBORNE RANGERS
FROM: CENTRAL COMMAND
DATE:
SUBJECT: COMBAT MISSION REPORT AND ASSESSMENT

Enjoy! You've earned it.

GENERAL NORMAN PATTON: Your men have done excellent work and I'm putting you and your unit in for meritorious conduct and multiple citations. Please list a name of those who should be singled out. Congratulations on a job well done…

Echo Bluff

So let me tell you all about Echo Bluff before you take over, after I retire as head groundskeeper here. As you know, Echo Bluff is a sprawling 400 acres of rolling hills, greens and fairways. It was built in 1928. It was built by Judge Herbert Brennamen, businessman Charles Walker and lawyer Irwin Rosen. The course is historic and considered a kind of area landmark in back in the day.

As you also probably know and have heard, we have had our share of luminaries and famous visitors here.

Back in 1954 President Eisenhower visited and played nine holes of golf here. I guess it was quite an event.

Prior to the presidency we had then, Michigan congressman Gerald Ford golfed here a couple of times. Yes, he did trip over something too. There were also governors "Soapy" Williams, Romney, Milliken. Not to mention the Dodges', the Kresge's and several other business movers and shakers.

Hell, we even had Charlton Heston stop here briefly in the 1950's and Clint Eastwood a couple of years ago.

So, we've had our share of famous names here. Some were very nice and others, well, calling them assholes would have been a major compliment. I could tell you a few stories later. If you press me on which ones are good or bad, I will only nod or shake my head as to who is who.

Also back in the day and before all of the newer and more prestigious courses we had a couple of the majors here. You've probably seen the photos in the lobby with all of the past golf greats.

Echo Bluff has always been kind of unique, with its own style and atmosphere.

Unique, different and timeless.

That is Echo Bluff in a nutshell.

Just to give you an example, the original groundskeeper's quarters were, with the exception of the roof, built without ever using a single nail. It was all peg and tongue in groove. It was so unique, every owner since this place was built has refused to use this building for storage. It has been only been used for rentals, meetings and special occasions. This place is almost as well maintained and cared for as the golf course.

The building is on some historical registries.

All of this is pretty much public knowledge and you probably already know that.

Now, I need to fill you in on the little known or different history here at Echo Bluff.

This is unspoken and little-known history, that only a few know of and those who do never really like to speak of, especially in public.

It is the kind of history that nobody likes to talk about and even fewer believe. Nonetheless, it is part of Echo Bluff. You could say it is the dark underside of things here.

I will start with the builders of Echo Bluff. First off, this property had gone unsold for a year before they bought it up for a song. In spite of this successful venture, the builders were not without misfortune.

Judge Brennamen who was known as a "law and order" judge who showed little mercy to most of the defendants who went before his bench. About a year later, he was basically assassinated by the mob. It was strongly suspected to have been the Purple Gang, because he had given stiff sentences to a couple of their friends and colleagues, but it could not be proven.

Charles Walker took charge after the judge's death. Unfortunately, that too was short-lived because the stock market crash of 1929 ruined him. He was one of those people that you heard about jumping from office building windows because they had lost everything. I guess his wife took her own life too shortly afterward because she had gotten used to that lifestyle as well.

Irwin Rosen who was the last one left of the tree, immediately sold off his portion. He believed they were cursed or something after his partner's deaths and wanted to get out. It was said that he went to Europe after that, finally settling in Holland. When the war broke out, it was believed he had been executed by the Nazi's who were implementing their Final Solution against Jews.

So, he too met with tragedy. Albeit much later.

Eventually it was sold off to the current owners.

There have been other events here that have been strange and somewhat uncanny things that have happened here.

Some fifty years ago, according to one of the "old timers" that I replaced a long time missing person's body was found in a wooded area near the ninth hole. He too was thought to have been a victim of the Purple Gang.

In 1964 there was a Halloween party here and a couple went out on the green, feeling a tad bit drunk and horny. People thought they had left to find a no-tell motel somewhere. Unfortunately they were found dead out on the golf course. Their faces seemed contorted in shock and horror. There were no wounds or traces on their bodies explaining why or how they died. It was all hushed up, and after a short time it quietly went away.

It was one of those long forgotten and unexplained mysteries.

But, the strangest event or thing had to do with the area near Hole Number Three. It's the one near that old abandoned road. We use that road as an occasional service drive when we need to do heavy duty work. It's basically a well-maintained two-track, but it was once a road that people used before more and better side roads were built.

Anyway, for years people always claimed to have heard kids playing and a school bell. These people said they heard them screaming, hollering, and yelling, as if playing outside.

The only problem was there were no kids playing anywhere.

There wasn't a school within two miles of here and the closest neighborhood is by some pretty thick woods. So, the acoustics are dulled. On top of that, there was no neighborhood of any size until the late 1950's.

Still we had complaints.

These dated back to the very opening of the park.

In fact, the very first one to hear the sounds of children was Irwin Rosen himself. From what I was told by a couple of the "old-timers" he heard the sounds of children. This really disturbed him. It bothered him so much, that he would never play golf there again. I was told he never really ventured out on the golf course again, at least when he was alone.

There were countless others. But the next person of any notoriety to complain about this, or in this case have an event was an up-and-coming professional golfer named Mark Scherzen.

From what I heard and have read, he was an intense golfer and fiercely competitive. He was so competitive that he really did not have much to do with a lot of the other professionals, and they him. He wasn't much liked. It seems he had a fiery and hair-trigger temper. Even when practicing Scherzen was known to lose his temper and even punch people for interrupting his practices. Anyway, when practicing for an upcoming tournament that was to be held here, he complained that he was distracted by a lot of loud, screaming kids that were disrupting his concentration. Apparently it became so bad to him that he threw his golf clubs and even attacked a groundskeeper. He basically had a nervous breakdown and needed to be physically restrained.

I don't think he ever golfed again.

Then a few years ago, a lady school teacher named Judy Sheppard and two friends told of how they could hear children playing nearby, but could not figure out where it came from. They just continued playing on figuring that it had to be coming from somewhere nearby.

There a lot of others that were just like that. Only a few had an effect on people like they did Rosen and Scherzen.

It wasn't until and old guy named Jess Carver entered the picture. Jess was lived in the house his parents had built that was right next to the golf course. He had been here long before the golf course was built. As it was, he was practically a hermit, keeping to himself. But it was after Scherzen went nuts that he broke his silence and filled the people who hired me in on the history and lore of the area.

According to those who told me, Old Jess said part of the area had always been a bit of a mystery. There was an area he and his parents once suspected of being a grave for a couple of Native Americans. There was no proof, and he was no longer sure of where it was, but there had been a kind of rock formation that was clearly man-made.

While this seemed inconsequential at the time, Old Jess was said to have told the "old-timers" that this site was in the area of Hole Number Three. On top of that, back in 1920 there was a one-room school house built where Hole Number Three is. The old abandoned road was what led to it. It was the Echo Bluff School House.

Anyway, on May 17, 1927, the teacher named Helen Blakeslee and her class of 12 were killed when the school was blown up with them in it. It seems that a former suitor named Albert Buttermaker was still very angry about being jilted or rejected by her for another man named Frank Sullivan. From what Old Jess told the guys, the school was blown up just after the morning bell.

When pressed on how he knew this, Old Jess said he was supposed to be in class but, due to his chores, he was late as were two other friends, George Stenner and Henry Jones. He said they were all a few hundred yards away when they heard the school blow up. According to the guys, he said they could see the debris from explosion in the sky ahead of them.

Anyway, I guess old Albert Buttermaker hung himself in a tree near the school as well, thus making it a multiple murder-suicide.

It seems that it is always on May 17, when people hear the sounds of children and a school bell. The guys retraced the all of the complaints that were recorded and discovered this fact. Somehow, they were able to find that was when Irwin Rosen first heard them as well.

The property had the school had been on was left vacant after that tragedy. It wasn't until the men who wanted to put golf course here that the property was bought. According to Old Jess, The builders being outsiders and not from around here, didn't realize what had really happened here. I don't think it would have made any difference to the men who built Echo Bluff.

The reason this is so forgotten is an even bigger and more tragic event happened in Michigan the very next day on May 18 with the Bath School Massacre that killed over 40 people, with 38 of those being kids and injuring more than 50 other people. The irony was that both men killed themselves.

According to the guys, Old Jess told them the new school was built about three miles away. He said every May 17 for years he would hear children playing out there and the school bell. At first he thought they were haunting him for not being with them when it happened. But then after a while, he said that he realized that wasn't it at all.

Old Jess died in 2005. Nobody was quite sure how old he really was, but we figured about 90. The surviving "old-timers" and myself attended his funeral. The golf course bought up his adjoining property soon afterwards and razed the house.

I guess they wanted the history and lore surrounding this forgotten as well. I guess I cannot blame them in a way, since it is not good for business.

Sadly, the Echo Bluff School tragedy was a forgotten moment in history, overshadowed by an even bigger and more terrible one.

Except when you're golfing on May 17 and near Hole Number Three.

So, now let me tell you about some of our regulars who golf here.

SAND TRAP

He stood quietly, admiring the neatly-trimmed and manicured lawn and fairways of the golf course as the early morning sunlight greatly enhanced its natural beauty. The landscape was magnificent, with a nice mixture or trees, bushes, and grassy areas.

To him it was almost heaven.

Then again, golf had always been his escape and respite. It had always been his way to deal with the pressures of his job, his wife when she was nagging and unhappy as well as the demands of his being a father of three kids.

Whenever the demands of daily life became too much or unbearable, golf was his salvation and his way to deal with them. While he did not want to admit it and probably never would, he enjoyed golfing more than spending time with his wife and kids. Golf was a continuous point of contention between them.

He was so into the sport, that in a store like Carl's Golfland, he was treated like the Norm Peterson character from the television series *Cheers*. Almost all of the employees knew his name and said it every time he came in.

Now he was in his element. Away from the claptrap and distractions the problems that everyday life offered.

He stood studying the terrain on how to do his next shot.

It had been the same routine for each hole. Hit the ball to the next hole, size up the distance and terrain, decide which club to use, crouch down and decide how much force to use on the ball. His routine had been set since the first hole and nothing was changing that now.

His wife had told him that he put more thought and consideration into a golf shot than he ever did with his kids on a daily basis. While it was probably true, he figured he was entitled to since he earned the money that paid for almost everything. He felt he had earned that right.

He deserved his "me time."

This was the first time that he had golfed at Mystery Hills. It did not bother him in the least that it had once been a landfill. He was quite impressed by how different it looked and all the changes that had taken place. He thought the developers had done an excellent job of turning a vacant piece of land filled with all kinds of junk into the current golfer's Eden it was now.

Even though he had heard a few stories and some talk about the area near the thirteenth hole he paid it little attention. He totally ignored one groundskeeper saying there was something wrong with that holes sand trap area and while he couldn't see it he could feel it.

Talk is cheap, he figured. *The world is filled with gossip and stories about all kinds of things*, he figured.

The fact that a couple of people came up missing after visiting this particular golf course fell on his own deaf ears. It proved little or nothing.

One disappearance was that of alleged mob lawyer Tom Ginardo. He was a burly, strong looking man who prided himself on being his own bodyguard. He had gone ahead of some clients to retrieve his ball never to be seen again.

It was thought that he had run afoul of some mob bosses and knew way too much for their own good. Near as anybody could figure he ended up like Jimmy Hoffa, probably at the bottom of one of the lakes in cement, a mystery for all eternity.

The irony was how many mob hit victims had ended up here when the place was a landfill. That did not take into consideration any other criminal activity too numerous to mention.

The other person had been a businessman named Allen or something like it. He could not remember exactly. He was last seen where the mob lawyer was said to have last been seen. Supposedly, he had some financial problems and discrepancies. He too was last seen at the golf course and not heard from again.

None of that mattered as he was fixated on his golf game, even as he was getting closer to the thirteenth hole.

With the sparse amount of people at the golf course, he decided that he would take his time and enjoy the peace and quiet and solitude. He planned on enjoying every minute of his time out there.

The further he went along, the better and more invigorated he felt.

He stretched a bit and took a few practice swings as he tried to gauge how hard he needed to hit the ball. It wasn't the longest drive he had to make, but it was still a lengthy and somewhat challenging shot.

But that was what he enjoyed about golf. He relished its challenges.

And right now nothing else mattered. Not his wife, his kids, or even his job. They were but mere distractions to his game and enjoyment. None of those things were going to ruin his private outing. No sir. Not on this day.

He felt too good for that to happen.

As he continued sizing up his next shot, he tried to gauge the distance. He took some more practice swings before finally lining up to take his real swing.

Finally, he swung mightily at the ball, driving it towards the thirteenth holes green. Initially he thought he had a good swing, but quickly realized it was slicing.

The ball sliced towards the sand trap, landing dead center with a dull, unmoving and noiseless thud.

"*Shit!*" he thought, thoroughly disappointed at his worse stroke of the day.

After a bit, he figured if that was his worse stroke of the day, then he didn't have much to complain about. He was still under par. He got in his golf cart and drove to the sand trap. Once there, he got out and surveyed the situation. He spent a few minutes trying to figure out logistically and strategically.

He dreaded having to venture out into the sand trap. He always seemed to get sand in his shoes and he hated that. It was irritating. Irritating, because he could feel it the rest of the day.

But, he knew it was inevitable.

It was just a matter of when. He needed to think about how he was going to approach the ball.

Beneath the sand the creature was stirring. It felt the vibration of the ball landing in the sand trap. That usually meant prey was nearby and immanent. It sensed that where the ball landed its prey would follow it for no other reason than to retrieve it.

So it waited.

Knowing that it would soon feed.

It was ready to pounce the first chance it got.

Finally after a few minutes of figuring out which club to use and how hard to hit the ball, he approached the sand trap.

For a moment he hesitated. He thought about just leaving the ball for someone else and taking a Mulligan. He started to turn then stopped. "*To hell with it,*" he thought. He decided that he needed the challenge anyway. Finally, he began to stomp across the sand trap towards his ball.

Finally he was standing astride of his ball. He positioned himself to drive the ball on the green.

As he stood measuring the ball with his club, he felt a slight movement somewhere beneath the sands under his feet. At first he attributed it to the soft and shifting sands and ignored it as he continued to plan his next putt. He felt the movement again, this time a little stronger. Then again, this time even stronger. He moved a few feet and looked around.

Nothing.

Then when he lined up for his putt again, he felt the sand move under his feet again.

Soon the sand began to give way and he began to lose his balance. He fought hard to keep his footing and balance, but could not. He tried to move and stumbled into the sand.

Whatever was happening, he sensed that he had to get off the sand trap and began to crawl. As he crawled across the sand, two large mandibles came up through it. He tried to scream, but only managed to gasp.

He had trouble making any headway as he frantically tried to crawl to the edge of the sand trap. Before he could reach the edge, the mandibles had grabbed a hold of him by the legs and began to pull. He fought to get free of them, but was only dragged deeper into the sand.

Even with his heroic struggle to get away, he was waist deep in the middle of the sand trap. He fought in futility as he was dragged deeper into the sand. He was now breathing hard and crying out in pain and agony. Unfortunately, there was no one around to hear him.

Soon, only his head was above the sand as he was being pulled down into the depths of the sand trap, by the horrid, unseen beast.

Finally in one last great heave, he was pulled down below the sand.

Like the others, his disappearance and subsequent death would remain mystery.

The creature had feasted, and once again, it waited in its home.

The sand trap near the thirteenth hole.

For there was sure to be another golfer. There always was. That was just par for the course at this particular sand trap.

Inferno

Inside Dell's Dive, Preston Forrester sat nursing his whiskey on the rocks. Even though it had been almost twelve hours since he and his crew helped to extinguish the Burke Lumber Company fire, he still smelled of smoke and fire.

While the fire may have been long extinguished, the memory of it lingered, much like the smell of smoke that continued to surround him. Fortunately for the bar owners, there were very few other patrons in to notice the unmistakable aroma.

He finally drank down the 80 proof liquid, exhaling as the burning sensation he felt continued downward. While he felt he needed the drink after what he had been through, it offered feeble comfort at the moment.

"Could I get another, bartender?" he asked hoarsely, his voice still affected by the smoke, he had inadvertently inhaled.

While not totally effective, it was the only way he could deal with the memory of the fire. It was as if the fire had seared itself into his memory and soul.

As he took a sip from his second drink, he was joined by fellow fireman Russell "Rusty" Donaldson.

"How are you doing, Preston?" Russell asked as he patted Preston on the back and sat down next to him. "You going to be okay?"

Preston quietly nodded and took another sip of his drink. "I'm alright," he finally replied. "I'm just fucking peachy, can't you tell?"

"Sorry," Russell apologized. "I know you've been

through a lot. You've been through a real close call."

"Yeah," Preston muttered hoarsely.

"Yeah, we thought we almost lost you tonight, too," Russell continued. "Thank God we didn't. Bartender, can I get a Stroh's?"

"Yeah," Preston muttered again.

"The Chief wanted me to tell you to take an extra day if you needed it," Russell said. "He thought you could use it. So, how are you holding up?"

Preston nodded again and was staring straight ahead. "Thanks," he finally said. "I could use it."

"You sure you're alright?" Russell asked after taking a drink of his beer. "You seem a bit out of it."

Preston took a deep breath and then exhaled. After coughing, he finally cleared his throat a little. "It was tough," he finally admitted. "In fact, the whole ordeal was quite terrifying."

"Really?" Russell asked. "We've been in fires before and were separated or trapped for longer periods of time. How was this different?"

Preston took a large drink, then grimacing as he felt the whiskey burn on the way down. "It may have only been about fifteen minutes, but it was an entire lifetime too."

"I know," Russell agreed. "Every minute you're trapped can seem like an eternity."

"No, that's not what I mean," Preston explained. "It was nothing like that. It wasn't so much being trapped in a burning building but where I found myself."

"You were in the lower storage area, down a few steps, right?" Russell asked.

"No," Preston said. "I was in some kind of passageway."

"A passageway?" Russell asked confused. "To where?"

"To Hell," Preston snapped. "To Hell. I found a passageway to Hell."

"You've gotta be shittin' me!" Russell almost bellowed, in disbelief. "Are you sure it wasn't the inferno you were in?"

Preston looked at Russell with a dead-serious, no-nonsense look that seemed to pierce through him. "I shit you, not," he finally said. "It was hell."

"How can you be sure?" Russell asked, skeptically. "It could have been fumes from the paint and lacquer thinners in there."

"How can I be sure?" Preston said, repeating the question. "Well, Rusty, it's like this when I was trapped back there, I had been checking the office and then I saw another door."

"And that's when the interior wall collapsed and we lost sight of you," Russell added.

"Yeah," Preston continued. "At first it was pitch black in there and there were no lights to speak of. Anyway, I entered to see if it was clear. I stepped inside and fell down. After I fell I rolled a few feet. When I was able to get to my feet I saw light. Only it was all orange and yellow from burning flames that were all around.

"So what else did you see?" Russell asked, before drinking down his beer.

"There was all of this moaning and groaning," Preston answered. "No, it was worse than that. It was like some kind of tortured and painful moaning and groaning. It was all around and echoing. Like tortured souls and eternal pain. I could also hear all kinds of sinister and evil sounding laughing and insane cackling."

"So what did you do next?" Russell asked. "What happened?"

"At first I was frightened and also mesmerized, I guess," Preston admitted. "I could not move at first."

"That sounds reasonable," Russell said, as Preston finished off his drink and ordered another.

"I then heard some very agonizing moaning and groaning that was close by," Preston continued. "I turned around to see it was Warren Burmeister."

"You mean the old firefighter that was here in the 30's and 40's?" Russell asked. "What? No! Why did you see him? He was one of the old guard, for Chrissake."

Preston nodded. "I saw him," he said. "He was being tortured and prodded by a number of smaller demons. They were so involved in and enjoying what they were doing that they ignored me. It was then I realized why I was seeing this. Warren had committed murder many years ago and I let him get away with it."

"What are you saying?" Russell asked, startled by the accusation. "That Warren Burmeister committed murder? What in God's name are you talking about?"

Preston nodded, took a drink and then exhaled. "It's true," he finally said, spitting out the words. I hired in after getting back from the war and Warren, well he was already one of the respected veterans in the firehouse.

"Didn't he hire in during the 20's?" Russell asked.

"Yeah," Preston replied after taking a drink. "He knew his shit and was a great firefighter. But the man had his demons too. Or should I say his dislikes."

"What do you mean?" Russell asked.

"The man hated blacks," Preston answered directly. "He was a bigot in the worst way. Blacks, Indians, Orientals, Mexicans, Italians, Greeks, you name it. He hated them and had a name for them. A couple of other guys in the house, John Blake and Tom Morgan gave him Hell for it, but they knew it was kind of a lost cause with Warren."

"Wow and he never got in any trouble over it?" Russell asked.

"You're pretty young and this is only your third year here, but things were different back then," Preston explained, before taking another sip of his drink. "Things were a lot different back then. Some guys we knew had no problem with going on "coon hunts" where they beat the shit out of them. Most of the guys had some kind of prejudices. Especially, the ones coming back from the war. There was an intense hatred for the Japs, but that was understandable because we had just fought the rotten fuckers in a war. But, while the guys might have had their prejudices, they kept them in check when it came to saving lives. We were there to help. That was our job. But not Warren. That man was racist, mean and hateful to minorities."

Russell ordered another beer. "What does this have to do with murder, though?" he asked.

"He let people die," Preston answered. "He could have saved them, but let them die. All because they were black."

"Man, that's bad," Russell commented. "He was really that bad?"

"Uh,huh," Preston grunted. "He was. He had more names for black people than any other race. Niggers, spooks, raisins, you name it he called them that."

"Wow, that sounds like my grandfather," Russell observed. "So what happened, exactly?"

"A black couple, named the Smith's bought a house just inside the Waterford, near the Pontiac border," Charlie continued to explain. "Which considering the times was not exactly kosher with the generally white population at the time, if you know what I mean."

"What happened?" Russell asked. "Were they burned out? He wasn't one of the guys who did it was he?"

"No, I don't think so," Preston answered. "But, I

think he knew who did. I always had my suspicions."

"Bartender, can I get another?" Russell asked. "That makes sense. So then what?"

"We had to answer the call," Preston continued. "When we got to the house, Warren was in no hurry to get in and help. He took his own sweet-ass time putting on his gear. When we finally get in we head upstairs. I took one end of the hallway and Warren took another. Anyway, I check two rooms, finding nothing. So, I headed down to Warren, as he was checking two rooms. It was then I thought I heard calls for help. I went to open the door and Warren stops me, and shakes his head and says "There's nothing in there."

"Don't you hear that?" I said.

"I don't hear shit," he laughed.

"It was then Sam McCready warned us to get out of there. Once outside we watched the house become engulfed in flames despite our best efforts. It was then we saw the couple in the window of the upstairs bedroom that Warren had supposedly checked and said he did not hear any cries for help."

"Oh, my God," Sam exclaimed, horrified.

"Jesus Christ!" John Blake yelled. "Who the fuck checked that room? Was it you, Preston?

"No," I replied, shocked at the sight of the two people. "I checked the other end of the house upstairs."

We all looked at Warren. "Do I really need to ask if it was you?" John asked, as he glared at Warren.

"Serves them niggers right for moving in here," Warren commented. "We don't need them here."

It was then the roof collapsed on the people, as the flames burned uncontrollably.

John grabbed Warren by the front of his coat. "If I ever find out you left them people in there to die, I kill you!" John screamed as some of the guys tried to restrain him. "That, or I'll see you run out of the department. You better mark my words, goddammit!"

Being six-foot-four and two hundred-and-fifty pounds, that was no small feat.

"Calm down Blake or I'll suspend your ass now!" the chief ordered. "There will be an investigation Burmeister and you better hope they clear your ass!"

John walked away angry. We all knew John was the one guy you did not want to piss off. Physically he could handle almost anybody, even a couple of us at once. He had been a Navy Seebee and had personally killed about a half dozen Japs when they had nearly overrun some positions they had been reinforcing. He was a good and decent man. People were people to him. Their color did not matter.

"What happened next?" Russell asked, as he sipped his beer.

Preston took a deep breath and exhaled. "Things weren't the same after that," he said. "We weren't as close after that. There was an investigation, but nothing that could finger Warren. I said, I wasn't sure that I had heard anything. So my testimony helped him. Still everybody wondered whether he had their backs or not. John, Tom, Sam, and a couple of the other guys did not invite him to their parties. He was kind of ostracized."

"No, I mean the people," Russell countered. "What happened to John, Tom and Warren?"

"With no real investigation, or should I say one that cleared Warren, John grew frustrated, and left," Preston explained. "He decided to go into construction and made a great amount of money in the postwar housing boom. John did very well."

"What about Tom and Warren and Sam?" Russell asked.

"Tom joined John," Preston continued. "He did well

too."

"And Warren?" Russell asked.

"That's the strangest part," Preston continued. "Basically his life went to shit after that. About six months after that call, we got another one. It was a farmhouse. Anyway, we get most of the family out and can't find two of them. So, Warren goes down the ice shoot and into the cellar to see if they are there. Anyway, we find the family members in the backyard and Warren gets cut off."

"Really?" Russell asked.

"Yep," Preston explained. "The roof begins to collapse and we're trying to find out where Warren is and how we can help him. Then somehow he comes out the front door in shock, babbling incoherently and his hair has turned all white. Needless to say, we rushed him to Pontiac General Hospital for shock and smoke inhalation."

"So then what?" Russell asked. "What happened to him then?"

"Well, he spent a week in the hospital," Preston added. "He began to drink heavily after that. Sometimes the cops would give him rides home, so he didn't have to spend a night in the drunk tank. For all intents and purposes he was a functioning alcoholic after that. Anyway when we were alone and during one of his more lucid times, he told that when he was in the cellar of that farmhouse he found a door."

"Let me guess, it was a door to Hell, right?" Russell asked skeptically.

"Yes," Preston said, not changing his expression or demeanor. "He said he found a doorway to Hell. Warren said he did not realize what it was at first and when he discovered what it was, he barely escaped with his life. He was a nervous wreck after that and really not the firefighter he was. But, most of the guys took piety on him."

"So how soon afterward did he retire?" Russell asked.

"I think it was 1949," Preston admitted. "Maybe 1950. No, it was '49. Because he was dead by 1950. He was killed in a house fire."

"Wow, that's ironic," Russell commented.

"That's not the half of it," Preston added. "The house fire that Warren died in was on the anniversary date of the house fire the Smiths died in. His burned remains were found with his hand on the bedroom doorknob. It appeared he tried to get out, but something kept him from getting out. We couldn't figure out how he couldn't get out since there was nothing in the way of the door."

"Boy that's pretty amazing, or should I say coincidental," Russell commented.

"Uncanny, might be a better word," Preston suggested.

"So what does this have to do with you and you seeing Hell?" Russell asked.

Preston downed the last of his drink. "I'm an accomplice," he admitted. "I knew what happened and never reported it. Hell, I even lied about it. Denied it. I am equally guilty. I let a guilty murderer walk because I decided not to rat on a co-worker."

"Yeah, but don't be so hard on yourself," Russell trying to ease Preston's conscience. "You were young and probably didn't know what to do next."

Preston silently shook his head. "But, I did," he admitted. "I knew better and I did know what to do. But, I failed. I am as bad as Warren was in that regard."

"So, what can you do about it now?" Russell asked. "That was twenty-five years ago."

Preston took a deep breath and exhaled. “I plan on doing the right thing,” he said. “I am going to the authorities and confess everything. I have to. I would rather go to jail than end up where Warren did. I want to keep my soul, my sanity and what little humanity and integrity I have left.”

“What happens if they don’t do anything?” Russell asked. “I mean it has been twenty-five years, after all.”

“I go to the Pontiac Press and tell them my story,” Preston said, as he got up to leave. “I need to confess this in order to save my soul. I have to. Will you drive me?”

“If that is what you want, man,” Russell said.

Preston left a twenty-dollar bill on the bar for their tabs. “Come on, I got this one,” he said, as he led the way out of the bar. “This is long overdue.”

Grandma's House

It wasn't a haunted house in the traditional or classical sense. It wasn't like the house in the movie "*The Haunting*." We didn't have to worry about bumping into Hugh Crane and whoever else "walked alone" there. Still, there was a silence that did lie steadily against the wood and stone. Sometimes too much so. It was not major pounding like in the scene from the movie '*The Changling*'. It was the little creaks that you thought you heard. Like any old place, with a bit of a history, there seemed to be a few things you saw out of the corner of your eye that were not really there. Little squeaks and creaks……soft, subtle, but still noticeable. Yep, things that were not there, but you *knew* they were.

There weren't really any apparitions, visions, or noisy poltergeists. No, nothing like that.

Still, there were some strange and eerie occurrences in that house. I should know. I experienced a few of them. As did my brother and some of my cousins. I think even some of the others in the family experienced a couple here and there as well, though they haven't mentioned it or whether they will even admit to it is another story.

Most haunted houses have a penchant or a history for tragedy. This one didn't really.

This was grandma's house. The ancestral home.

In spite of my grandfather being a terrible, abusive drunk, the good memories outweighed the bad.

There was the fact that neither I, my brother nor my cousin liked the upstairs back bedroom to the house, even in the daytime. Something up there gave us all the creeps.

No, in all actuality, it *terrified* us, to be more exact. We never wanted to be alone up there. With somebody, we were fine. Alone, forget it.

The fruit cellar in the basement and the back bedroom were the other areas. The fact that all three of these areas were directly over each other makes us wonder if there wasn't something there. Or at the least buried there before the house was put there.

For the most part, the rest of the house was pretty comfortable to be in.

Grandma's house had a little history before my grandparents and aunts and uncles lived in it.

From what I was told by my grandmother, and she was quite the area historian, and my mom: they both said the house had at one time been the town hall or public office in Orchard Lake about a hundred or so years ago, and this was back in the 1960's when they told me. It had also been on Apple Island, the small island in the middle of Orchard Lake. It was later moved, most likely in the winter time when the lake was frozen over. That was the only opportinity they could have made such a major undertaking.

The house was later moved to its current spot along Pontiac Trail where my great uncle Burt, my grandfather's older brother, worked on it, renovating the place back into a house.

When it was a town hall, I suppose some public official dropped dead on the front steps and somebody got caught having an affair at the turn of the century and was shot, but other than that nothing. That was the extent of the tragedies.

The affair just goes to show you that you don't eat where you shit, even back in the good old days.

The house was moved to its present spot some time before the great depression, but after the end of World

War One. It was remodeled, with a green wooden siding with white trim. It was set into a hill that had been excavated that gave the house its basement and combined garage. We can't help but wonder if there was something else here first before the basement and cellar were excavated. I mean, hundreds of years ago, Indian tribes traveled through this area regularly. Anyways, a coal furnace in the basement was the house's source of heat that fed up to a three-by-three-foot heavy metal-screened vent on the floor between the dining room and the living room. Vents in the ceiling went through to the upstairs floors. You could see through them from upstairs to downstairs. The coal furnace was in place until about 1972, when it was replaced by fuel oil.

As kids we used to melt our Hershey bars on the furnace vent to get them soft and eat them. Man that was good. Forgive me for digressing. But, like I said the house had many great memories to it.

The first occupants of the house that I was told of were the Gardners, Emily and Francis.

I'm not sure whether they were the ones that had the house moved to its present spot, but my great uncle did a lot of work for them. My grandmother couldn't tell me a lot about them. She said there were rumors. I guess she had a mother that got into trouble during the great war, World War One, when she kept saying stuff like "The Kaiser will show them." I guess she was a little off her rocker and a true-blue Bundist. I bet if she lived long enough she would have been a loyal Nazi. A nice little old Bundist. I guess they threatened to deport her, if she didn't shut up.

I guess she was later committed to Clinton Valley, where she died. Story has it, she died saying "Kaiser will show 'em."

Go figure.

Grandma said even Burt didn't mention much about them, except that they were very secretive, dark and kept to themselves a lot. Nobody knew much about them. Grandma said Uncle Burt was always a little afraid of them. Not the intimidation type of afraid, but the leery, *I-think-they're-weird* afraid. They always dressed in black. But Uncle Burt kept working for them because they paid well and in cash and in those days that was what put bread on the table so to speak. They were never seen much, except on weekends and evenings. I guess they were a bit eccentric.

When they moved, I guess Grandma said that the neighbors felt like some cloud had been lifted from over them. I tried to come across any public information on them and I couldn't find any records on them anywhere. It was as if they had never been here.

Looking back in old news pages, I guess a couple of people disappeared locally. I guess authorities thought that they drowned in Orchard Lake or one of the other nearby lakes. They were last seen in the vicinity of Pontiac Trail and Old Orchard Trail.

Grandma and my mom did mention one *other* thing: that the Gardners were killed in some kind of freak accident. This just six months after selling the house. Not much was known about it, how or what exactly happened. We don't know if they had family, kids or relations that survived them. There weren't any records or anything.

It was as if they never existed or fell off the earth. That in itself was pretty spooky.

The next family to own the house was the Webbers, Max and Eliza. They stayed for about a year and then moved to New York. I guess old Max Webber killed himself when the stock market crashed. He shot himself. Eliza, his wife, distraught, soon joined him by turning on some gas in her room and lied down and went to sleep…forever.

I guess I can't blame her. First she loses her lifestyle and all that she has ever known and then the main person in her life. I can't imagine how it was back then.

Uncle Burt bought the house and then rented it to my grandparents. My grandma thought they bought it outright and paid Burt the money directly because of the bank situation. It wasn't until 1970 she found out they had only rented and decided to put the money up for what Burt originally wanted for the house.

Grandma herself loved the house, but I do remember her saying that she hated a couple of rooms in it. She did not like the upstairs and the very back bedroom. We didn't think much about it at the time until years later when we realized we didn't care for those rooms either, as I was saying.

The first grandchild to spend a lot of time there was my cousin Janet. She liked the house. She would ride the upstairs wooden banister like a horse and pretended to play post office with junk mail in the railing posts. It was almost a second home to her. As it would be to me and my brother a few years later.

Janet said that she would ride the wooden banister make-believe horse only when the doors at the top of the stairs were closed. Something up there bothered her too.

The most striking thing Janet had to tell me about the house was years later in our forties: in the back of the basement near the fruit cellar, as a girl she kept telling our grandma that she kept seeing people down there. She said she kept telling her, and Grandma would almost get mad at her, as if she were making it up.

Then one day, Janet said Grandma asked, "What do these people look like?"

Janet responded, saying, "I don't know. They're see-through. I can't really see 'em very good."

Janet told me later she thought Grandma never really believed her.

I don't know. Sometimes I think Grandma may have had her own little sightings or instances, but she just wouldn't let on. She always thought Harry's spirit was the one turning on and off the lights. I can't help but wonder if it wasn't someone else. Because some of this happened when he was alive, but not in the room.

Getting back to my cousin, Janet, she had more to tell....

The day before our grandma died, Janet visited her at her home, before going up north. Janet said Grandma always walked her out to her car when she was ready to leave. That day, Grandma didn't. Her coloring was bad and the food didn't agree with her at lunch. Janet thought it was strange how Grandma didn't walk her out to her car. How she only walked to the front porch and waved.

Shortly after Grandma died in 1986, Janet said she had a dream. A very disturbing one that dealt with the upstairs bedroom.

We sat down and talked one day about this dream.

"Grandma wanted to lead me into a bedroom. I had to go upstairs to use the bathroom. Grandma opened up the bedroom door without speaking and tried to lead me into that room. I thought it was because I was so close to her she wanted to take me with her. I fought her and pulled back because I did not want to go with her. I broke out in a cold sweat and was shaking. Tom, my husband, had to calm me down, I was so upset. I was upstairs."

Janet later figured that it was Grandma trying to warn her about our Aunt Faye's death, just two short years later.

I might have poo-pooed the idea of this, but my brother had a similar experience. So did a few others, as I would find out later. When we managed to compare notes, a number of us had some similarly eerie stories to tell.

After Grandma died, Faye moved her bedroom into Grandma's bedroom. Janet said that every time she walked passed the bedroom, it was cold. She couldn't bring herself to even go in there because of the cold. We think this is because it was where Grandma died. She must have gotten up early, lied back down and died. Just like that.

Janet said that she saw her, looking out one of the upstairs bedroom windows. It used to be Faye's room, until our aunt Judy moved out and Faye took over her bedroom. This kind of freaked Janet a little bit.

But I believe her. My brother saw her looking out the kitchen window. I was given a double treat. At different times, I saw both, my grandfather and grandmother looking out the kitchen window not long after both of their deaths. I saw Grandpa when I was mowing the lawn and Grandma, Faye, Timmy and myself were outside. This was in 1976 or 1977. I saw Grandma one day when I stopped by to visit Faye. Faye was on the porch and I saw Grandma in the kitchen window.

Faye mentioned one time how Grandma's room was also so cool and almost cold, even in the summer. I don't think she thought it had anything to do with where Grandma died. I think she thought it was because it was on the shady side of the house.

I don't know how she lived in that house by herself for the next two years. That house can be pretty creepy at night when you are by yourself. I have been in it. Me and my cousin Tom, not the one married to Janet, were there playing when Gram and Faye when away for a couple hours one night. The upstairs was really spooky then. The trees rustled closely against the house making for some interesting noises. This was especially true during storms. At times, it was as if the trees were reaching out and hitting the house for being next to them. We would run up, use the bathroom and run back down. I couldn't have done it. I couldn't have stayed in that house by myself. Not overnight and not by myself.

There were way too many creaky floorboards and squeaky door hinges that one heard when alone. They are all so subtle. Nothing slammed, but you knew that you heard somebody walking upstairs when there was nobody up there. You were almost positive you heard something in the basement and the cat wasn't down there. Little things like that. It was all shadows, movement, sounds and the twilight. One hell of a mix, if you had an active imagination. Even if we did have that, that still does not discount the events we witnessed.

I was the next grandchild to spend a lot of time there, usually weekends and whole weeks at a time in the summers. I mowed the lawn and did a lot of odd jobs out there. I was there to mainly to keep Grandma company, so my aunt Faye who lived with her could go on vacation or just go out without worry.

My first experience was when I was about five. I went upstairs to use the bathroom. With the bathroom at the very top of the stairs, you could see to the right the next two bedrooms. When I went up there, I could see that the bedroom doors were open and could see the bedrooms plain as day.

Grandma and my aunt Faye were working so only my grandfather and myself were there. He spent the day out at the kitchen table playing solitaire all day. This was one of those rare exceptions where he had to watch me. Anyways, an hour or so later, I had to use the bathroom again. I went upstairs only to notice that the bedrooms door was now closed. This gave me the chills. The windows were open to let a breeze come through them. But, there was no breeze. Besides, if there were, how is it that when I opened the first door nearest the bathroom, that the next bedroom door was now closed as well? Either way the wind was blowing, a closed door would have cut off the wind to another door. It wasn't possible.

Needless to say, I went to bathroom as fast as I could and hurried downstairs with my pants around my ankles, because I knew there was something else up there. I couldn't see it or hear it. But, I sure as hell felt it. There was something else there and I knew. I still know it. It's a miracle I didn't break my neck going downstairs with my tangled-up pants. Grandpa helped me get them resituated later. But I didn't go back up there until somebody else got home. I have heard the breeze go through before and close the doors up there. Usually one or the other, but not both. The doors usually slammed shut, though. I didn't hear the doors shut at all and I was in the living room that led to the stairs watching TV.

Trust me, it wasn't the wind.

I know that. I spent too much time in that house.

I had spent as much time as almost anybody in that house and it wasn't the friggin' wind. I knew that house about as well as anybody else. I knew it better than almost all of the other grandkids. Later, when my brother and myself were older, we were leaving

Grandma's house to go to one of our twenty-plus cousins' birthday parties. I remember Grandma asking my aunt if she turned off the light upstairs in the middle bedroom. Aunt Faye said she did and we were off. It was when we were headed down the driveway that we noticed the light she'd said she turned off was on. Grandma was mad, cursing and muttering she thought she turned it off when it was still obviously on.

My Aunt Faye replied, "I did mother! I did!"

"It's probably Harry or some damn short," Grandma said.

That was the room we slept in. My aunt's room was next door. When we returned, the light was off. For years, Grandma and Faye would say and in some cases even swear that the lights would flicker and go on and off at certain times because it was Harry, my grandfather, who had come back to haunt them. I could believe it, he was a mean old bastard. But, in his defense, some of the strange goings-ons happened when he was still with us. What's surprising is that even they commented on these things from time to time, figuring that the wiring was just old and obsolete. That was always the excuse though.

Some nights when I spent weekends, I had no problem there, even at night. Other times, I knew damn well that there was something there. My brother was the next one to spend time there. He was about six years younger than me, so when I graduated from high school, he took over the lawn mowing and spending time out there to keep Grandma company. Timmy didn't like the fruit cellar in the basement, the back bedroom or the upstairs back bedroom any better than the rest of us. It bothered him. He didn't tell me some of this until after Faye died.

He said that "We were never alone in that house. There was always somebody in that house." He said this after Grandma and Grandpa had both died and he was there physically by himself.

The one event that he had that really bothered him and still does happened before Faye died. He was older then, not some little kid. Timmy was going to OCC when he stopped off to use the bathroom on his way home. Timmy had a key to the house, just as Janet and I also had one. He stopped in, went upstairs to the bathroom and took a leak. As he was standing there, a magazine caught his attention. He started to read it. One thing about Grandma's bathroom, you never had to worry about reading material up there. As he started to read the magazine, he distinctly heard Grandma yell "Did you fall in up there!" Timmy hurried up and got the hell out.

Faye would live only a little while longer in that house. She would later sell it and buy a house next to our Aunt Bonnie and Uncle Fred. She never got to enjoy it. She died before everything was totally finalized on it. She was, sadly enough, the youngest of ten children and the very first to die. That was pretty rough. It still is. Even after all these years.

My mother mentioned how the earlier occupants sold the house and then shortly afterwards died as well. That was what basically got a few of us talking about the house. A kind of comparing notes and memories. One day I may write about all of the stories in detail about the house. But not right now. That's not why I am here. Some of us always thought that it should stay in the family or be a historical place of some kind. None of us had the money to do that. Now we do.

I know you probably think this is bullshit and I am just telling you this to put an idea in your head about the house being haunted. Honestly, I am not. Like I said, we had fond memories here, my family and I. It was home. We just believe that it should stay in the family…..that it should come back to us. We want to buy it back. It was a big part of our extended family history. There are over a hundred of us now. I've made my living for the last few years writing books. I'm not a millionaire like Stephen King, but I do all right. I just believe the place should come back to the family. The furniture that we were familiar with is spread throughout the family from this place. We would like to put it all back together. We are now our parents' and aunts' and uncles' ages, when Grandma died. So, are you interested in our offer?

The Countess Corardesa

What I am about to tell you is really second-hand at best, and that comes from my partner who was told this by another person, who was our client. So, in fact it could be even more removed than that, but I also believe it to be true.

As unbelievable as it is....

My partner John Mathews and I hire out as personal bodyguards to those willing to pay the price with our company: Lifeguards, Inc. Individually, we are very adept at martial arts, hand-to-hand combat, assorted small arms and weapons. This comes from our Special Forces backgrounds from our Armed Forces service.

So, we are very well-versed in all facets of personal protection.

We have been and are hired on anything from a daily basis to long-term. In fact, we have protected everybody from pop singers and rappers to movie stars and politicians. So, we have had a nice clientele the last ten years. Not bad for two guys from Michigan.

One evening last year, we had an appointment with a possible client whose name was Countess Corardesa Varcolur. We were somewhat taken aback and more than a little flattered by this, especially since we had nothing remotely close to royalty as a client.

When we first met her, it was towards evening. She arrived in a large black limousine, short in stature, yet very shapely.

Countess Corardesa had light brown hair and looked to be in her mid-to-late thirties, yet she seemed younger and a bit more vivacious. If I had to gauge her age, I'd say thirty-five.

She wasn't what I would call ravishingly beautiful, but she was attractive.

Very attractive.

There was a sexiness and allure to her that was very pleasant to the eyes. Her curves were in all the right places and shapely enough, while her facial features were almost mesmerizing. It was hard to look away from her. You were almost swallowed up by those eyes of hers.

The Countess was immediately taken by John's mature good looks. But why wouldn't she? He was about her age, perhaps a little older and in great shape. We both were.

"Countess Corardesa, it is a pleasure to meet you," John said, shaking her hand gently. "I am John Mathews, and this is my friend and partner Lee Corey."

"Please to meet you, Countess," I said, as I shook her hand. "Please have a seat."

"Please call me Desa, gentlemen," she replied. "Countess Corardesa is so formal, and I prefer to keep things simple."

"Can we get you anything, Countess, er I mean Desa?" I asked.

"No, thank you," she answered, as she sat down.

"So what can we do for you?" John asked as he sat down across from her, and I sat down next to him.

"I need bodyguard protection," she replied.

"Could you tell us your situation?" I asked. "How do you feel threatened?"

The Countess looked at us both warily, then nodded her head and looked directly at John. "I need twenty-four hour protection for a lengthy period of time and I am willing to pay handsomely for it."

"Okay," John replied. "I am sure that can be arranged."

"Is there something wrong?" I asked. "I mean, something that has happened that has made you believe there is a reason for a bodyguard?"

Tears welled up in her eyes and she took a deep breath. "Yes," she said, as she exhaled. My sister was murdered a month ago."

"By anyone you know?"

"I am uncertain at this time," she replied.

"That seems reasonable," I said. "What do you think, John?"

"I agree," John said. "Look, Desa, could I confer with my partner on this alone for a moment?"

"Please do," she answered, as she dabbed her eyes with a tiny handkerchief.

John and I went into the next room and talked. He admitted being attracted to her. (Both of us, on occasion, had physical relationships with our clients.)

We also knew that we had to settle on a price and find out how long of time period she would require.

When we returned, we asked the good Countess how long she needed our protection.

"Indefinitely," she replied. "Basically, until I feel safe and there is no longer a substantial threat."

"What price were you thinking of paying?" I asked. "I guess, I mean what sounds fair to you?"

"I will gladly pay twenty-five thousand dollars a month," she admitted. "If I need you longer than six months, I will pay an additional ten thousand dollars a month. But that is for continuous, round-the-clock service. You have to be at my side day and night."

"All right," I said. "What do you say, John?"

"Fine," John agreed. "When do I start?"

"As soon as possible," she responded. "How soon can you start?"

"Okay," John said. "I can be ready tomorrow. Okay enough?"

"That is fine," she replied. "I can send the payment tomorrow as well. I shall pick you up in my limousine here tomorrow night."

"What about clothes and other belongings?" John asked.

"Just take what you would need for a week," I suggested. "I can bring the rest or have them sent to you."

"That would be ideal," she agreed.

"Well, it looks like we are in agreement…Desa," John said, extending his hand to shake hers.

"Yes," she said. "I think we are."

We all shook hands and she signed the paperwork. That was it. The deal was done. John Mathews was now Countess Corardesa's personal bodyguard.

Later that week I was bringing the rest of his belongings and some weaponry to Countess Corardesa's place in the hills. It was a long and winding drive up to a very secluded and almost hidden place. It was a rustic chalet style building with a garage excavated into the hill it sat on.

As I made my way up the walkway that ran from the driveway, I noticed some closed circuit cameras that were very well camouflaged. If I hadn't been trained as I was, I might have missed them myself. I could see John had already used his time efficiently well. Once I reached the door, the front door had a large knocker on it. I decided to forgo using it and gently wrapped on the door with my fist.

A few moments later, John answered. Immediately, I could sense something different.

"I just brought you the rest of your stuff," I said.

"Including some weapons you requested."

"Thanks," John said as we both grabbed the remainder of his belongings and lugged them inside. "Come on in."

I quickly entered as John scanned the walkway one more time before closing the door.

"I have some important things to tell you," he announced. "Follow me. Do you want a drink?"

"No, I'm good, thanks," I replied as I followed John to a deck that was on the back of the chalet which overlooked a wooded gorge.

"Have a seat," John said, pointing to an Adirondack patio chair.

"Very nice," I commented, as I sat down. "So, what's going on?"

"I think the job is bigger than either of us could have figured on," John admitted. "What I am about to tell you is true. Or what I know and believe to be true. Don't laugh."

"Don't worry, I won't," I replied, skeptical by John's sudden seriousness.

"Good, because there is no easy way to say what I am going to say," John explained and then paused. There was a long, difficult silence. "Countess Corardesa is a vampire."

"A what?" I asked, shocked by John's sudden revelation.

"Desa is a vampire," he repeated.

I looked directly at John's eyes. "You're not shitting, are you?" I asked.

He shook his head slowly. "No, I'm not," he replied. "She admitted in bed a few nights ago. In fact, she told her whole life's story the other night, too."

"Say what?" I asked. "In bed? Shit, I thought they only slept in coffins. In bed, though?"

"I'm afraid I have indulged in those fringe benefits we

discussed earlier," he admitted. "I have indulged almost every night and multiple times. Does that answer your question? And to answer your coffin question, not all. Some can exist in daylight too. I don't know all of the specifics, of the ins and outs of vampires, but I am learning."

"Has she?" I started to ask. "Uh, you know…"

"Bitten me?" John asked, cutting me off in mid-sentence. "No. Still, the sex has been almost intoxicating. She has an almost insatiable appetite for it. She said I remind her of a long lost love. A warrior protector of hers."

"You can nix this deal," I suggested. "You need to get out of this situation before it goes bad."

"I wish it were that simple." John admitted. "But I can't."

"You're in love with her," I surmised.

"I'm afraid so," he admitted. "I am almost as surprised as you are at this, but I am."

"So, what do you plan on doing?" I asked. "You're mortal and she's….like, a thousand years old, or at least thirty-five forever."

John simply nodded in agreement. "Well, I think you had better hear the rest of her story and what she told me. Maybe this will give you some more perspective on things."

"That, maybe," I responded. "Anyway, I think I need that drink now."

"Okay," John said, as he went inside.

A few moments later he returned with two drinks. "Here, Captain and Coke," he said.

He then began telling me about the Countess and her history. He began by telling me that she was born into a unique clan or family in Transylvania. Her family was allied with Vlad Tepes who was otherwise known as Vlad the Impaler. He mentioned that their lineage began some time before Vlad II Dracul. She said that an old alchemist named Vurdalac gave them a potion that could give them eternal life, but that they need the blood of others to survive. Their clan was basically the equivalent of the Vlad family cheerleaders and supporters. Kind of like boosters for a school. The women of the clan were nicknamed the Blood Widows. They would throw pre-battle festivals to encourage Vlad and his men as they went into battle. When they returned victorious, they would have blood orgies and celebrations

"Blood orgies?" I asked, somewhat taken aback.

"Yes," John explained. "Apparently when Vlad and his armies were victorious, they would bathe and even drink the blood of their enemies and the vanquished. They would take the prisoners and the women humiliate and in some cases torture them to death. Much like a cat would a mouse before eating it."

"Jesus, that's pretty extreme isn't it?" I asked.

"You do have to consider the times and what they were like," John said.

"Yeah, but still," I protested mildly. "How did she survive all of these years?"

"How do you think?" John asked.

"Drinking blood, of course," I responded.

"Yes, but one does not need to kill in order to do that," John replied.

"That may well be," I said in response. "But, that still makes her a kind of predator of sorts."

"Aren't we all when you come right down to it?" John asked. "Think about it, everything is in its own way a predator."

"True," I replied. "You got me there."

"That's why I said it wasn't quite so simple as all that," John admitted as he turned and looked out off of the deck. "I have never felt this way about anyone. Until now, no woman ever has."

"Boy, that is really something," I said. After a long silent pause, I finally spoke again. "Well, now that you've got me curious….."

John turned and smiled. "I thought you would be," he said. "Especially knowing how much of a history buff you are."

"You know me too well," I laughed.

"Well, after twenty years, and ten of those in the army, that does help," John confessed.

So John started up again. He began to tell me how after Vlad the Impaler was forced out the first time, that they decided it was time to move on. They could see that his power was waning and thought it was for the best. They knew their safety could no longer be guaranteed under him and headed west to the Kingdom of Hungary. The worst of it was that Desa and her family lost two of her brothers Alexandru and Petre when Vlad reclaimed his throne.

A short time later when the Ottoman Turks caught up with and slaughtered their parents and another brother Andrei. This was when they were hunted by another faction of the Ottoman's that had a blood feud against them. A feud that continues to this day.

Desa and her sisters, being wealthy and royalty, were familiar with others of the like in Europe, to ingratiate themselves with them. After several decades of relative peace and tranquility in Hungary, they found a friend and ally in Elizabeth Bathory.

I was astounded by this, and yet not surprised. They had made friends with the "Blood Queen" who was said to have bathed in the blood of six hundred virgins. I was noticing a kind of a trend in their friendships, but I listened as John continued.

John went on to say after Bathory was imprisoned for her crimes, they were no longer welcome there, so once again they were nomadic royalty for hundreds of years. They basically found that they could exist on the victims of all of the European conflicts throughout the years.

It was at that point they decided it was best to roll with whatever prevailing wind was strongest. Especially since they knew they had enough potential enemies around and they did not want to compound that.

In a sense they became political opportunists to stay alive and wealthy.

According to John it wasn't until the Thirty Years' War with the fragmenting of the Holy Roman Empire that their sister Esmerelda was destroyed. Apparently she was killed when a building she was in had been burned to the ground. They did not know for sure whether it was deliberate or on purpose, but with so much conflict going on, they had their suspicions with the possibility of their enemies being nearby.

John continued to tell how Desa and her remaining sisters split up into groups of two where they never spent more than a few days in one place. Being wealthy and in considered royalty helped to garner them allies and friendships that helped provide them protection and security.

Apparently the royalty and upper class in Europe had a lot of strange and eccentric way as well. Many were as bad or worse than Desa and her sisters. From what John said, they were opportunists who made the best of their situations. He continued to tell me how they spent the better part of two centuries continuing their nomadic ways, traveling from Germany and France to smaller and lesser known Central European kingdoms.

"So, basically they lived out of a suitcase," I surmised before sipping my drink. "Or should I say coffin?"

"You could say that," John remarked.

"So, what happened to her other sisters?" I asked. "Please don't tell me she's the last one."

John quietly nodded. "I am afraid she is," he admitted. "Her sisters were eventually destroyed throughout the ages. Picked off one by one."

"Well, Wilhelmina, or Mina as she was called was killed around the time, that the violence and turmoil were going on after the Archduke Ferdinand and his wife were assassinated," John explained. "From what Desa told me it was during the ensuing turmoil that someone impaled her and then cut off her head."

"Did they think it was someone associated with the Ottoman's?" I asked. "Or their allies?"

"They're certain of it," John replied before sipping his drink. "But there was no real proof, other than the staking and beheading. Someone had to know what she was to kill her that way."

Then what?" I asked. "That left Desa and who?"

"That left Desa, Hildegarde, and Magdalena," John replied. "Desa called them, Hilda and Lana. During the First World War, they acted as nurses. Naturally, they were able to survive on the dying."

"Naturally," I commented.

It made sense. They could feast on the dying and critically ill who eventually would die. They were, as John said, opportunists.

John turned and looked back out off of the deck. "The next to go was Hilda. She was killed in the war during the bombing of Dresden," he said. "Unlike Esmerelda, that was thought to have been a case of being in the wrong place at the wrong time with all of the napalm."

"I kind of figured," I admitted. "It makes sense. That leaves Desa and Lana."

"Yep," John said.

"So what's the history there?" I asked. "What happened next?"

John walked over to the railing and leaned against it as he stared out into the wooded gorge. "They had helped some of the wealthy Jewish people they had known and befriended to escape," he continued to explain. "Unfortunately they could not save all of them, and the very old and the infirmed were taken care of."

"Don't you mean put down?" I asked.

"According to Desa it was painless and very fast," he responded, somewhat defensively.

"She said that the families realized this and had to make some tough choices. They promised that they would be dealt with painlessly. Anyway, after the war they made their way here. Several of the people they had helped vouched for their character so they could enter the country."

"I guess everybody does what they have to in order to survive," I surmised.

John turned to me. "You know that already," he said. "We both have been in combat and had to do what we had to do in order to survive ourselves."

I nodded in agreement. "Yeah, you got me there," I admitted. "Remember that firefight in that Afghanistan shit hole? My God, that was horrible."

"Yeah, I remember," John confessed. "At least a couple of times a month, I remember."

I took a deep breath and commented." Everything you told me makes everything appear to be justified. So what happened next? I assume they arrived here in 45 or 46 with a lot of other refugees."

"She said they arrived in June of 46," John continued. "They arrived in New York. From there they continued their nomadic ways."

"So what happened next?" I asked. "They prey on the New England blue bloods?"

Before John could speak were joined by the Countess Corardesa. "No, we continued to live our lives," she said.

I could not help but stare at the Countess Corardesa was in an opaque white nightgown. She was beautiful and looking sexier than when had first met. I had trouble turning my gaze away from her. For a moment I felt almost envious of John.

She seemed to glide over to John, lean upwards and kissed him tenderly, as he held her in his arms and then turned to face me. "You see Mr. Corey, we lived amongst the wealthy and powerful," she said. "We kept a low profile as you might say. That was for our own self-preservation."

"That's understandable," I said, with some uncertainty.

"You see, Mr. Corey, that lifestyle gave us protection," she admitted.

"Lee," I said. "Please call me Lee. I figure we are on a first name basis, Countess."

"Desa," she said. "Since we are both on a first name basis."

"Alright," I said. "Desa, please tell me the rest of your story, or I mean history."

The Countess smiled at me. I was surprised at the warmth and friendliness that she exuded with it. I had been expecting a sinister one. Then again, I imagined she reserved that for her victims. Right now, I was an ally and friend. Or at least the friend of a friend with benefits.

"After we arrived, we basically lived out of hotels," she admitted. "We were incredibly wealthy and very discreet. We were able to pay for silence and security. Nobody knew how much we had, but they knew we were quite wealthy."

"Like the Rockefellers and Waltons?" I asked.

"Yes," she purred. "In that area, and probably more so. Especially since we had accumulated wealth from a number of centuries."

"I see," I said, before finishing my drink.

"John, please fix Lee and yourself another drink," she suggested. "This is a lot to take in and he might need it."

John quietly nodded and left momentarily to make us another drink.

While John was inside, the Countess Corardesa continued. "I understand your ambivalence and hesitation. In fact, I expected it. Hopefully by talking to you I can alleviate some of your misgivings."

"It's just that he's my best friend and partner," I explained. "We've been buddies for twenty years, since we joined up at 18. We've saved each other's lives in combat. In fact, I owe him one. So that's why I'm like I am."

The Countess smiled at me. "We both love him," she admitted. "He's your brother and he's my long lost love and soul mate reincarnated."

I could only nod. I understood what she meant. While John may not have been my actual brother, he had been the only brother I had left. He was my brother in arms and best friend that I'd lay down my life for.

"You are right," I confessed.

"I am a lot of things, Lee," she continued. "Some say I am evil. I have done a lot of things that could be construed as that. I have committed some very bad and horrible acts. I drink blood to exist. That is a fact and I will admit to it. But I have never betrayed a friend or an ally. And in John's case my protector and lover. I will never turn on that. Ever."

Somehow in spite of everything I believed her sincerity. It was hard to explain. While I was usually suspicious and leery, my gut told me she was being honest. Deep down, I knew she was being honest not only with me, but John. I did not know whether to be flattered or frightened by this.

John returned with our drinks. I immediately took a drink of mine.

"Once Lana and I arrived in the United States, we immediately applied for citizenship. Being connected, we had no problem and were able to cut through the red tape. Through our proxies we donated money to charities and political campaigns. Whatever offered us the best protection and security we made sure that we backed it financially."

"That makes a lot of sense," I said.

"We mingled with the many movers and shakers of all the different industries. We were acquaintances of the rich and powerful. Some of whom were every bit as bloodthirsty and malicious as we had been. A few were even more so. The only difference was they preyed on different victims. Most were decent, kind and even generous."

"Such is mankind," John commented after being silent for a while.

"Yes, that is true," she agreed. "Living for so long we witnessed much. We had made allies and friends with many that were rich and powerful. Some cruel, some kind. After arriving here, we continued to do so. Eventually we made friends with the Kennedys….and others."

"That makes sense," I said. "It always helps to have friends in high places."

"Anyway, Lana struck up an intimate relationship with a young congressman named John Kennedy," the Countess continued, as she crossed the deck, almost appearing to glide over it.

"Whoa, really?" I asked. "Did they..uh, well..?"

"Yes, they were lovers briefly" she replied, almost anticipating the question. "Six times as congressman and once as president."

"Whoa, that's something," I commented.

The Countess quietly nodded. "It's just too bad his father was such a rotten bastard. You think my kind is bad; we only do it for food to survive. Believe me, he was just as bad.

He tried to make advances towards me, and when I rebuffed him, he threatened to expose us. Thankfully, John and Robert stepped in and prevented him. But, we helped to insure the old bastard had a stroke, so he couldn't hurt us."

"Wow, so that bastard really was a douchebag," I commented. "I had heard stories, but never really imagined how bad."

The Countess laughed. "And how. He was terrible. What an atrocious man."

I took another step of my drink. "So what other characters have you met?" I asked. "I hate to ask, but you got me curious. What happened next?"

"My, aren't you the curious one?" she replied, more as a statement than a question, with a whimsical smile on her face.

"Guilty as charged," I replied. "I guess I am. But inquiring minds want to know, as they say."

The Countess laughed. "You are very amusing, Thomas," she snickered.

"Well, thanks, I guess," I said, before sipping my own drink.

"Believe me, that is a good thing," John said, before sipping his own drink as well.

"Let me just say this, the sixties and the seventies, especially the early part of the seventies, were a great opportunity for Lana and myself," she continued. "With all of the turmoil and free love of the era, we definitely took advantage of the opportunities that were afforded us. With all of the drugs the people taking then, well they were in a stupor when we took blood from them. They did not know who it was and some had little memory of it, other than feeling weak and tired."

"That makes sense," I commented. "They in all likelihood did not know what was happening and were even less likely to remember it."

The Countess nodded in agreement. "Given our wealth and position we were able to attend parties and orgies with many actors and actresses. We met and even partied with the Beatles and the Stones to name just a few."

"It must have been almost like a second Renaissance for you," John commented. "With all of the artistic figures of the day."

"It truly was," she agreed. "With all of that going on we were able to feast and have fun at will, while remaining almost totally anonymous. I will gladly tell you more about that era later."

"Good," I responded. "I'll hold you to that."

The Countess went on to explain how for the next forty or so years they moved all over the country. They continually moved from all over. East and west, north and south, they moved throughout the different regions.

"That's a lot of moving around," John commented.

"Yes, it is," I agreed.

"That is what we had to do in order to survive," she admitted. "Now, this brings us to today, the very present. My sister, Lana was destroyed. She was destroyed by those who have had a generational blood feud with us and have been trying to end our existence for centuries. They are descendants of the Ottoman Turks."

"Do you know exactly who they are?" I asked.

"Craven," she spat, the words almost disgusting here. "Craven. Dr. Craven. He is a slayer, much on the order of a Van Helsing. His family had a generational blood oath."

"Craven?" I asked. "Does he have a first name?"

"Does he really need one?' she asked me, almost seething with anger at mentioning the very idea of him. "He is only known by one name and that is only Craven. He is horrid enough to be known by that."

"No, I suppose not," I replied. "But could you tell me more about him. The more we know about your enemies the better we can protect you."

"Craven and his clan or tribe was a group of ritualistic berserkers," she explained. "They were not only slayers of us, but Christians, Jews and others who were not them. They were every bit as bloodthirsty and brutal as Vlad. Many of them had raided our and Vlad's villages we joined forces to be rid of them. They joined the Ottoman Turks, acting as their spearhead for attack. When we had killed almost all of them, Vlad let a couple of them live as a warning to any others of their ilk. Unfortunately, they vowed an eternal revenge on us for what we did."

"Wow, that is one hell of a generational blood feud," I responded. "Are they immortal like you?"

"They sound like some of the bastards we dealt with in the Middle East," John opined.

"They are of the same deplorable ilk and persuasion," the Countess replied, with tears welled up in her eyes. "They are vile and unworthy. I hope to see all of their destruction. And no, they are not immortal. For us the blood is the life, for them, and their animalistic ways, were not."

"So, how many are we dealing with?" I asked.

"There have never been more than thirteen ever since then," she explained, still sounding sad and somewhat angry. "As our numbers have dwindled so have theirs. They have killed us, our servants and even our allies, but we have eliminated many of their lines and lineage as well. There is also the fact, that many of them have found another enemy that is more current and accessible."

"Still, we need to gauge their numbers," I said insistently. "And who exactly they are."

"They are Craven's servants," she replied. "It is of little consequence who they are since Craven is the one who leads them. They are in a sense powerless without him."

"So take him out and they're leaderless," I suggested. "As well as useless."

"Something like that," the Countess replied. "He used to have better lieutenants but they were eliminated. I know Lana was able to get his brother eliminated by one of her acquaintances a couple of years ago."

"Do you at least have a ballpark figure?" I asked. "How many can we expect? A dozen or so?"

The Countess and John looked at each other knowing something that I did not.

"More like half that," John finally responded. "I was forced to take out a couple of them out a couple of nights ago. They tried to jump me when I checking the parameter."

"He killed three of them single-handedly, protecting me," she said proudly. "He showed great expertise in doing so."

"Really?" I asked. "So, that's why you told me to bring more weaponry like Bushmaster AR-15's and enough ammo for a week-long patrol."

"Exactly," John replied. "Fortunately it was not here, but it was still too close to here. Besides, I believe it was a probing action. They sent three men who were not very good. Unfortunately, it forced my hand and might have exposed us eliminating them."

"What did you do with the bodies?" I asked. "I hope you hid them somewhere good."

"Desa drained them and showed me where to dispose of them," he answered. "If they're ever found the authorities will think it was a mob hit. But to answer your question, that might leave us with about six, give or take. It's hard to gauge."

"Hopefully, take as far as numbers are concerned," I laughed. "So, I take it these guys are somewhat Middle Eastern-looking?"

"You've seen them?" the Countess asked.

"No, I am assuming," I replied. "I figure if they are part of the Ottoman Turks they usually have dark features, so it only goes to figure."

"He's right," John agreed. "The ones I killed were in spite of their changed hair color. On top of that they were inexperienced and young. I guess that is typical, of those types, to sacrifice the young."

"Gentlemen, may I suggest we head indoors," the Countess suggested, calmly, as she led the way inside. We decided to quietly follow her lead. "They are here."

"What?' I asked.

"They're here," she repeated.

"How do you know?" I asked, taken aback by this

knowledge.

"I can smell them," she said coldly. I looked at her in amazement and confusion. "Every blood has its own unique trait. A vampire like myself can smell the difference in each person's blood and that each person has a very unique blood taste. We pick our victims by their individual blood scent. However there are times, when beggars cannot be choosers. Still, we can tell whose and what your scent is."

"Wow, kind of like a human blood hound of sorts," I said, as John shut off any lights and we moved stealthily away from any of the windows.

"This was the same scent as the other night and what surrounded my sister's body when she was destroyed," the Countess explained.

John and I grabbed the weapons from near the front door and loaded them with quickly with our many years of expertise. "I think they'll move in soon. Before dark, thinking that is when she is at her weakest. The ones I took out made the mistake of coming at night. "

"So what's your plan?" I asked.

"We let them come in so far and try to spring a trap as best as we can," John replied. "We both know that they will be on their guard and fully alert so we try to give them a false sense of security."

"Maybe then we can surprise them," I suggested.

"Hopefully," John responded. "But they know we're here. If Desa can smell them *or* their blood, they know we are here and probably how many of us. I build a kind of obstacle course or barrier in the basement garage. I also booby trapped the stairs halfway down, so if any kind of weight is put on it, they will collapse."

I could only smile. That was a big relief.

After safely navigating the stairs, we took up positions in the basement and garage area where it was darker and there were large crates piled up in positions to allow us cover. We both knew from our experience to expect a flash grenade or even a real hand grenade.

We waited in the relative darkness for what seemed an eternity. The Countess took up a position somewhere behind the stairs. It seemed as if she instinctively knew where she needed to be. Even in the dark I could see that her eyes blazed with a fury of hatred and revenge. It was somewhat intimidating. On top of that for me personally, I had not been this nervous since our last firefight in Afghanistan. I knew John was by the way he was chewing some gum that he had put in his mouth before coming down here.

We soon heard some scurrying upstairs as multiple pairs of feet made their way through the chalets first and second floors. The wood floors betrayed their positions with every squeak of the floor boards.

John was hidden directly across and about twenty feet from the stairs, while I was positioned parallel to the wall just left of him. Now we waited for an unseen enemy.

After a while our wait was over and as expected the door opened and a flash grenade was tossed down the stairs. We sought shelter from the flash as we heard the men begin to stomp down the stairs.

From that point on, the rest was a kind of blur as the action became both fast and furious. The first two men crashed onto the landing below as the steps underneath them gave way. Once they hit the ground, the Countess quickly took care of them. Since she was out of my view, I could only assume that she dispatched them the same way vampires did in the horror movies.

The next ones were much more careful, doing a kind of acrobatic tuck and roll move where once they hit the ground, and came up firing as they brought their weapons to bear. We quickly dispatched them.

The last few threw some kind of explosive device of some kind, perhaps a grenade that exploded into the crates that John was hidden behind. Even with the effects of the flash grenade, smoke and debris, I could tell the crates were badly damaged and shattered, as the force of the explosion pushed John backwards and out of my sightlines.

I fired, hitting the last three men and mortally wounding them.

I came out from behind my position with my AR-15 still pointed at the dying men. I was soon joined by the Countess Corardesa, who looked down at the men with blood still dripping from her lips and mouth.

"Craven," she muttered disdainfully, as if spitting out a foul taste from her mouth.

"You bitch," the man, she identified as Craven, muttered softly with his dying breaths. "You…wh… as he began coughing and wheezing, cutting himself off.

"You shall pray for death before I am done with you," she promised.

"No," he gasped, between coughs.

Then it occurred to me that John was not with us. "John?" I called out, as I moved towards his position. "John, are you all right?"

There was no answer. I headed over to where I thought he might be. Finally I saw him, sprawled out onto the floor, with his head and back leaning against another crate. Almost immediately I noticed a large, broken piece of wood sticking out of his abdomen.

"Holy shit, John!" I yelled. "Are you okay?"

John muttered some inaudible reply as I moved in to comfort him "Stay with me buddy," I said, trying to comfort him. "Stay with me."

I pulled out the wooden shard and clasped my left

hand over his wound. I knew it was serious. I was focused on trying to save my friend that I failed to notice what the Countess had done to the other men as she finished them off.

"Damn!" I muttered as I tried to treat my rapidly fading friend.

Then I heard a heartbreaking tormented scream of "No!" coming from the Countess as she noticed what had happened to John.

She looked at me, as bloody tears fell down her cheeks and I could only shake my head negatively. "I'm afraid this might be it," I said.

"No," she responded. "No. This is not the only way. I can save him. I can give him life. I can turn him and he will live."

I was immediately torn. I understood what she meant. I was hesitant at first, but he was my best friend, partner and the like a brother to me. He had after all saved my life. I thought maybe it was my turn to do the same. I owed him that chance.

"Do whatever it is you have to do," I groaned as I turned away, lowering my head into my hands.

I heard a soft slurping noise coming from her as she did what was needed to preserve John's life. After a few moments I turned around and John appeared to be resting as the Countess gently brushed his hair off of his forehead and back into place.

"You shall be back with me, my love," she cooed gently. "You will be restored to me."

"You really do love him," I observed.

"Yes," she replied, not looking away from John. "I do."

After a few minutes I could see John take a deep breath, then exhale. I knew he was going to be alright. I finally relaxed a little, knowing he was still with us. "So what do we do now?" I asked.

"I think I'm going to have to move around with Desa," John surmised. "You can dissolve the partnership if you wish. The business is yours."

"Hell, no!' I retorted. "You will be her bodyguard on a continuous status.

"I'm not the same," John warned me with some concern. "I am like Desa now."

"Yeah, so," I answered. "Regardless, you are my best friend. You are like my brother. I told her to save you. Besides, I won't do that."

"Thank you," he replied.

"So, the partnership stays intact," I said. "Besides, you will need some of my help in logistical support from time to time."

"We will need to move soon," John said. "So, we could use your help there. Probably not for a month or so."

"Of course," I said. "Whatever you need, buddy."

Soon we were rejoined by the Countess, who had finished taking revenge on the men. She had drained them all dry, impaled them and then cut off their heads.

"Are you alright, my love?" Desa asked.

"Never better," he remarked, as he touched her cheek tenderly. "Thanks, Desa."

She smiled warmly at him. "Well, at least now it will not be an awkward forbidden inter-species kind of romance," she half-joked. "We are the same."

"Yes," he said. "We are."

A short time later, when he was fully recovered. That night we hid the bodies along with the weapons in a very desolate and hidden spot in the gulley. We carefully set up a scene that made it look like drug deal gone bad, just in case.

We sat around and plotted out a strategy for their

security and safety. We plotted out a strategy for them to follow. They joined the Vampire Society and other associated and related groups and clubs which would help provide and fulfill some of their needs.

We also devised a kind of plan where Desa and John could seduce and feed on some of the nerds that attended comic book conventions. So far, it's worked beautifully. Desa would seduce the nerds at after parties, get them excited, drug them, and both would drain them enough to leave them tired and exhausted, but not kill them. Best of all, they'd little memory of what happened. Since there are enough of these in every state, it has been a very effective way for them to get blood. This would also give them friends and allies as well as additional security and protection.

On top of getting my usual twice-a-year visit from them, I usually receive a postcard or a letter every year from where they are at. Last year they were in New Orleans, this year they are somewhere near Traverse City, Michigan, where they live in relative obscurity.

Some unwary hikers found the badly-decomposed remains of Craven and his men several months after the fact. With some drug drugs planted on them and the condition of the bodies, the authorities suspected it was due to the casualties of the drug war or competition between gangs.

With John and Desa now safe and somewhat sound, I have another potential client that has an interest in my services. There is one thing that is making me hesitant, and that is the fact that she claims to be a witch. It helps a lot that she is very beautiful. But, I don't know.

Decision, decisions.

Dirty Rotten Bastards

I guess you could say it all started on Friday night.

We were all hanging out in Kirk Howard's parents' basement. There was me, Kirk of course, Dennis Caldwell, Rick Seitz, Ben Frye, and Rollie Bostick.

Kirk, Ben and Rollie were hanging out, smoking a dime bag. I arrived about the same time as Rick to see what was going on. I was handed a beer and we sat around drinking and getting high. I didn't do marijuana or smoke. It wasn't me and I'd gladly take a drug test to verify what I am saying. But, I digress, once the bag was gone, the guys had the munchies and we all kicked in a few bucks to order five large pizzas.

Once we were eating we sat around, shooting the bull about our day and week. It was basically a gripe session about how bad we all had it in dealing with certain individuals.

Kirk was bitching about his parents' rules and how they'd come to expect him to do more since graduating from high school, while Rollie complained about his boss at the oil change place. Ben tried to play psychologist, to it all like he always did after feeling enlightened by the marijuana. He failed miserably. Dennis kept crying the blues about his ex-girlfriend who broke up with him over his constant cheating, and was now going out with someone he could not stand. Rick was one of these guys who thought the whole world was pathetic and did not really care what happened to it.

As for me, I was grumbling about how it seemed at times how my parents and bosses had little empathy for my working my way through school. At the time, it kind of pissed me off, but that would change later when they were more helpful.

Dennis kept going on how he'd like to kill the guy who was now dating his ex-girlfriend.

When it was suggested that she wouldn't have broken up with him if he hadn't been nailing everything thing he talked to, he spat, "Fuck you!" very loudly. Somehow, he viewed himself as some kind of half-assed Romeo.

As we sat eating pizza and bitching about life and people, we watched the movie '*The Wild Bunch*.' Kirk made the comment that would be the life. He mentioned how he loved the idea of boozing it up, whoring around, stealing money and killing people at times that pissed you off, or ones you did not like. He even included his parents.

I wasn't surprised by this. But when the others all agreed and thought it was a cool way to go, I was a bit shocked and concerned. I expected this out of Kirk and Rollie, who were always pissed off at someone, but not the others. When Rick mentioned he wouldn't mind randomly shooting someone for kicks, I wondered what in the hell had happened to these guys and what I'd gotten myself into.

We had all grown up together and gone to school with each other since elementary and at times had not always been close, but we'd remained friends. We had all changed from one degree to another, but this was beyond the pale.

I was taken aback when Kirk asked me what I thought. I told him, while I had my gripes and complaints with things, none of the rose to the point where I wanted to kill someone over them. None of my complaints were that important. In fact, looking back on it, they were quite trivial.

When I mentioned that I was taught that we made our own breaks, and most of our personal hurts and wounds we suffered in life were usually self-inflicted, Dennis and Rollie quickly jumped me and told me how stupid I was. *To which*, I pointed out, that Dennis would still have his girlfriend Kristen is he hadn't kept cheating on her. I then asked him how long he expected her to stay with him if he kept doing that.

He wanted to fight me right then and there. I told him that I could kick his ass and the guys knew it too. They quickly told him he was wrong to want to fight over this.

At that point I had enough. I finished my last beer about the time of the climatic final battle of The Wild Bunch.

"That's the way I want to go out," Kirk announced.

"Yeah, that," Dennis agreed, raising his beer bottle to Kirk's to toast that comment.

Soon, Ben, Rollie and Rick joined in. It was like they were all of one mind.

A chill ran up my spine. I announced that I was out of there. I told them that I probably would see them tomorrow. That was a promise I did not intend to keep. I could see some trouble brewing and I did not want to be a part of it. Somehow the thought of dying in some horrific, bloody gun battle wasn't my idea of glory and seemed kind of warped.

If not warped, then seriously insane and stupid.

They had gotten worse in the three years after high school graduation. I think it had to do with their dead-end thinking and lack of responsibility in working towards a goal, I guess.

Individually, the guys all had their roles. Kirk was kind of the unelected, defacto leader. Why, I don't know. But, the others all deferred to him. The only other one who might be considered that was myself, and I wanted no part of it really. He was not a tyrant or anything, though he could be, but he was the leader.

Ben was, at the time, a kind of second in command. He was the rule setter. He always thought of himself as a real strategist or a psychologist type who could get in people's heads. I think he became that way from playing too many strategy games. These of course did not help, and he was not as smart as he seemed to think he was. He was a genius with numbers and technical things, but had trouble reading. I still remember the time, I called his sister a thespian, because she acted in a play, and he got mad at me and yelled that she liked boys. So Ben had trouble with some words. In spite of this, he knew how to build pipe bombs using chemicals and other objects. He did this to blow up mail boxes on occasion for kicks.

Rollie was the real enforcer and group hothead. Ben might have enforced the rules, Rollie made sure you did. He kind of reminded me of a guy named Eddie Temple I had heard about. He hated most authority figures, even though he acted like one himself. He was also our resident bigot. He had a tendency to use racial slurs every now and then.

Dennis was the group's self-proclaimed Casanova or Romeo. In reality, he was a man-whore. He always seemed to be with a new girl, but that was due to the fact he ended up getting dumped for cheating on them. In reality, he probably didn't get laid any more than the rest of us. In fact a lot of his women were not really that attractive either.

Rick was the intellectual snob of the group. Every group seems to have one. He seemed to have disdain for everybody. He would speak about the downtrodden while at the same time he looked down on them. He wouldn't tip a waitress because he thought it was their own stupid fault that they were working as a waitress in the first place. He was basically a hypocrite and either did not realize it or did not care. Many of his pontifications were out there to say the least. On top of that he acted like he was so above the fray and so much smarter than everybody else, when he really wasn't.

They were a mixed bag of personalities. We had all grown up together and were all from basically middle class households.

It was a few days after that I found out the guys were actually planning something.

I figured that the euphoria of going out like the Wild Bunch had worn off and I stopped by Kirk's place. I discovered that the guys had "borrowed" weapons and ammo. There were two twelve gauge pumps and hundreds of rounds of ammo, an old M-1 rifle with a few hundred rounds and two pistols with ammo, a Winchester and a 30.06 hunting rifle. According to them, they were borrowed for a hunting trip and nobody would miss them.

I had also heard Rollie's grandfather was found dead around that time I had my suspicions. Supposedly, he had fallen down the stairs and broke his neck. He was old, and he had fallen before, but something told me his accident was manufactured. Nothing ever came of it. The authorities did not investigate it.

I did not know what was going on, but I knew there was something going on.

I decided to stay away for a while. After almost two weeks I decided to go back and see what was going on.

When I finally returned to Kirk's house, the guys' mood was even more sullen and angry than before. Kirk had been having arguments with his parents and was wishing they were dead. He was even trying to think of scenarios for their deaths and how he could pull it off. At the time I figured it was all talk. Rollie wanted to kill his boss. But then, he always did. Dennis was wanting to shoot his ex-girlfriend and her new boyfriend. Ben laughed about it all and just thought killing people for kicks would be something different and even exciting. He was funny that way, in a sick sort of way. Rick wanted to just be rid of everybody he viewed as rabble.

There was a lot of thought, planning and seriousness to their conversation. But that was typical of him as well.

Initially, they were a little suspicious of me being there, but after I hung out a while, they were still loyal to me. Somehow though, things had progressed further than I could have imagined. What they were talking about was disturbing and a bit frightening to me.

I had a couple of beers with them and told them I had to go because I had a date. This was the truth because I had a date. This made for a good excuse. Besides, I was to the point that I'd rather be with some pretty girl than a bunch of guys.

I was in no hurry to return.

A few days later I ran into two guys who hung out at Kirk's on occasion. They were Jeff Fadly and Ted Anderson. Both told me that while they were sitting around smoking some weed, they were talking about what they would like to do.

Jeff mentioned that a couple of them were talking about shooting some people they did not like. Ted said he thought Rollie mentioned he actually shot a couple of people, but wasn't really sure.

While both admitted they didn't mind talking about shooting people they didn't like, they were hesitant to be cold-blooded murderers.

Something did not sit right with me. I felt like I was being played. I had never been close to Jeff or Ted and had always been leery of them because they were always on the shady side of things. They bought and sold drugs, while mostly marijuana, they had been known to beat up a few people and slash a few tires. They also had a habit of not caring who they might have hurt by what they said or did. I did not trust what they were telling me and wondered if they weren't trying to set me up somehow.

I felt like they were feeding me information to see if I blabbed.

I thought it was some kind of test of my loyalty. But these two weren't exactly the best ones to keep a secret either. They both had a tendency to talk too much.

Fortunately for me I had a date and had more important things to do. By that time I had been seeing a girl named Dannette Gauthier, a real hot babe if there ever was one. Dannette was better to be with than those losers and assholes.

It was a real easy choice for me. I could either spend time with a real hottie, or those Wild Bunch wannabes.

Even though I was seeing Dannette, I was able to keep tabs on them. It wasn't hard since we lived so close. I stopped by one day to hear Rollie and Ben laughing and taking great pleasure in "coon hunting" about the same time as four black people had been randomly shot in Pontiac where one actually died.

Kirk said they'd do it again soon.

Though I could not prove it was connected to them, there had reportedly had been more larcenies and robberies in the area. My first clue it was them was when I heard they were throwing money around and they were having parties.

I was invited to one. It was a big one they called Cosmic Weekend Party. While hesitant, I thought about it and decided to put in a token appearance. By then, Dannette was my girlfriend and I thought we could go for a while together. Having her with me, at least, gave me an excuse to leave early just in case something bad was going to happen.

The party was as wild and surreal as any I have ever attended. On top of the loud music, there were kegs of beer, drugs and even hookers, or should I say professional escorts and dancers. Supposedly, there was an orgy going on in the basement.

We decided it was best not to stay. After about an hour we left. This wasn't a party you brought your girlfriend to. We both could party and had done so in the past, but even we had our limits. We also could tell that this was one of those parties where someone gets arrested, hurt or even dies. As far as we could tell the only thing missing was a potential human sacrifice. That pretty much describes how bad it was.

The next day we heard there had been a couple of near overdoses; someone was said to have been left on their lawn, passed out drunk in their underwear; a fistfight over one of the escorts or dancers and two people that had been there were rumored to have come up missing. The party had also severely depleted the money they had accumulated to this point.

When I ran into Kirk a few days later, he hardly batted an eye or acted surprised when I asked about the two people who came up missing. Once again, I couldn't prove it. I knew that it was probably Jeff and Ted who had been taken out for talking too much. Given their track records and run-ins with the law, they weren't going to be missed by many people except maybe their immediate families, and maybe not even them.

A few days later they found Jeff and Ted's bullet riddled bodies out in a gravel pit in Lapeer somewhere. Jeff's car was badly shot up. A lot of people speculated that it was a drug deal gone bad, like in the movie *No Country For Old Men*. They did buy and sell drugs, so a few people expected it.

I thought differently.

I knew it was those guys. With every fiber of my being, I knew it was them.

A couple of weeks later, I heard about some local business owners being robbed at closing time or as they were going to make the day's cash deposits. The business owners were people we had all known for a long time. They were really good people.

From what the news reported, they jumped the owners from behind, knocking them unconscious, and were able to get away with over a hundred thousand dollars. Not a bad take for a bunch like that. One business owner who resisted was shot in the ass.

That is not me showing them respect, but commenting on how lucky they were. Especially since they were not that smart or good. They were a bunch or retards. Or damn near.

Because of these acts, they were called the Dirty Rotten Bastards by the business owner's friends and workers. This was a name they wore with honor.

The way they acted after the robberies was even more stupid. They'd go around singing, "Were the Dirty Rotten Bastards. Bastards of the night. We're the dirty, goddamn sons of bitches who'd rather fuck than fight. So be careful what you do or ask or we'll shoot you in the ass."

By the third one they had gotten pretty cocky and were throwing money around. Kirk even bought our dinner one night when Dannette and I were out on a date when he ran into us. He seemed magnanimous and friendly. Part of me thought it was last act of friendship towards me. I think he knew that things had changed and would never be the same after that. He told Dannette to take good care of me and hoped that we had a good life together.

Fortunately for me, Dannette and I had gotten pretty serious at that time. When I wasn't working or going to school, I was with her every moment. So, in a sense she saved me, and got me away from my former friends' criminal element.

However, I did manage to keep tabs on them. I did it for my own sake and piece of mind. Mainly because I no longer trusted them. If they were able to bump off their drug dealing buddies, who else might they decided was a threat?

I figured I was not high on the list.

They knew I did not approve and that I thought it was wrong. They also knew that was part of the reason I had distanced myself from them. Fortunately, I also had Dannette, and that was another big reason I was not hanging out with them as much.

Like I said earlier, it was an easy choice of spending time with a real hot chick or sit around drinking beer with the guys. For me it was no contest. It was Dannette.

While I still had the better part of a year of college left, it did not matter and I decided to propose to Dannette. My mother gave me her mother's engagement ring and I asked her. I asked her when we were having a dinner date at the Lion's Den. She accepted. Shortly after dinner we ran into a Ben and Rick who had been drinking.

When I asked how the guys were doing, they said everybody was fine and that they had a lot of plans in the works. Ben even said that people would see what they, Dirty Rotten Bastards were about. Rick echoed the sentiments agreeing that it would be soon.

I knew it was no good and that it was possibly something potentially big.

A kind of chill ran up my spine at the thought.

Yet, there was nothing I could do until I at least knew more than I did.

I strongly suspected that they were committing crimes, most of which were robberies in the area. Though I have to admit I suspected they were in on a few shootings as well. They had become more cunning, more efficient and more deadly.

I suspected that they had obtained some automatic weapons, by the kinds of ammunition they had lying around the last time I had been over. And while I couldn't prove it I suspected that they were responsible for some panhandlers being shot to death.

I stopped by and quickly realized I was now an outsider. I was viewed with skepticism and suspicion. While I did not know what to expect when I arrived, I was not totally surprised by this.

From what I could gather by the various conversations and innuendo, they had been pretty active. From the way they were freely brandishing weapons around me with no fear or concern whatsoever, I could sense they were confident to the point of cockiness.

Then again, what could I do? Kirk's parents hardly ever came down the basement. They gave Kirk his space. Plus the guys had me. They knew I would not say anything because they kind of had me on the spot.

"Shouldn't you be with that girlfriend of yours?" Dennis asked, snidely.

Before I could answer Kirk spoke up.

"We're not the same people you were friends with," he pointed out, almost ominously. "Like you, we've moved onto other things. Have a good life man."

I quietly nodded in agreement and left. I knew our friendship was officially over at that point. I left with his words still running through my mind. They were disturbing to me.

I could see trouble brewing on the horizon and there was nothing I could do to prevent it.

Then again, maybe it was best to let whatever was supposed to happen just happen. Maybe guys like Kirk, Ben, Rollie, Dennis and Rick deserved to be left to whatever fate had in store for them no matter how bad it was.

A few days later, we heard about the gruesome murder of local area businessman and well-known, all-around asshole Carl Snow. Someone shot him in the face and robbed his office for an undetermined amount of money that was believed to be in the thousands.

A few days after that all hell began to break loose. It started with Dennis running into his ex-girlfriend Kristen at a Sonic Drive-In. She was there with her new boyfriend. It turned out he was an off-duty-undercover cop. Well, from what I heard and was later told by some of the guys, Dennis saw her kiss the new boyfriend, he lost his temper and nearly emptied his handgun into her. He also shot the boyfriend once in the side and left arm.

Being a cop, he pulled his firearm and shot Dennis in the head and side. Amazingly enough, Dennis was still alive and able to get away with assistance from Ben and Rollie.

I can only surmise from there that the guys realized they were living on borrowed time, and decided to take out as many people as they could. This was reserved to those that pissed them off, had problems with and even hated.

I know this because they stopped by our house in Kirk and Rollie's cars, demanding I give them bandages, cotton and any other medical stuff we had. They told me what had happened and what they were planning. They had decided to go down in what they viewed was proverbial blaze of glory.

Even Dennis who was bleeding profusely and had a bullet wound in his head went along with the idea.

"That's crazy!" I protested in vain.

But, I knew their minds were made up.

After stopping by our house, the guys went on a kind of homicidal kick. It was all a blur to me. Kirk killed his parents, while Rollie killed his boss. I even heard that Ben killed old man Latimer, a crotchety, mean, old bastard we had known and dealt with since we were little.

After they had gotten the bandages and medical supplies, I contacted the police and told them all I knew about them. From there I know only what was pretty much reported.

Somewhere between Kirk killing his parents and the other killings, they were confronted by the authorities. From what I heard Dennis already being wounded like he was, acted as a kind of rear guard of sorts. He was basically a suicide by police, since he charged at them firing automatic weapons.

From what I heard he was riddled by at least a couple dozen bullets.

After that with the information I had given the authorities, they were able to get a better idea of who they were, how they acted, what they might do and where they were more likely to go. Plus, it didn't hurt that those guys were idiots and doing everything stupid. They left of path of death and destruction that was easy to follow.

Somehow all four ended up at a nearby abandoned house to try and hole up in. From what I heard Rick, the intellectual snob and jerk suddenly got "cold feet" and tried to surrender, until Kirk shot him in the back several times.

Somehow Kirk, Rollie and Ben had been able to make it into the house with almost all of their guns and ammo.

The authorities informed me that involved a horrific shoot-out that involved SWAT teams as well as three different police agencies, ranging from the sheriff's department and even the State Police.

From what I was told, Ben tried to throw a pipe bomb and was shot multiple times, causing him to drop the pipe bomb onto his bag of other pipe bombs and was blown all to Hell. I heard he was shredded by the impact of the explosion.

I guess when the bomb went off the shrapnel hit both Kirk and Rollie.

I guess Rollie was blinded by the blood and shrapnel, and while firing blindly at the police was hit by several shotgun blasts.

Kirk, now the world's biggest jerk acted like he was going to surrender. He walked out with his hands and arms raised. Then according to the police he gave everybody the middle finger and pulled two pistols from the back of his pants and began firing away.

From what I was told, he was shot so many times at that point that the gunfire that riddled his body somehow kept it up for a few seconds before falling to the ground in a bloody heap.

It was a fitting ending to guys like this.

I found the real irony to be, unlike the characters in the movie *'The Wild Bunch'* who killed most of a Mexican general's army in a blazing gun battle, no police were wounded or killed. The only one who was wounded was the one who shot Dennis and he was off-duty.

The other thing was these guys could have had decent lives and careers had they not gotten the insanely stupid idea it would be cool to do these things for kicks.

Not only do they come off as the ultimate assholes, but stupid as well. They were not the cool folk heroes they desired to be thought of. Instead they were viewed as pieces of shit that killed and stole for no other reason than they were bored.

They were monsters of their own making. Nobody else gets the blame for their actions. Nor should they. When it comes to being Dirty Rotten Bastards, Kirk, Ben, Rollie, Dennis and Rick were self-made men with only themselves to blame.

Music in the Night

"Do you hear that, Morgan?" Al Burnette asked. "It sounds like music."

David Morgan finished drinking his Coke and listened closely. "Yeah, I do," he admitted, while nodding. "It must be coming from somewhere on the lake."

"What is that?" Burnette asked, as he leaned against the porch railing as he tried to listen more closely to the music.

Morgan tilted his head and listened intently. "It sounds like a jazz tune," he finally replied. "I can't make out what it is exactly, but it is definitely coming from somewhere on the lake. The music sure carries on a hot summer night."

The two men continued to listen from the porch as the evening began to get darker.

"Yeah, it sounds like jazz," Burnette finally agreed. "I wish I knew where it was coming from."

"Wherever it is, it sounds close," Morgan observed.

Burnette and Morgan were soon joined by the much older Roger Dennison. "So did you guys enjoy the fishing on this beautiful Fourth of July?" he asked upon walking out onto the porch.

Morgan raised his finger as if to shush, Dennison. "Listen," Morgan replied.

Dennison raised his head and listen. He sighed and quickly lowered his head, then shuddered as if he experienced a chill. "It's nothing," he commented. "Just ignore it."

Morgan and Burnette looked at each other quizzically, then at Dennison.

"It sounds like jazz," Morgan replied. "Where is it coming from?"

Dennison nodded. "It's *Ain't Misbehavin'*," he finally said.

"I never knew you were a jazz aficionado," Morgan commented.

Dennison walked over to the porch railing. "I'm not," he admitted. "But that music ain't exactly what you think and I've heard it every year since I can remember."

"What?" Burnette asked. "What in blue blazes do you mean by that?"

"I mean it is music from another time and place," Dennison explained.

"Say what?" Morgan asked. "What do you mean?"

"You better grab yourselves a drink first," Dennison answered.

"I'll get it," Burnette said, as he went into the house to retrieve some Budweiser's they had on hand. He soon returned with three of them, handing them out each of them. "So continue."

Dennison opened his beer and took a drink. "You might not believe this, but it's true," he explained. "I only know what I know. But it is true."

Burnette laughed, pulling out a cigarette and lighting it. "Try me," he said, before taking a puff.

"The music you hear is from the twenties," Dennison continued.

"Well, that's obvious," Burnette snapped. "I can tell by the tune."

Dennison took a deep breath. "You see there was a party at a beach house down the road."

"What beach house?" Morgan asked. "I didn't see a beach house anywhere."

"Like I was saying, there was a Fourth of July party at a beach house down the road," Dennison continued. "The party was many years ago. Back in the Roaring Twenties."

"So what are you saying there was some kind of tragedy?" Morgan asked, before finishing off his Coke and leaning against the railing. "This is some kind of ghost music from it or something?"

"Well, not exactly," Dennis answered as he walked over to the porch railing, staring into the darkness. "Not exactly a tragedy, more like a massacre of sorts. You see the party was with mobsters. Supposedly it was some of Capone's boys or another rival gang. Anyway they were having a party with a jazz band, prostitutes, bootleg booze and whatever else you can think of. Anyway at the height of festivities the Purple Gang struck."

"So what happened next?" Burnette asked, before taking a drag off of his cigarette.

"From what I heard, they mowed everybody down," Dennison answered. "Because of the holiday, nobody knew they were dead for a couple of days."

"Wow," Morgan muttered. "So you're really saying this music is ghost music, then?"

Dennison nodded. "Yeah," he finally replied. "In a way."

"Did anyone survive?" Morgan asked.

"Yeah," Dennison replied. "One jazz musician, a saxophonist, played dead, and a couple who were skinny-dipping in Orchard Lake."

"So what happened to them?" Burnette asked snidely.

"They couldn't tell the police anything," Dennison answered. "The couple was out in the lake making love, and the musician was underneath the dead bass player. The musician said that he hadn't seen any of the men before and was on his stomach immediately after the bass player was hit."

"Wow, that is something," Morgan commented.

"I'd say so," Burnette agreed. "But, it sounds kind of like bullshit if you ask me. Tall tales and such."

"You can believe what you want," Dennison responded. "I know it's hard to believe, but you yourself heard the music."

"So, what?" Burnette answered. "Someone could have their radio turned up high or a band is actually playing somewhere else. Sorry, but call me skeptical."

"Sounds plausible," Morgan surmised.

"So why don't we go check this out?" Burnette asked. "Just to see what you're telling us is true."

"I'll tell you this," Dennison said. "That would be foolhardy. A few people in the past decided to do exactly that, they went to investigate and were later found dead. They had been machine gunned to death. One man went about fifty years ago and he staggered all the way here. He was shot and bleeding and managed to tell what he saw."

"First off, there ain't a beach house there anymore," Burnette argued. "There is now a house there. So what happens to the people who live there now?"

"They know the history too," Dennison explained, before taking a drink of his beer. "They are never home the week of the Fourth."

"So finish telling us about the man who staggered here," Morgan said. "What happened?"

"He said he arrived at the party where everybody was dressed like flappers, and old-time gangsters," Dennison explained. "He walked up and someone let him in. He said he had some drinks, food, listened to some jazz and was watching some fireworks when all Hell broke loose. He then went on to tell how as soon as the fireworks went off outside about a dozen men with Tommy guns and shotguns came in shot everybody. When we called the police and went back with him later, there was nobody there. There was no party, no bodies, no bullet holes. He had witnessed something from the past. It happened. But many years ago. He somehow witnessed and became part of it."

"You said the people who actually were there did not tell the authorities anything?" Morgan asked.

"Yeah," Dennison said, just before finishing off his beer. "The couple said they were outside swimming in the nighttime lake and only heard the noise. They also said they hid from the gunfire and were unable to see anything. The jazz musician said he couldn't really identify them because of the three hundred pound bass player that was lying on top of him."

"How convenient," Burnette said, skeptically.

"Yeah, well nobody messed with the Purple Gang," Dennison said. "Capone wouldn't even fuck with them. That's how bad they were. They supposedly sent some of his guys back to him in pieces before they had a truce. Hell they pretty much controlled the Great Lakes."

"I know about them" Burnette snapped. "I just have trouble believing with what you're telling us. Especially when it comes to this hoo-hoo, ghost bullshit, that's all. I mean to believe this happens again and again every Fourth of July is a bit tough."

"I know that," Dennison said finishing off his beer.

"So who exactly were these people who ended up shot that went to investigate the music?" Burnette asked.

"Burt Yeardley and George Hansen," Dennison replied.

"And how do you know this?" Burnette asked.

"My grandparents told me," Dennison answered. "According to them the two men's wives asked if they had seen them when they did not come back from checking on the party. They had not seen anybody at the beach house, and wondered who had suddenly showed up there.

Anyway, the next day, a couple of people went over there and they found them riddled with bullets. I was told they found Yeardley with a part of a ladies white boa in his hand."

"So what?" Burnette argued again. "That could have come from anywhere."

"Possibly, but I don't think so," Dennison said. "As a kid, while staying at my grandparents, I too decided to investigate one night with my brother. We snuck out after we heard the music. We got real close and listened. We could see people dressed like what we thought were mobsters, and ladies dressed up in old fashioned clothing. We even started to go closer when our grandfather came and grabbed us and quickly led us away. He was scared and we were scolded to never go there again. A few minutes later we heard what sounded like machine gun fire. That was when were told everything."

"Hey, you hear that?" Morgan asked. "It's a different song. The music has changed."

All three men stopped talking and listened for a moment.

"Yeah, so, you can't play the same song forever," Burnette snapped after a long period of silence.

"What song is that?" Morgan asked, looking at Dennison.

"*Ain't We Got Fun*?" Dennison replied. "It will be followed by the likes of *Making Whoopee*, *Rhapsody in Blue, Stardust, Sweet Georgia Brown, Toot Toot Tootsie, When You're Smiling, Second Hand Rose, and Charleston*. The last song to be played and will stop in mid song will be *Farewell Blues*."

Both men looked over at Burnette who still had a skeptical look on his face. "I still say we need to investigate," he argued.

"No!" Dennison snapped. "Please do not do that! Trust me, it's better you don't."

"You expect me to believe this story?" Burnette asked. "It all sounds too unbelievable. I really need to check it out. Just for confirmation."

"No don't," Dennison said. "I beg you not to."

"I don't know," Morgan suggested. "I think he's right. Better safe than sorry as they say."

Burnette shook his head in in disagreement. "Alright, yeah, whatever," he finally conceded.

How do you know so much about this?" Morgan asked. "You seem to know a lot of details. Did you know the people who survived?"

Dennison looked down and nodded. "Yeah, I did," he admitted.

"Let me guess," Morgan said, trying to guess. "You either knew the musician or one or both of the couple in the lake."

Dennison nodded. "The couple in the lake were my grandparents," he confessed. "It seems they were working for the caterer or whatever they were called. Anyway while on their break, they snuck off to well, you know."

"Wow, that makes sense," Morgan commented. "Good thing for you they decided to get frisky out in the lake, huh? What do you think Burnette?"

Both men turned to Burnette to see what he was going to say only to find him no longer there. He was gone.

"Burnette?" Morgan called out. "Burnette? George? For Chrissakes where are you? Oh God, you don't think he…?"

Dennison shook his head then looked downward. "God help him, I think he's gone over there."

"Shit!" Morgan cursed and started to leave. "I should go get him."

"No!" Dennison said, physically stopping Morgan. "You can't."

Morgan stopped. He knew Dennison was right. "Damn," he finally muttered, and let out a sigh of deep resignation.

Both men went back to listening to the music. Just as Dennison had earlier stated the music was played in that exact order. They went back to listening to the distant music that was floating in the night air as the fireworks began to go off.

Soon *Farewell Blues* stopped abruptly.

"Was that machine gun fire?" Morgan asked, after the music stopped and hearing some noise between fireworks blasts.

Dennison could only nod as they stood listening at the porch railing. The music in the night had ended.

So had their friend's life.

Tom Sawyer

Night of the Skinwalker

The trip out west had been both enjoyable and eventful. It was to have been our last hurrah after college and before new jobs, careers and life in general took over. For us, it was to be a kind of personal celebration. It was a kind of treat to ourselves.

My friends and I decided that we would head out west to try and see everything from the Grand Canyon to possibly even Las Vegas. It was to be our last guys' trip anywhere together for some time possibly ever. After this it was our careers, the army and our futures looming ahead and us heading in different directions.

There were six of us: myself, my best friend Mike Collins, Andrew Forbes, Brad Simmons, Dean Pritchard and Ken Childress. It was Westward Ho, about a week after the last graduation. We had been invited earlier by Mike's Uncle John to come out and work his Arizona ranch for a few weeks, so we decided to finally take him up on it. In exchange for our work we would be paid cash, all the beer we could drink and fed some of the best barbecue and largest, not to mention freshest steaks that side of the Mississippi. Like any other young men, we were also enticed with the promise of a popular bar in town where there were lots of girls and women.

So, with visions of living life for a while like it was the promise of a beer commercial, we took the red eye flight out to Arizona and were there in three hours.

As soon as we landed, things felt a lot different. I can't explain it, other than it was almost like an adventure in a way. I knew Mike was every bit as excited as I was about being there. Dean and Andrew were still talking about drinking and getting laid like they had been since before the flight. Brad and Ken were mixed bag of excited to be there like we were and wanting to get laid too.

Once we were picked up by Mike's Uncle John, Mike introduced the rest of the guys and we were driven to his place. After meeting his wife, and family we stowed our belongings in the bunkhouse and were given a tour of the place.

I had met John's sons John, and Matt, as well as their daughter April before when they visited for their grandmother's funeral a few years ago and we got along well. They were all close to Mike who had visited a couple of times before college.

April then introduced us to her friend Callie Longtree, who was the daughter of one of their friends. She was very attractive and friendly. She hugged and kissed Mike and myself. From what Mike's uncle said, she was almost like an extra daughter.

Andrew later muttered about having one less in competing for the girls when we hit the bar.

Needless to say, even working the ranch, we had fun and enjoyed the time out there. We put up fencing, baled hay, rode horses and even helped to herd cattle. We worked hard and had fun afterwards.

While Andrew, Dean, and Ken had hoped we would go to the bar every night after work, reality set in. We were too tired and sore afterwards. Mike, Brad and myself didn't really mind because we were fed great food at night, given beer and it was just nice to hang out by the fire pit, relax and enjoy the night sky. Besides, Callie and I were becoming closer. She seemed to always be sitting next to me at the fire pit. Also half the time Andrew and Dean were either asleep or dozing off from the work by the time we sat down after dinner.

John's sons complimented Mike, Brad and myself on our ability to keep up, work smart and be able to do a lot of the work. They said how well suited for the work we were. I replied that we had all done landscaping, or roofing to help get us through college in the summer which helped.

In the course of the first week I think a few of us lost five to ten pounds and still bulked up our muscles. I know Mike, Brad and I were pleased with this. Especially Brad, who was due to go into the army in September.

The first Friday night we went to the bar, along with all of John's family. We had a great time playing pool, darts, drinking and dancing. Andrew, Dean and Ken put on their best pick-up lines and acts only to be just plain rejected and shot down in flames by the ladies. All three tried to be something they were not, were basically laughed at, and ended up just drinking in frustration and getting very little action.

Meanwhile, Mike, Brad and I were asked to dance by the ladies. Callie pretty much filled my dance card.

After a couple of weeks, we picked up supplies and ferried some cattle and horses to people outside of Flagstaff, Tuba City and Gray Mountain. Eventually we became familiar enough with the area to do it ourselves a couple of times. On a day off we drove to Flagstaff to check out the city life for ourselves.

It was fun, exciting and very enjoyable. So much so that we did not arrive back until about dusk. When we arrived back Mike's, Uncle mentioned they were getting a bit concerned because driving at night in and around the desert could be difficult, especially because of how dark it became.

The next day, Callie admitted to being a bit worried about us and getting back in the dark. That evening after dinner, we managed to sneak off somewhere to be alone. It was the first time we managed to get anytime by ourselves together without everybody else being around. We had sex a couple of times. Afterwards, Callie mentioned to me to be careful while driving at night out on the desert highways near the reservations because there were many strange and unexplainable things out there. Things that could be very dangerous to us.

When I asked what she meant, she only said that it was too hard to explain, but they regarded legends of her people, and these legends were bad and very capable of hurting us. She called them skinwalkers. She explained they were witches or werewolves of some kind…..it was hard to remember what she'd said because we had sex again a few minutes later….after which she awarded me a cool sort of Native American necklace meant for protection.

After that, we headed back to join the others. While her words weighed greatly on me the rest of the night, it was hard to not think of her, her body and our earlier lovemaking. After a couple of weeks, and more private rendezvous between us, I had almost forgotten what she had told me.

Mike asked me about her and our relationship. I told him I really liked her and that I was going to hate leaving. He said it was possible to maintain a long distance relationship if we wanted it bad enough. He was right, but I knew we both had to wait and see.

Things continued pretty much like they had. We were up early helping to work the ranch; Callie and I would be together whenever the opportunity arose.

Andrew decided to be an asshole once while we were sitting around having some beer after working, and asked how the "squaw pussy" was. It was all I could do to contain myself, and I asked rather angrily "What?" with Mike, Brad and even Dean holding me back.

About two weeks later, we were told that we needed to drop off some horses. Mike's cousin Matt had to have an abscessed tooth removed and he couldn't do it. Plus Mike's uncle and Cousin John had to go see about buying some livestock and would be gone most of the day. Naturally, we were all too willing to do so, since it let us see the beautiful countryside and gave us a much easier work day.

Before we left, Callie instructed us to be careful and for me to remember what she told me earlier.

We went to drop off some horses and a trailer to a friend of Mike's uncle's near the town of Kayenta. After we did that, we visited Monument Valley Navajo Tribal Park. Then we headed back to the ranch.

We took route 163 through the Navajo Indian reservation that night. Mike wasn't thrilled. "I've been told when I was out here by my uncle and cousins that many strange things happen out here. Especially at night when going through the reservation."

"That's funny, so was I," I admitted. "By Callie."

After stopping off for a few drinks, we headed back to the ranch. It was after nine p.m. with Mike driving. Ken and Dean had dozed off.

The moonless night made everything look alien and unfamiliar from what we had earlier passed through that day. With the lack of moonlight, the pitch black night, made visibility limited. At best we could see maybe a few feet in front of the headlights.

We stopped along the route at a lonely gas station convenience store to use the bathroom, get some cokes, and stretch our legs. When we entered there was the soft din of country music playing on the radio inside the store.

The store itself was a mom and pop place that was filled with everything from rakes and tools to soft drinks and beer. It was nothing special and it looked old and a bit decrepit as far as buildings went.

The clerk, an older Native American looking man, eyed us somewhat suspiciously when we walked in and merely grunted.

The place was dimly lit and decrepit. I suddenly felt very uncomfortable being there. I knew something wasn't right. The clerk had a strange look and kept eyeing us. I could not describe the look except that he was watching at us with a kind of hunger in his eyes.

"Man, they don't really have anything here," Dean announced.

"Yeah, there ain't Jack shit here," Ken agreed.

Before I could turn to leave, Mike grabbed me and muttered. "Let's get out of here. I don't like it."

I nodded in agreement. The guy behind the counter gave me the creeps. We grabbed Brad and left the store very quickly.

"There was something wrong with that place and that guy," Mike said, out near the truck, to us. "I don't know if walked in on a robbery or what, but there was something not right going on there. Let's get the fuck out of here."

Once we went back out the vehicle, the darkness made the area surrounding the store look very strange and unsettling. From outside the place was lonely and desolate, almost creepy. Mike and I thought we had seen something out in the darkness as we climbed back into the truck, but were unsure.

"Maybe it's a coyote," he said to me.

"I don't know, Mike, but it looked too big and like it was on two legs," I replied.

Needless to say we quickly got out of there. I don't think any of us liked being out there too long. Only moments after we started on our way again, Brad noticed headlights behind us in the distance. "We've got company." he announced.

"Must be another lonely traveler," Ken surmised.

"Shit!" Andrew said. "I hope it ain't the store owner."

"Why?" I asked. "Why would he?"

"I took some trinkets when he wasn't looking," Andrew said. "I don't think he saw me. At least I didn't think he did."

"What the fuck his wrong with you?" I asked. "Is there some kind of major malfunction in that brain of yours? Why would you do that? Are you stupid?"

"No," Andrew protested. "I just didn't think they would miss them, that's all."

"Thanks, asshole," said Mike, more than a little pissed. "When we get home we're done after this. I will not travel anywhere with you again."

"If we get pulled over, I'm not lying for you," I said in agreement with Mike. "You're on your own."

"I don't blame them for being pissed, Andy," Dean said. "You always pull some kind of bullshit. This time it's worse. You could get us all in trouble with this one and that ain't cool."

Andrew always had a habit of doing things like that. It would start with little things and then escalate them until the point of really irritating people. He never seemed to learn that there was a limit to people's patience to things like that.

One example of this was when we were playing football and he kept hitting people in the nuts when he was blocking them. Finally, after warning him to stop he did it again, this time to me, and I punched him in the mouth. He was stunned and surprised by my actions. I told him if he did it again, I would kick his ass.

He finally stopped.

But it usually took one of us to get very mad at him and damn near have an altercation. The only thing that saved him from being killed by one of us was we had known him since elementary school.

However as we got older and had grown up, his act had gotten old and very stale. We wondered whether he was stupid, and asshole or just a stupid asshole.

After a few minutes of silence and our anger had dissipated, we continued onward down the road, each of us in our own conversations

Andrew was still pretty silent. He knew that he had screwed up and pissed us off to boot.

We kept watching, the headlights some distance behind us and they didn't get any closer. We concluded it wasn't the store owner or the police, just another traveler on the dark road.

"Hell, as dark as it is, it is kind of reassuring," Andrew admitted. "Even if it is the cops."

Mike had to agree with him. This stretch of road as dark as it was bothered us. We could tell they were still behind us, the same distance that they had been earlier and were not getting any closer. As we crested hills, we momentarily lost sight of them, only to gain it once we both had done so.

We watched in a kind of anticipation as we watched the headlights behind us crest a hill, and then disappear. As we waited for them to reappear, there was no sign of them. They did not show up. The headlights had not crested the hill as we had done earlier and were gone. It was as if they disappeared into the black abyss of night.

"I still don't see them," Brad announced.

Mike and I looked at each other in amazement.

"Maybe they had to take a piss, or something," Andrew suggested after his long silence.

"Why do it at the bottom of a hill?" I asked. "Nobody would see them out here, regardless. That doesn't make sense."

We kept turning back to check for any headlights, but they never did reappear. They had disappeared completely. It was as if they went into some kind of black hole.

"Maybe something happened," Mike suggested. "Maybe they had an accident. You think we should go back?"

"I don't know," I replied. "Maybe we should. Or should we go to the next town and get help."

"I'm for that," said Andrew. "Besides you can't see good enough to turn around out here. It's too Goddamn dark around here."

"Hell no!" Ken snapped. "This place is too damn dark and spooky."

Brad and Dean kept turning around in hope of seeing the other vehicle again.

"Nope nothing coming," Dean announced.

"Just darkness," Brad added. "Just pitch black darkness. No sign of anything at all. I wonder if they crashed."

"Too bad if they did," Dean snapped. "After that store, I'm in no hurry to stop and help anyone out here."

It was then the darkness seemed to get darker and take on surreal quality. Each of us exchanged glances as this weirdness seemed to permeate the vehicle. Then as we were cresting down another hill something leapt at the vehicle, hitting it with a dull thud.

As we all turned to look, we saw something outside of the vehicle. It was some kind of hairy black creature with glowing yellow eyes and an open snarling mouth. It was humanoid, but no man. Almost in unison Andrew, Ken and Dean all screamed and yelled. "What the fuck is that?!"

Mike swerved to and fro as he drove the vehicle down the road in the smothering blackness. The creature raised its clawed hand and scratched against the driver and the rear passenger side windows. Finally, Mike swerved once more and the creature was gone. It had either fell or jumped off. We were not sure which. Even though it was gone, we did not feel any safer out in the middle of nowhere. We still had some distance before getting back to the ranch.

After a few minutes, we came to another gas station and convenience store that looked a lot like the one we had quickly left. We climbed out and inspected the truck. It looked fine. No damage or scratches.

"I have to take a leak," Andrew announced. "That, or spring one."

"Me too," said Ken, as he followed Andrew to the bathrooms outside of the gas station.

Mike, Brad and I all went inside. Much to our surprise, this was the same gas station with the same owner we had left some time ago. The place was identical to the earlier gas station and convenience store we had visited earlier. Even stranger, the clerk at the counter looked the very same.

"What the he…" I started to say.

"Are we lost?" Mike asked the store owner. "I could have sworn we just left here."

He nodded. "You could be. Then you could be not." he said. "You boys, look like you saw something horrible. Are you alright?"

"We left here an hour ago," I said. "Did we drive around in circles?"

"Some do that," the store owner replied. "But, I doubt it. You said you left a store like this one?"

"Yeah," I said. "And there was a guy who looked just like you there."

"On top of that, we saw something pretty damned frightening outside our vehicle," Mike explained.

"Can you describe it?" the clerk asked.

We all exchanged looks. Finally Dean, Ken and Andrew all came running inside, frightened.

"Man, there is something out there," Dean said, excitedly.

"Yeah, there was something running along behind that supply shed out there," Ken exclaimed.

"You saw something?" the clerk asked, concerned. "Can you describe it?"

"Look, Sir," Mike said. "Something horrible…it was all hairy and like a man that attacked our vehicle. I don't know what it was."

"It scared the shit outta of us," I added.

"Skinwalker," the man replied.

"What in the fuck is that?" Andrew asked.

"A *what*?" Mike asked.

"A skinwalker," the man repeated.

We just looked at each other.

Then we hurled bloodcurdling howl from out back that jolted us. We ran to the door to see what it was. The hairy thing we had encountered earlier was now on top of the vehicle.

"What the fuck…" Dean muttered.

The clerk pulled out a shotgun from behind the counter, walked to the door and fire it at the creature. The creature then took off into the night making a painful kind of a howl in the distance.

"You boys were lucky," the clerk said matter-of-factly. "That first place you stopped at used to be our store. We had to move. My brother was killed one night by that thing about five years ago. The place was later burned to the ground. That man you met there was the skinwalker who made himself look like my twin brother. Did you take anything from there?"

At first we did not answer then we all looked at Andrew. He still had the trinkets on him. The clerk could tell by our body language one of us had taken something.

"That is only half of it," Mike announced. "There was a vehicle behind us. We could see its headlights, but then after a hill they disappeared."

The clerk nodded and took a deep breath. "You boys got lucky," he muttered.

The clerk called the Reservation police. Meanwhile, Mike called his uncle to let him know we were alright and that we would be back after the authorities checked on the vehicle we had thought had an accident. Needless to say, they were greatly relieved to hear from us.

When we returned with the Reservation Police to the site of the first store, it looked as if it had been partially burned out and deserted for a long time. According to the police it had been closed since the owner was mysteriously killed by what they thought was a cougar or a mountain lion ten years ago. We later met the Arizona Highway Patrol about where we thought we last saw the other car. The Highway Patrol said they found two bodies in the car that were torn apart by a wild animal of some kind. According to the Reservation Police, they were in the shame shape as the store owner was ten years ago.

While the Arizona Highway Patrol speculated it was a wild animal like a cougar, we knew differently.

Our story checked out and we were released. Andrew was held for further questioning because he somehow had valuable trinkets that were once the deceased owners. We basically left him to be questioned and picked him up later. He wasn't thrilled that we deserted him as he called it, but we told him he deserved it for his own stupidity.

Callie and I got together again as soon as I returned. She was glad I was safe. It was a very memorable summer being with her. Eventually Dean, Ken and Andrew were able to see a few of the local Arizona girls when we went to the bar.

We continued working the ranch, but never did any of us go out at night by ourselves. After that we made deliveries and hurried right back to the ranch with little or no sightseeing. The only time we really went out at night after that was when we were near the fire pit with all of us around it. Whatever it was we encountered had really frightened us.

Mike's uncle told us that they may not have totally believed the Native American legends they definitely paid them heed and were cautious nonetheless.

Callie told me more about the legend and that because of the necklace I was safe.

We returned back to Michigan and went about our lives. Callie and I stayed in touch and kept a long distance romance going for a while. She visited me in Michigan and we visited all of the key attractions. We visited everything from Mackinaw Island to Pictured Rock and from Tahquamenon Falls to Alpena. It was great. We talked about getting engaged and decided to wait a few months until I became more settled in my position.

A short time after Callie's visit she was killed in a car accident. It wasn't by a skinwalker while driving out on the reservation. It was from something more ordinary and just as tragic. It had been a drunk driver just outside of Flagstaff. She died instantly.

Mike and I went flew out to the funeral. I was going to go alone, but Mike decided to join me, since he was my best friend after all. We flew back after the funeral. I presented Callie's family with the necklace she had given me shortly before our encounter with the skinwalker.

They in turn blessed Mike and me for our own protection. They had known of our encounter and thought enough of us to do so.

That was perhaps the saddest period of my life. I had lost someone I truly loved. But I carried on with my life and eventually had the career I had always wanted.

That was twenty-eight years ago. A whole other lifetime.

About a year later, Mike and I met girls about the same time, got married and had kids the same year. In fact, our children ended going to school together, much like we did. Naturally, we stayed close and maintained our friendship that endures to this day.

Brad joined the Army and stayed in for twenty-five years until a brain tumor forced him out on a medical discharge. But he is fine with a family of his own. We cross paths on occasion and sometimes have a drink or two when we can.

Dean and Ken were kind of changed after our encounter with the skinwalker. Dean became more serious. He quickly distanced himself away from Andrew as soon as we got back. He found a job. None of us had seen him since our ten year class reunion. It was as if he disappeared.

Ken he became even goofier, if that was possible. He finally was able to get a regular girlfriend. After bragging about how much sex he was getting, he went out and cheated. His girlfriend dumped him and he spent quite some time crying blues over 'losing' her, all while trying to hit on other women. He began to drink heavily and eventually became an alcoholic. He died at 35 from acute cirrhosis of the liver. We always thought it went back to that night we encountered the skinwalker.

Andrew, well he seemed even more destined to continue his thieving and dishonest ways after leaving Arizona. None of us had anything to do with him after that. He served five years for his part in robbing a bank. After his release, he was found torn to pieces in what the authorities called a possible drug deal gone wrong with some Mexican drug smugglers. Somehow he still had that trinket on him, along with a dime bag of marijuana, an illegal firearm and all of his money. Even more ironic is the fact he and his van were found out near that deserted store on that stretch of road in Arizona.

None of us believed it was a drug deal that had gone bad. We knew he was killed by what we encountered that night. We knew better. We also knew it was the skinwalker. There was no doubt in our minds about that.

As for us survivors, and except for Callie's funeral, none of us ever went back to that part of Arizona again for obvious reasons.

Tempting Fate

The witching hour was approaching with much fanfare and festivities as the Halloween Party had reached its zenith. As the clock chimed two a.m., the anticipation and excitement grew for a small number of party attendees.

"It's time," Ashley Lancaster announced to her small group of friends outside on the deck. "Do we have everything for the ceremony?"

"Yes," her best friend Samantha Tanner replied. "I am pretty sure we do."

"The board?" Ashley asked.

"Right here," Jamie Farnsworth exclaimed holding up the Ouija board.

"Candle?" Ashley continued to ask.

"More than enough," Brianna Holtzman answered. "As well as flashlights."

"What about the lighter, the book, the blanket and the other stuff? Ashley continued to ask.

"Relax, Ashley, Samantha exclaimed. "We have it all."

"Yeah," Brian Lindemann replied. "I have the blanket, the book and the knife."

"And I have the incense and the lighter," Brooke Salinger announced. "So we're all set."

"Good, good, that sounds like everything," Ashley said, almost gleefully. "Are we all ready for this?"

"I guess," Jennifer Rycroft muttered. "I'm just not sure I want to be in a cemetery at midnight conjuring things."

"It'll be cool," Samantha countered. "Even fun. Should we invite any of the others here?"

"No, too many will be a problem," Ashley commented. "We're pushing it now."

Jennifer just shook her head. "I don't know about this," she mumbled.

"Don't be a party pooper," Jamie chided, Jennifer. "It will be a real experience."

"Count me out Ashley," Chris McAlister commented. "I don't do cemeteries. Especially on Old Hallows Eve and with the intent of summoning a spirit. That is tempting fate if you ask me. Nothing good will come of it."

"You wussie," Ashley chided.

"Yeah, you sound like a chickenshit, man," Brian agreed.

"Call me what you want, but I'm not doing it," he repeated. "You couldn't pay me enough to do it. You're venturing into the unknown and none of it is good, if you ask me."

"Would you at least drive us there, then?" Brianna asked.

"Okay," Chris agreed. "I will pick you up later even, but I'm not doing what you guys are planning on doing. Just call me."

"Who else is interested in going?" Ashley asked. "Oh, yeah ask Carl. I think he's in the bathroom."

"Nope he's right here," Brianna announced. "Hey Carl you want to go summon spirits in the cemetery tonight?"

"Sure," Carl Henshaw replied. "Sounds like it could be fun."

"Let's go then," Ashley barked. "Onto the cemetery."

As the small group started to head to their vehicles they were approached by a couple.

"Hey wait up!" the girl shouted.

"Who in the hell is that?" Brooke asked.

"It's Conner and Melanie," Samantha announced.

"Shit!" Brianna muttered.

"Hey guys what's up?" Conner asked. "We heard you guys were going to a cemetery to have a séance or something."

"You heard right," Ashley said.

"We'd like to come along," Melanie exclaimed. "It sounds like great Halloween fun."

"Well, I don't know if we have the room," Ashley explained. "We already have eight of us."

"No problem, I have my own ride," Conner replied. "If it gets boring or we get in the way we'll leave then."

The small group looked at each other, nodded a bit and finally Ashley spoke. "Okay," she said. "But we're serious about this and no screwing around. We're going to summon the spirit of Abram Brown."

"Cool," Melanie said. "We'll follow you there."

"Sounds like a plan," Samantha commented.

Ashley, Samantha, Brooke and Brian piled in Chris' vehicle to be driven to the cemetery, while the others climbed into Carl's jalopy. They were soon joined by Conner and Melinda, who followed them to the Milford Cemetery.

The small caravan of vehicles pulled into the Milford Cemetery service drive, each car turning its lights off as they passed the entrance and the fence that encircled it. As they reached their desired location, the two following vehicles pulled off to the side as much as possible. With the exception of Chris, everybody piled out of the vehicles.

"Are you sure you won't join us?" Ashley asked, almost pleading.

Chris shook his head. "Hell, no," he responded. "You're lucky you got me this far. Once I get turned around I'm outta here."

"Okay," Ashley replied, a bit disheartened.

Chris waved as he then drove his car up to another service drive that crossed paths with the one they were on, turned around and quickly sped back without stopping. Once he hit the main road, his tires squealed loudly as he accelerated away.

"Chickenshit," Carl muttered to Brian who snickered.

"Oh be nice," Jamie laughed. "Some people just don't like cemeteries."

"Okay, let's go," Ashley commanded. "Everybody got their flashlights?"

"Yep," Brianna said.

"Nope," Conner admitted, speaking up. "We didn't figure on it."

"I brought our blanket," Melanie announced.

"Here, I got two, anyway," Samantha said, handing Conner a flashlight.

"Are we ready, now?" Ashley asked, somewhat perturbed. A chorus of 'yes's' and 'okay' erupted from the small group. "Then let's go."

Ashley led the way, with Samantha close behind as the small group trekked through the cemetery. Every so often one of them would trip or stub their toe on an unseen flat or small headstone.

"Do you know where you're going?" Carl asked, as he crept closer to Ashley.

Ashley glared. "What do you think?" she finally asked, sarcastically.

"Just asking," Carl said, defensively.

"We've been here a few times, scoping out the place," Samantha offered. "We wanted to be able to find it even in the dark. That's how we know."

"Oh," Carl grunted.

Once again, the group quietly muddled through the cemetery.

Conner and Melanie were falling further behind the others.

"Will you two keep up?" Brianna asked, as they lagged further behind because of their constant kissing and groping of each other.

"We will," Conner replied, as he waved Brianna onward.

"Jesus," Brianna muttered in disgust at the couple's overly amorous behavior.

After a few more minutes of walking in the darkness the group arrived at their destination.

"Okay, we're finally here," Ashley announced.

"So, this is it, huh?" Brian asked, shining his flashlight on the aged headstone. "Abram Brown, huh? Who the hell was he exactly?"

"A real bad person," Jennifer replied. "I don't like it here."

"Okay, let's start spreading the blanket, and setting up the other stuff," Ashley ordered.

The group silently placed the blanket on top of the grave and the Ouija board in the center of that, while the others lit the candles. Brian silently handed Ashley the knife.

"Okay, gather around," Ashley said, looking at the others. It was then she noticed Conner and Melinda were not with them. "Where are Conner and Melanie?"

Everybody looked around, shrugging their shoulders.

"They were lagging behind," Brianna announced. "They're probably off getting their freak on somewhere."

"Should we check?" Carl asked.

"Leave them be," Brianna barked. "They just came along to find a good spot in the cemetery to have sex in, that's all. Besides do you really want to see them screwing?"

"Only if we can film it," Carl joked.

Brian and some of the others laughed.

"Okay enough of this," Ashley said loudly, let's get down to business.

Soon the group was seated on the ground with hands clasped as they began the séance.

"Okay Brooke, get us started," Ashley said.

"We summon the spirit of Abram Brown," Brooke began to chant. "We summon the spirit of Abram Brown. Join us this night. We seek your presence. Join us Abram Brown. Join us now."

Dead silence.

"Keep trying," Samantha implored. "Maybe try another spirit or something."

"Abram Brown we continue to summon your spirit," Brooke continued. "Make your presence known. We summon you here and now."

Once again dead silence.

Suddenly all of the candles' flames shot upward into the air for several long moments before dying down.

"Jesus!" Carl exclaimed as the flames shot in the air.

"Holy shit!" Brianna said, shocked.

"Wow!" Jamie said, excitedly.

Finally after the flames died down, back to their normal state of burning, the Ouija Board planchette moved as everybody sat in stunned silence.

"We're not alone," Brooke observed.

"No kidding," Brianna muttered softly as Ashley glared at her. She knew immediately to shut-up.

"Abram Brown, are you with us?" Brooke continued to ask. "Are you with us Abram Brown? Is that you?"

The planchette slid across the board to the word 'no'.

"No," Ashley stated.

"If it's not him who is it?" Jennifer asked, more frightened than she already had been.

"Find out who it is," Ashley said, shaking her head.

"If this is not the spirit of Abram Brown, then who is with us?" Brooke asked. "Is this Abram Brown? Are you still with us spirit?"

There was no answer, just continued dead silence as an eeriness now hung in the air.

"Spirit are you with us?" Brooke asked.

The planchette slid across the board to the word 'yes'.

"Are you Abram Brown?" Brooke asked.

The planchette quickly slid back over to 'no'.

"I guess that answers that," Carl muttered. "So now what?"

"We find out who this is," Ashley responded.

"Spirit, are you still with us?" Brooke asked. The planchette then slid back over to 'yes'. "Will you communicate with us?"

The planchette slid back over to 'no'. It was followed by an eerie quiet and stillness.

"What just happened?" Brian asked. "Did it leave?"

At that point the group could hear something moving around nearby, but could not see anything.

"It is still here," Brooke announced. "It is nearby. Spirit, will you communicate with us? What do we have to do to communicate with you?"

Soon the planchette moved over to the letter 'S'.

"S," Ashley observed, as she watched it move to 'A', and then 'C' then onto the letters 'R', 'I', 'F' 'I', 'C' and finally resting on 'E', with her repeating each letter.

"What does that spell?" Carl asked, uncertain of what the word was.

"Sacrifice," Ashley announced.

"Sacrifice what?" Brianna asked. "An animal or what?"

"I'm outta here, guys," Jennifer announced as she stood up and broke the séance circle. "I'm not sacrificing anything. Anything that requires a sacrifice is not good."

They watched as she quickly marched away into the night.

"We don't need her anyway," Brianna commented.

"Find out what the spirit needs," Ashley said.

"What kind of sacrifice?" Brooke asked.

The planchette slid across the Ouija board and spelled out the word: *human.*

"Human?" Brooke announced. "It wants a human sacrifice."

"This is nuts," Brian snapped. "That is murder. We can't do that."

There was an uncomfortable silence amongst the group as they looked at each other dumfounded and uncertain of how to proceed and what to do next.

"But we've come this far," Ashley said. "We have to do something. Maybe we can find someone. You know like a homeless person or something."

"How do we do that without getting caught?" Brian asked. "And how do we do that and get back here in time?"

"Ask it if some other kind of sacrifice will work?" Ashley asked. "Ask if we can do something else?"

"Is there anything else we can do other than a sacrifice?" Brooke asked.

The planchette quickly returned to 'no'. It then proceeded to move across to the letters that spelled out V-I-R-G-I-N.

"Virgin?" Jamie exclaimed. "It doesn't just want any sacrifice, it wants a virgin one too."

"Everybody looked at each other with doubt and uncertainty. Almost everybody in the group knew or suspected which of them had lost their virginity, but weren't entirely sure.

"It looks like truth or dare time," Ashley announced. "I'm not. Haven't been for some time and that was before I began seeing Chris."

"Me either," Brooke admitted.

"Same here," Brian confessed.

"Ditto that," Carl muttered.

Jamie shook her head no, while Brianna and Samantha did the same.

"The only who was I know was Jennifer," Brianna said. "She always wanted to wait."

"And definitely the Melanie and Conner are not," Brooke said. "Those two are always doing it somewhere."

"So that leaves Jennifer," Ashley surmised, as everybody looked at each other.

"I'm not so sure about this, guys," Brian opined. "This has to be truly a bad spirit or a demon or something. Do you realize what this is asking us to do?"

"We made contact with the other side," Brianna argued. "And we've never done that before in any of our séances. This is a big chance."

"It means we have to kill somebody," Brian contended. "And not just anybody but somebody we know. Jen and she's our friend."

"I agree with Brianna," Ashley said. "If we want to continue we need to do this,"

Brian shook his head. "I ca…" he started to say, as some invisible force suddenly grabbed his body and hurled it somewhere out into the darkness with him screaming in the darkness.

Brian's sudden upheaval caused everybody to stand up in shock and panic.

"What the hell?" Brooke yelled.

"Oh, my God," Jamie exclaimed.

"Shit!" Carl yelled.

"Look," Brianna said, pointing to the board as the planchette once again was on the move. This time it spelled out Jennifer's name.

"It wants Jennifer," Ashley announced.

"But what about Brian?" Carl asked.

"We'll look for him while some of you get Jennifer," Ashley said. "Sam, you, Brianna and Carl go get her. Tell her we aren't going to do this and we'll contact someone else. Brooke and Jamie and I will look for Brian and see if he is alright."

The group split up and went in different directions. Sam, Brianna and Carl were able to eventually catch up to Jennifer. After much coaxing they were able to talk her into coming back.

Ashley, Jamie and Brooke looked around for Brian with their flashlights.

"Brian?" they called out every so often.

"Do you see any sign of him?" Ashley asked,

"No," Brooke muttered.

"Where could he have gone?" Jamie asked aloud.

"Who knows?" Brooke asked. "He was thrown pretty far."

"We're in the general direction," Ashley commented. "He was thrown this way."

As Jamie continued to shine her flashlight across the ground and through the trees, the beam of light came across something hanging from some tree low lying tree limbs as she caught a glimpse of the object.

"What the hell," Jamie gasped in horror, as she shined the light in the area where she first saw the object.

Once again her flashlights beam fell upon the object. It was Brian. His body was unnaturally contorted and broken as it was dangling from some branches.

"Oh, God," she gasped.

"Look at his face," Brooke muttered.

Brian's jaw was agape, with his tongue hanging out and his head was turned in such a way that they immediately knew his neck was broken.

"Gross," Ashley muttered. "Let's go. We found him. There's nothing we can do for him. Besides, he tried to stop what the spirit said it wanted."

The three women headed back to their séance spot. They arrived just before the others returned Jennifer.

"Are you alright," Ashley asked Jennifer.

"Yeah," Jennifer nodded. "I'm okay. I'm just not doing any human sacrifice. Or any sacrifice of anything for that matter."

"That's fine," Ashley said, trying to reassure her. "We can live with that."

"Good," Jennifer said, somewhat more at ease.

"Did you find Brian?" Brianna asked.

"No," Ashley said, quickly before the other girls could. "We'll find him later.

"Let's resume the séance," Ashley suggested. "Brooke get us started. Everybody sit back down."

"We have returned, spirit," Brooke began. "We summon you back. Will you communicate with us?"

Once again the Ouija Board planchette moved, slid over to the word 'no'.

"Is there nothing else we can do?" Brooke asked. "What do you want?"

The planchette moved to spell out the words *human sacrifice.*

"See, it's still demanding a human sacrifice," Jennifer said, very upset.

Ashley looked at Brooke and some of the others and nodded. They knew what she meant and what they had to do.

"Spirit, we have our human sacrifice," Brooke stated.

A chill ran through Jennifer who started to get up to leave. "Hell, no," she exclaimed. "I said…"

"No, you said you wouldn't sacrifice anybody," Ashley said. "We didn't say anything like that and we need a sacrifice."

Before she could say anything else or leave, she was grabbed by the others and held down on the ground. Ashley then pulled the sacrificial knife from her pocket.

"Okay Brooke, continue," she ordered.

"We sacrifice this virgin unto you," Brooke commenced, as Jennifer screamed and Ashley stabbed her in the center of her chest, piercing her heart. "Communicate with us, spirit."

Suddenly, the candle flames rose into the night and stayed there for several moments causing everybody to look around in awe and wonder.

"Whoa," Carl muttered.

Brooke lowered her head and appeared to be asleep or unconscious.

"Brooke? Brooke?" Brianna called out.

Soon a guttural groan emanated from Brooke before she raised her head. Her eyes had rolled up into her head as she laughed deeply and hoarsely.

"Brooke?" Ashley asked.

Brooke continued to laugh. "No," she said in a deep, sinister sounding voice. "Guess again. I am what you have summoned. There are many like me here. Your sacrifice is not enough. For we are legion."

"Holy shit!" Samantha exclaimed. "We've summoned a demon!"

"I'm outta here," Brianna announced.

Whatever dwelled in Brooke laughed loudly, as Brianna was thrown like a rag doll into a tall cemetery monument nearby by another unseen force. Her body landed with a horrible thud, and ended up lying in a clump at its base.

"Oh, my God!" Jamie screamed. "She's possessed!"

Ashley stabbed Brooke in the chest with her knife, only to have whatever was in Brooke laugh and slap her, and sending her sprawling across the ground unconscious. Brooke's body then collapsed on top of the Ouija board.

Once again the candle's flames rose into the night as the sounds of other diabolic spirits lurking around and stalking the remaining three.

"Let's get outta here!" Carl yelled.

"Run!" Jamie shouted.

All three took off towards the service drive pursued by whatever they had summoned. Part of the way, they became separated.

Carl was in a dead run when he tripped and fell over a small headstone and hit his head on the ground and became unconscious. Samantha became lost and ended up spending the night huddled in sheer terror next a family crypt for the rest of her night. Jamie made her way back to the road where she bumped into Connor and Melanie who had finished their cemetery sex and were next to their car getting ready to leave.

"We've gotta get outta here!" she exclaimed, terrified. "There's something chasing me!"

All three jumped into the car and quickly drove out of the cemetery.

"What do you have on you?" Conner asked.

"I think its blood," Jamie confessed, crying.

"Good, God," Melanie said.

They decided to meet up with Chris and they all drove to the nearest police station, where Jamie explained her story of the events.

By daylight, the authorities found Samantha next to the mausoleum, her hair turned pure white and babbling incoherently. They found Carl who had no memory of anything whatsoever.

When they found Ashley she was sitting next to the dead bodies of Jennifer and Brooke near their séance spot just staring into space, void of any acknowledgement of anything. Eventually they found the mangled body of Brian.

About six months later, Chris ran into Conner and Melanie at McDonalds. "You two okay?" he asked, approaching them in the parking lot. "How have you been since that night?"

"Okay," Melanie admitted. "We didn't really see anything. So we couldn't testify too much."

"Yeah, me either," Chris confessed. "Though I had to admit the knife was Ashley's. I could only tell the authorities about my misgivings about the whole thing."

"We were lucky," Conner admitted. "I'm glad we were more interested in sex than séance. They didn't really grill us much."

"I can't say the same for Ashley and the rest," Melanie said. "I think they're in for a long jail sentence when the trial gets done."

"Yeah," Conner agreed. "Ashley will probably get life and the others will get at least twenty years or more. That's what I've been hearing."

"And poor Samantha is nuts," Melanie commented. "Boy how sad. She still hasn't spoken a word since that night, I heard."

"I don't plan on ever going to a cemetery again," Conner confessed. "At least not at night and for nothing other than funeral."

Chris and Melanie laughed somewhat uncomfortable, but knowing all too well what he meant.

"I tried to keep Ashley from doing that," Chris admitted. "But she had to do it. She had to tempt fate, as they say. I've never understood the appeal of tempting fate."

A Long Dark Night in a Very Haunted House

He moved silently up to the casket that held his old friend, John Thomas, a person he had grown up with and known for years. A man who was perhaps the best friend he ever had. Now he was dead. A victim of cancer.

Even though it had been years since he had seen him, they had shared a closeness and a kind of brotherhood few could ever admit to. While their friendship had been forged at an early age, a bond had been sealed later that made it permanent and timeless.

Try as he might to keep his composure, tears welled up in his eyes as he got closer. Finally, he was able to look upon his old friend. After wiping them dry, he closed his eyes and said a silent prayer.

"*Had it really been twenty-five years?*" he asked himself, shaking his head in grief and sadness.

Once again he raised his hand to rub his eyes. He took a deep breath, and sighed. "I'm sorry old buddy," he muttered softly. "So very sorry."

Before he could turn away, he was approached by a man and a woman in their twenties.

"Excuse me, sir?" she asked.

"Yes," he replied hoarsely, still a bit shaken by seeing his friend.

"I don't believe we've ever met," she said. "I, or we've met almost all our dad's friends and co-workers and don't recall ever meeting you."

He nodded as he eyed the two young people. "My name is David Franklin," he replied.

"So, how did you know our father?" she asked.

"You must be Mary," David surmised. "And you must be…"

"David," the young man exclaimed. "David Franklin? I know your name from somewhere. Let me think."

"So, how do you know us?" Mary asked.

"I heard your name mentioned a couple of times," Mary admitted. "And of course I came across it when I was going through Dad's things."

"I moved away right after you were born," David said to the young namesake. "In fact your parents named you after me. We were that close. We kept in touch. I was here when your mother passed away too."

"Oh, yeah, now I remember," the younger David said. "You were here, then you left afterward. Wait a minute now I know. You were the other guy we heard about. The other guy who was with our dad when he….you know, Mary, the story. The story. The one story."

Mary looked at her brother, puzzled at first. "You!" she exclaimed. "That's right. Now I remember. Our parents didn't talk much about it, but we heard pieces here and there. "You and my dad were the ones who went to that haunted house out on the point."

David quietly nodded. "Yeah," he admitted. "I'm that guy."

"The Westcott Place," Mary snapped. "That was it."

"We heard stories from other people," David said. "Or at least parts of them. Dad never talked much about it. But we moved around quite a bit too. It was like he could never get comfortable in any house after that, mom said."

"Yeah," David said. "I know. We talked a lot."

"Wow," Mary said.

"Look, Mr. Franklin," David said. "The funeral home is about to close would you be willing to go out with us afterward for dinner and some drinks?"

"Yeah, we would really love it," Mary said.

"Okay," David nodded. "That would be fine. I think I owe it to you both."

Thirty minutes later the three ended up at a nearby bar that the elder David and his friends had frequented many years earlier.

"Wow, the place hasn't changed much," David observed as he looked around. "The last time I think I was here was for young David's birth."

"Wow, that has been some time," Mary commented.

"So, Mr. Franklin, could you tell us the story?" David asked.

"Please, just call me David," the elder David replied. "But we need alcohol first."

"That sounds good," Mary agreed.

David and Mary ordered beers while, their father's old friend ordered a Maker's Mark and Canada Dry.

"Alcohol," David said holding up his drink, and eyeing it. "Because no great story started with someone eating a salad."

David and Mary laughed, while the elder David took a drink.

"Okay, believe it or not, this story starts right here," Dave began. "Only it was over twenty-five years ago. We stopped off right here after work. We sat and drank with friends talking over the usual shit like, jobs, sports, girls, and sex. We were as my cousin Jim would say, young, dumb and full of cum. Sorry, I hope I didn't offend you."

"No," Mary laughed. "My dad said shit like that all

the time."

The elder David laughed. "Yeah," he muttered. "Anyway, we were sitting around having a good time when a Harold J. Boyle walks in and plants himself at the bar. We knew him as Harry Boyle. Now at the time Harry Boyle was perhaps the loudest, rudest and most insufferable loudmouth and bully the town ever had."

"Harry Boyle?" laughed the younger David. "Really? Wow, what a name."

"His name was fitting, alright," the older David continued. "It was the perfect moniker for such a terminal and blatant asshole as he. We had to deal with him all through school and he seemed to get worse with age."

"With him was his toady and sidekick Larry Lawson. While he wasn't as big an asshole as Harry, he could call 'Jerk' his middle name. Neither one were people we liked to hang with or trusted as far as we could see them."

David took a sip of his drink then continued. "Things stayed pretty peaceful until Stanley Groves walked in. He was the caretakers' assistant at the Westcott Place. He was a nice quiet, man who was a little slow. I guess you could say it was special needs."

"I heard that name too," Mary admitted, holding her beer.

"Well, Harry and Larry took great pleasure in picking on him and calling him 'half-wit' and making fun of him and his fear of the Westcott Place. They kept threatening to take him out there and leave him locked inside of it."

"Wow, that's terrible," the younger David said.

"Yeah, well your dad and I had enough of it," the elder David continued. "Especially when they started to get physical and kept picking on him when he tried to get away. John, your dad decided to really intervene and being his best friend, well, I had to have his back."

"Alright Boyle, enough's enough already," John snapped. "Leave him alone."

"Yeah, and who's going to make us, asshole?" Larry asked, acting all tough and bad because they thought they had the advantage.

"I guess we will, asshole," I said.

Harry Boyle laughed, but the whole place became quiet with everybody watching to see if anything was going to happen. Some were anticipating a fight breaking out. I have to admit I was and believe me, I would have taken great pleasure in pummeling Larry Lawson.

"Boyle, you know we can take you and your sidekick here," John said. "So, I suggest you stop."

Harry just glared at John and I. Even though he was bigger, he knew it was true and that we were serious.

"Alright, alright, already, we'll leave the retard alone," Harry said, finally giving in. "Jesus Christ, all of this bullshit over a dummy."

"You got that right," I said, looking at Harry. "Stanley shouldn't have to deal with a dummy either."

John and the others laughed at my comment, while Harry and Larry just glared.

"What is it with all of you, fuckers?" Harry exclaimed. "Everybody is so terrified of that place. It's ridiculous. You wouldn't see me that scared of anything. Shit, I'd put a whole paycheck up about spending a weekend there."

"Sure, that's why we see you spending so much time out at the Westcott Place," John said, as Harry glared. "As brave as you claim to be I'd love to see you spend a weekend there. Shit, even one night."

"Fuck that!" Larry spat.

"And yet, you and Harry pick on Stanley for being afraid of the place," I said. "What's the difference between you two chickenshits and him? At least he admits it."

"Not a damn thing," John commented.

"Shut up!" Harry snapped. "That's horseshit! There's plenty. I'd spend a night in there anytime. Would you? Shit, I bet me and Larry would last longer there than you would. I'd bet a whole paycheck we would."

"Tell you what?" John replied. "How about this Friday? That way it's soon enough so you pussies don't get cold feet and back out. What do you think, David?"

I didn't really like the idea, but I had to support and have the back of my best friend. "I'm in," I said. "I'm game. I'll put my paycheck up too. How about you Toady, I mean Larry?"

Larry looked like a man caught in a trap. He was stuck and everybody knew it. The look on his face was priceless. All of the blood and coloring ran out of his face. Fear emanated from every pore of his body. He had to say yes, or look like a complete coward. Finally after a long silent pause, he managed to hoarsely gasp an "Okay."

"So what happened next?" Mary asked, excitedly.

"Waitress, I'd like to order another drink," the elder David said. "Okay, where were we?"

"You and our father just challenged Harry Butz or whatever the hell his name was to spend a weekend in the Westcott Place," Mary said.

"Oh, yeah, we all agreed to do it," the elder David recalled. "We had some ground rules about being in sight of each other at all times, where we would pair off. We decided to meet up with the caretaker and have him let us in. Your dad and I decided to treat this like a camping trip in the wild unknown. We brought our sleeping bags, flashlights, and rucksacks full of supplies, food, drink and first-aid. While we weren't sure why, we decided to bring our hunting knives. We figured they might come in handy and it had nothing to do with the people we were staying with."

"Here's your drink, sir," the waitress announced as she placed it in front of him.

"Thank you," David replied. "When we arrived Harry and Larry were already there waiting for us. We suspected they were hoping that we wouldn't show up. Much to their disappointment, we did."

"We were wondering if you pussies were going to show up," Harry commented.

"Sorry to disappoint you, but we're here," John responded.

"It was classic John," David continued.

The Westcott Place was really a mansion. A pocket mansion if you will. Not as large as some, but big for this area. While it looked dark and foreboding to us at the time, back in the day we knew it had to be magnificent. It reminded me of a nicer version of the Addams' family house only not quite as ornate or large. It just had a bad history from its very start.

"Bad history?" the younger David asked.

"Yeah," the older David continued. "The place was built on what had been an old Native American burial ground. The man who had the place built was Captain Francis Westcott. He was warned not to build it there and did it anyway. He was a real piece of work. He made a lot of his money from human trafficking. Whether it was slaves prior to the Civil War or prostitutes from nations to other nations, he was said to have taken part in. Supposedly he was involved in the black market and other nefarious activities. That didn't speak to his own personal dealings."

"How so?" Mary asked.

"While your dad and I didn't know everything about him at the time, we did hear plenty to know enough about him," David replied. "We knew it was said that he was cruel and harsh taskmaster. Supposedly he lost at least one man every trip. It was said that he beat a man to death with a belaying pin."

"We were told he fled New Orleans when they found a certain place he owned was found to be a house of horrors with sex slaves, torture and murder. After he and his family fled from there and moved up here a number of strange things happened. First off some people came up missing."

"Missing?" the younger David asked "Really? Like who?"

"It varied," the elder David continued. "A vagrant here and there, some runaway kids or just some kids heading somewhere. They were people last seen near the Westcott Place. But that ain't the half of it."

Supposedly, the captain and his wife hosted some elaborate parties and celebrations with people from out of town and the area. Some were said to have involved Satanic worship. It was rumored the wife was involved in voodoo from her time in New Orleans. It was said by some of the old-timers we knew they allegedly sacrificed goats and well, humans too.

I can't remember which relative we were told it was but supposedly it was an aunt or a mother who kept saying 'Kaiser will show them' during World War I. It so outraged so many people that she was hardly ever seen after that.

It was sometime in the roaring twenties that Mrs. Westcott suddenly went insane. And in a very public way. We were told she attacked and stabbed some kids in the local store. As they took her away she was babbling something about being haunted by the ghosts of the children that were buried on their property. It was said they numbered in the dozens, and not just children.

"Oh, my God," Mary gasped. "So what happened next?"

"I guess the county and the authorities decided to investigate," David continued. "They found about a dozen children's remains ranging in age from about eight to late teenagers. They also found adults and even that aunt or mother."

We were told that after he was shown the search warrant, that the Captain quietly went upstairs and hung himself from one of the top floor rooms. He cheated the executioner so to speak or in this case the jailer, since there is no death penalty in Michigan. I guess his wife died about the same time in the insane asylum she was committed to.

After that only a few families moved in there. Those that did were not there for very long. I guess the first one somehow made it a year, but barely. The next one was a few years later and they lasted about six months. About ten years later another family didn't last one month."

"So the place was bad after that," the younger David surmised.

"You could say that," the elder David replied. "Throughout the years an occasional homeless person or bum would try to be squatters there and they'd be found dead. A couple weren't found until they caretaker could smell them from the outside."

"Oh gross!' Mary exclaimed as he brother laughed at her facial expression. "So what about the night you spent there? Tell us about that."

David took another sip of his drink. "Well, Old Nate Roberson, heard what had happened with his assistant, Stanley. He let us on the property and then let us in. He was not very happy with Harry and Larry and called them assholes and fools. He appreciated the fact that we stood up for Stanley.

"Welcome to Hell," Old Nate announced. "Enter at your own risk."

Once inside, we stood near the entryway. The light was dim, and it was dank and smelled like a place that had been sealed up for a long time. There was dust and cobwebs all around. The walls had yellowed with age. It smelled old and stale in there. We looked around, taking everything thing. It seemed to fit every movie stereotype of a haunted house. After a couple of moments of standing there we heard footfalls from the floor above.

"Is there somebody else here?" Larry asked.

Old Nate Roberson just shot him a look that spoke volumes. Without saying a word, he had basically said. "*Nobody that was alive and that you would want to meet.*"

We all continued to listen intently as we continued to hear the footfalls walk all around from the floor above. Nate looked upwards and just shook his head.

"I'm outta here," Old Nate announced. "See you in a couple of days. Hopefully you're still alive and sane. Especially you two fools. You two be careful."

"We'll try," John said.

Before anybody could say or do anything, we were locked in.

"Well, what do you think?" John asked me.

"I think we camp out down here, and ride the night our down here," I replied. "We only explore when it's daylight or have decent visibility."

Harry laughed. "Boy aren't we the brave one," he commented. "What a couple of pussies. What the hell do you think you're going to run into? Dracula, for Chrissake?"

"I don't see you doing any exploring right now,

Harry," John responded. "How about you lead the way, big talker! We'll gladly follow you big mouth."

"You talk too much," Harry snapped.

"Yeah, well, I don't brag like you do," John opined.

I noticed that after hearing the steps from above that Larry had grown quiet and a bit pale. He did not like being there and it showed. Try as he might to put on a brave face, you could see the fear in his face and eyes.

John and I looked at each other and nodded. "Let's go look around," he said. "It's still daylight. Come on Larry. Stick with us. There's safety in numbers."

So, we left our belongings in a room just off the entry way. As we headed upstairs, surprisingly Larry followed us. That was a hell of a non-verbal comment about his so-called friend and our situation. Lagging behind us was the dishonorable Harold J. Boyle.

Once we arrived to the second floor, it was surprisingly quiet. Even though the sunlight had shone through the windows, there was a darkness about the place. We were the only four individuals in the place, yet we knew that we were not alone.

"Maybe we should split up," John suggested. "David and Larry and you and me. What do you think?"

"Why the hell not?" Harry answered. "Only it will be me and Larry and you two homos can stick together. You deserve each other."

"Have it your way, Boyle," John muttered in disdain.

"See you on the flipside," I said, still feeling a bit bad for Larry.

John and I both suspected that the first chance Harry had and if the opportunity afforded itself that he would turn on his friend and sidekick. Deep down, we believed Larry knew it too, thus the reason he followed us.

John and I headed in one direction while they

headed in the other. The first room we entered had been a bedroom. It looked like it hadn't changed since the last residents lived here. The dust we kicked up caused me to sneeze a lot. It was terrible. The room was also very cold. Bone chilling cold. It was an almost unnatural cold. We knew there was a presence in it. We could feel it. As we scanned the room, our eyes caught the slight movement of an old rocking chair in the corner. It was moving just enough to know that it had been occupied and recently.

"Come on," John said as we decided to leave the room.

We looked at each other with uncertainty. Outside the door, we thought we caught the sound of the old rocking chair, rocking again. We quickly opened the door and the rocking chair was no longer moving, as if it stopped immediately. It was damned spooky. After a couple of moments we closed the door again. And once again, we heard the rocking chair moving.

Once again, John opened the door, only to see the rocking chair still idle.

This time decided to close the door most of the way, leaving his hand on the doorknob. When we heard the rocker in motion again, he opened the door quickly. The next thing we saw was the rocking chair fall over frontwards. Startled, John quickly closed the door.

"Can you believe this?" John asked.

"What did we get ourselves into?" I asked.

"God, forgive me for getting us into this," John said to me. "I am sorry."

"Too late to worry about it now," I said, trying to be reassuring. "Besides, I couldn't let you experience this alone."

"Well, let's keep going," John suggested. "Let's keep looking while we can."

From there we made our way to the next room. Like the other it was a bedroom. There was an old brass bed with a very aged and yellow mattress in the middle of it against the far wall and next to it was an antique wooden wheelchair. The room smelled like an old person or an old folks' home.

"Boy this room smells like my grandmother's before she died," John commented.

"That or Shady Acres Rest Home," I commented.

"It smells too fresh in here," John commented. "This smell should have been gone a long time ago. It is still so strong."

All I could do is nod in agreement. This room was equally cold. We both figured this room must have been the mothers' room that we heard about.

"Let's go," John muttered.

As soon as we left the room, and closed the door behind us, we noticed that the door to the first bedroom we had visited was now open. We looked at each other dumbfounded. When we went back to check we found the rocking chair in another corner.

"Are we closing the door again?" I asked.

"Nope," John replied. "Let them do it."

"Them?" I asked.

"Yeah," John answered. "You know who I'm talking about and it isn't Harry and Larry."

It was then we heard something roll across the floor from the room we had just entered. We looked at each other and then I opened the door to the room again. The wheelchair that had been next to the bed was all the way across the room. Once again, John and I looked at each other dumbfounded. I quickly closed the door.

We continued to look around until we came to the stairway that led to the third floor. The very top floor of the house. The main room where the Captain was said to have hung himself. We both looked up the stairs, hesitant to go any further.

"What do you think?" John asked.

"I'd rather not," I admitted. "There is a darkness up there. But, I think if we don't we both may kick ourselves for not doing so. I don't want to, but we need to. It's one of those things where you don't want to do it, but you have to do it."

John just nodded. Once again, we heard footfalls coming from above. We listened intently and kept watching for something. It was then we felt a kind of cool breeze of some kind blow past from the stairs. Only we did not believe it was a breeze. We knew it was something else.

Something unexplainable.

"Jesus," I muttered.

"Whoa," John said. "Let's go. If we wait any longer, we'll both lose the nerve."

I could only nod in agreement, knowing he was right.

So, with much fear and trepidation we slowly made our way up the stairs. I know for a fact we both thought about turning back, but somehow did not. Once we reached the top we found the third floor to be strewn with loose papers and odds and ends scattered about.

One thing we noticed was there seemed to be a kind of dread and foreboding that hung thickly in the air. It was almost overwhelming. I have to admit that I was scared shitless while we were up there.

We were in the room that Captain Westcott had hung himself in. The only furniture was an old wooden chair in the center of the room. Carved or inscribed into the wall to the right of it was the word 'Guilty'. The air, while still heavy, was also stale and musty, while cobwebs hung in the corners near the windows.

We walked over to look out the dusty windows. From up the third floor the view was great. As we gazed out the window, we caught the reflection of something behind us in the window. As we focused on the glass it looked like someone was hanging behind us.

"What the…!" John exclaimed, as we both turned around startled.

"Holy shit!" I yelled.

Once we turned around there was nothing there. No signs of anybody. We both knew that we had seen or caught a glimpse of something, but couldn't say for sure what it was. At that moment a cold draft hit us, causing us to shudder.

"Let's go," John said.

We then quickly headed back downstairs where once again, we then heard the footsteps coming from above.

"I don't believe it, but I think we caught a glimpse of the Captain," I said.

"If I hadn't seen it myself, I wouldn't have believed it either," John admitted.

Once we got over our shock and disbelief, we noticed all of the doors on the second floor near us were open. It wasn't too long after that, that we were joined by Harry and Larry.

Larry looked pretty pale and upset. He looked like a man who had witnessed something horrific, that or he was just pissed at Harry.

"I will say it just one more time," Larry snapped. "I did not fucking touch you. I was on the other side of the room."

"Well, someone did," Harry argued. "And you were the only other one in the room."

"I don't give a damn!" Larry spat. "It wasn't mean."

"Everything alright?" John asked.

"Yes," Harry replied.

"No," Larry answered.

John and I exchanged quick glances and Harry glared at Larry.

"Larry scared the shit out of me," Harry explained. "He touched me when I was not expecting it."

"It wasn't me!" Larry protested. "I wasn't even near you."

"Are you trying to tell me it was some ghost bullshit?" Harry asked.

"Yeah," Larry argued.

Harry just glared. "So what about you two?" he asked. "Or were you two queers freaking out with each other?"

You really are a piece of work," I said.

"Well," John said. "We heard more footsteps, doors opened and closed by themselves and were heard a wooden rocking chair move. Oh, and we thought we caught a glimpse of the captain in the window."

Larry just shook his head. He was visibly shaken. "This place is haunted like they said," he muttered.

"Aww, bullshit!" Harry scoffed.

"Think what you like, stupid," I said. "But there is something else here other than us."

"Did you see a bathroom anywhere?" Harry asked. "I have to take a shit."

"How should we know?" John asked. "We've never been here before either."

"I would guess that it's downstairs," I replied. "But there probably isn't any toilet paper."

"I guess I'll have to use something else then," Harry muttered. "Any of you ladies care to go with me?"

All three of us stared blankly at him. "Go ahead," John said. "I'm sure you'll have matters well in hand."

"Fucking wussies," Harry muttered under his breath as he headed downstairs.

"Maybe one of us should go with him," I suggested.

"Fuck that," Larry snapped. "Let him go by himself."

John and I looked at each other a bit surprised how fast their friendship appeared to be deteriorating.

We then heard the footsteps from above again and well as doors opening and closing. After a few minutes of listening to this we decided to head back downstairs. It was getting late in the day and we had no interest staying where we were.

As soon as we reached the bottom of the stairs, we heard Harry scream.

"What is it, Harry?" Larry called out. "What is it?"

We found the bathroom on the main floor and saw the door was closed.

"Are you alright, Harry?" John asked.

"Let me out of here!" Harry yelled from the other side of the door. "Goddammit, let me out!"

John turned the doorknob and the door opened easily. On the other side of the door was Harry looking frantic and terrified.

"What is it?" John asked.

Harry was breathing hard and still quite upset. "I had finished taking a shit and when I was washing my hands I looked in the mirror and saw something looking back at me. I tried to get out of there and the door was locked or something. I couldn't get out of there."

We all looked at each other.

"It wasn't locked," John said.

"It sure as hell was," Harry argued. "Either that or you fuckers were holding it."

"Nobody was holding it," Larry said. "We heard you scream and we came running."

"I didn't scream, I hollered," Harry protested.

"It sure as hell sounded like a scream to me," I said.

Harry just flipped me the middle finger.

"Is that your I.Q.?" I asked, sarcastically.

We decided that it was getting near dinner time and decided to eat. John and I brought a loaf of bread and a can of spam and made sandwiches. Harry and Larry soon joined us and began to eat their own food as well.

We sat on our sleeping bags, relaxing after that. The meal had made us more comfortable and a lethargic.

"So, now what?" Harry asked. "We sit around and look at your ugly mugs and sing *Kumbaya*?"

"Yeah, why not?" John asked. "Can you think of anything else?"

"How about we explore this place in the dark?" Harry asked.

"Go right ahead," I said. "Feel free. You can give us your report when you get back."

"Fuck you!" Harry snapped.

John and I laughed. Surprisingly, so did Larry.

"What are you laughing at?" Harry asked his friend.

As the daylight waned, the shadows and darkness in the Westcott Place grew more prominent. Soon, the only light we had were our flashlights and some candles Harry and Larry brought.

"Jesus, this place is spooky," Larry admitted.

He was right. Once darkness had fallen, the Westcott Place appeared to come alive. Even without the noises, the place was creepy. Now with nighttime the footsteps were louder and more frequent, we heard indistinguishable voices and doors creaking as they were opened and closed.

John and I sat next to each other on the floor, just listening. A few feet from me was Larry and about ten feet from him was Harry who was smoking a cigarette. We found it interesting that Larry was closer to us than to his friend Harry.

As we continued to listen, we thought we heard what sounded like something being dragged along the floor above us.

Larry nervously looked upward and let out a kind of suppressed sigh. We looked over to see Harry taking a drink from a pint of whiskey he had secretly brought along. All three of us were a little concerned with this since Harry had a penchant for getting mean when he drank. When he drank whiskey he was even worse and outright mean.

"You really think you should be drinking that now, buddy?" Larry asked.

His asking this really surprised John and I. It was different seeing Larry take Harry to task on things.

"What the fuck do you care?" Harry asked. "Besides, it's ain't none of your Goddamn business. Besides, spirits combat spirits right?"

Larry just shook his head in frustration and disbelief.

"Don't drink too much," John warned. "We may need you sober and with all of your faculties."

"Hey, you deal your way and I'll deal mine," Harry commented.

"Just try and stay sober enough in case we need you for something," I added.

"Terrific," Larry muttered. "Just freakin' terrific."

"What?" Harry asked, no hearing what his friend had said.

"I said, terrific," Larry repeated, sarcastically.

"Hey don't you start either, you little bastard," Harry warned. "I don't need shit from you too. So put a goddamn lid on it."

Larry just shook his head in anger and disgust.

We just sat there for a while listening for a while engaging in small talk. It was enjoyable. For the first time in our lives we actually enjoyed talking to Larry

Lawson. We got to know each other a little better. He wasn't as bad as we initially thought, and I imagine we appeared the same way to him. We may not have been ready to be best buddies, but we were at least respecting each other for a change.

After laughing about a bad joke that Larry told, we could hear louder but still indistinguishable voices from upstairs. It made our hair stand on end.

"Jesus," Larry muttered, as Harry took another drink from his bottle.

"I feel torn," John confessed. "On one hand I feel like we should keep on investigating the place and yet on the other hand, I just can't bring myself to do it. I'm too damned scared."

"I hear that," I agreed.

"Ditto that," Larry chimed.

"Chickenshit!" Harry laughed.

"That's easy to say, just sitting there," John replied. "I don't see your ass going around exploring the place. Why don't you go investigate the noise yourself, blowhard?"

"Shut up!" Harry snapped.

"You talk a good game," John continued. "You can't make fun of people when you won't do it yourself. Lead by example or shut your yap."

Harry just glared. Even in the darkness you could see and sense the anger and hatred in his eyes.

After a few moments we went back to watching and listening. Soon we heard what sounded like something like footsteps coming down the stairs. It then stopped abruptly. It was followed by what sounded like the muffled cries of children somewhere in the house.

John, Larry and myself all exchanged looks. Instinctively we all stood up and aimed our flashlights towards the doorway and where the stairway was.

We then heard something come down the stairs. It did not sound like footsteps, but one bump after another. Finally it stopped. A child's small red ball came into view of where we were shining our flashlights.

"Good God," Larry gasped, both shocked and horrified

"Oh, my God," I muttered, now terrified.

A chill ran through our spines like no other. Up until then we had been scared, but now we were totally frightened.

Harry just shook his head and laughed at us. Whether it was the alcohol or just his shitty personality, he was showing his disdain for us. Anyway he got up from his spot, headed over to where the ball was and picked it up. He took a few steps past the doorway and looked up the stairs.

We don't know exactly what happened or what he saw on the stairs, but a look of horror spread across his face, he just gasped something inaudible, dropped the ball and staggered back into the room where we were. He was in shock. Harry tried to say something, but couldn't get the words out.

"What is it Harry?" Larry asked.

He turned to say something to Larry, but could not speak. He staggered over to where he had been sitting, picked up his bottle, and chugged the remainder of it down before finally collapsing on the floor.

"Harry, are you alright?" John asked.

Harry was in shock and just staring into space. It was very unsettling. What had he seen that made him almost catatonic, we asked ourselves? We were not sure what to do next.

"Shit, he's lost it," Larry muttered. "Something scared the shit out of him. Now what do we do?"

"I guess we try to stick it out for the night," John

replied. "Other than that I don't know. What do you two want to do?"

It was then we thought we heard the mixture of children's laughter and cries coming from somewhere above us.

"I suggest we leave in the morning," Larry said. "You've proven your point. We were fools. Hell, I'll pay up."

"I think I agree with that," I admitted.

"You think the honorable Harold J. Boyle will go for that?" John asked.

"I don't know how he doesn't," Larry replied. "He's in no shape to disagree.

It was then we heard a guttural kind of moaning emanating from throughout the house. It sounded like it was coming from above and below us.

"Boy, I'm glad we passed on checking out the cellar," I commented. "I'd hate to imagine what's down there."

"I wouldn't even go down there in the daylight," Larry admitted. "Frankly, I wish we could just go now and leave this fucking place."

We looked over to see that Harry had either fell asleep or passed out.

"Well' he's definitely out," John announced.

"Yeah," Larry said, not very pleased. "Thanks for getting us into this place, buddy. I really appreciate it you fucking asshole."

John and were both stunned at Larry saying that. We knew that he was pissed at him, but we did not suspect how much.

"You alright?" I asked Larry.

"Yeah," he replied. "Look I don't know what you guys experienced or witnessed, but when we split up we had our own experiences."

While I cannot remember every small detail that he said, Larry went on to tell us that after we split up they had some strange things happen. He said the first room they entered had a large pentagram in the middle of the floor. It was etched into the wood. He said there was some other kind of writing on the walls. He assumed it was Satanic ritual stuff, but could not be sure. He said it really bothered him to see it. For him it was confirmation all of those stories about Mrs. Westcott were true.

He also said Harry teased him about being spooked by it. One thing Larry noticed was, there seemed to be a cold draft in the room. The problem was there were no windows open or anywhere that cold air could get in.

Larry went on to say when they entered the next room, that something touched him. At first he thought it was Harry accidentally bumping into him. But he said that wasn't possible since he was too far away. While not frightened, he was unsettled by the experience.

Larry mentioned that they went into a third room that appeared to have been used for storage. It was there that something touched Harry. Apparently, he thought it was Larry. Larry said it was not him and that he was too far away from him.

Apparently it unsettled Harry, enough for him to keep asking Larry if he was sure that it was not him who had been touching him. He kept accusing Larry of doing it because he just could not believe there was some unexplainable thing actually touching him. Larry suspected it bother Harry more than he cared to admit and that was part of the reason he kept accusing him.

When they left the last room, Larry said they both noticed all of the doors were opened. Doors that they had earlier closed.

Larry also admitted that he caught glimpses of things

out of the corner of his eye. He thought he saw people nearby, but when he turned to see who or what it was they were gone. Larry said the feeling of not being alone and that they were always watched was almost overwhelming.

As it grew later, we all yawned. It might have been a spooky place, but always being on alert and keeping our guard up was wearing us out and making us tired. I offered to the take the first watch while the others rested or tried to get some for a couple of hours.

So while John and Larry nodded off, I kept watch. It was a lonely and horrifying vigil as the noises grew louder and more frequent. The sounds of doors creaking, and other structural noises were not so bad. I had grown somewhat used to them.

It was the more human noises that were truly frightening. The cries and laughter from children no longer alive, the moans and groans and the inaudible voices were very unsettling.

At one point it felt like someone was in the room with us. I could hear what sounded like someone exhaling loudly in there with us. It went on for a while.

I don't know whether it was confidence, cockiness, or just being tired, but I shook my head no, and eventually I no longer heard it.

When my watch was over, I woke up your dad at one a.m. He kept watch until about three. From what he told me later, he experienced pretty much the same thing.

I guess Larry took his watch about three. Apparently Larry kept watch long enough to fall back asleep after a few minutes. The next thing we knew we were being jostled awake by him.

"Harry's gone!" he announced.

We looked over at where Harry had been and sure

enough he was gone.

"I thought I heard someone call my name, but soon realized it was Harry," Larry explained.

"Shit!' John cursed.

"Are we looking for him?" I asked, already knowing the answer.

"Yeah," John muttered.

"We could wait," Larry suggested. "You know he wouldn't look for you."

"Yeah, well I'm not him," John commented.

Larry just nodded in agreement.

Slowly and with a great deal of apprehension we made our way up the stairs. Initially our flashlight beams caught what looked like a couple of sets of eyes looking back at us, but they quickly disappeared.

Once we reached the second floor, we thought it best to stay together, shining our flashlights all around.

"Harry?" John called out. "Harry?"

There was no answer.

We thoroughly searched the second floor, checking the rooms we had just been in hours earlier. There was no sign of Harold J. "Harry" Boyle.

"Now what?" Larry asked.

"Third floor," I said.

We looked up only to hear some disembodied laughter above us.

"Shit!" Larry muttered.

"We have to," John explained.

So we made our way up to the floor. Once we reached the third floor we were greeted by a very cold draft.

"Harry?" John called out again. "Harry?"

"Oh, my God," I gasped as Larry and my flashlights shone on Harry's body as it was hanging from a beam in the ceiling.

"Damn!" John said.

"How in the hell did he get up there?" Larry asked. "There's no chair or ladder or anything. Someone had to lift him."

"But, by what?" I asked.

Larry then inadvertently shined his flashlight towards the windows and caught the reflection of several pairs of eyes and some non-descript faces looking back at him.

"Holy shit!' he screamed.

John and I both jumped back upon seeing them ourselves.

Suddenly, it was as if all the fury of hell, the house or some other supernatural force was released upon the room. A ghostly milk white light filled the room as a supernatural wind blew and howled throughout the third floor.

The wind was so strong that it blew Larry across the room as we were knocked off our feet.

"Let's go!" John yelled over the howling force.

We half-crawled and walked to the stairs. Just before we reached the stairs, Larry made the mistake of standing up and was thrown halfway down the stairs. Only his desperate reaching out to catch the railing kept him from being thrown the rest of the way and possible injury or death.

We made our way down the stairs, holding tightly onto the railing. When we reached Larry we helped him the rest of the way down the stairs. At the bottom of the stairs we looked to the top of the stairs and what we saw about froze our shit.

Standing at the top of the stairs was Captain Westcott and what we assumed was his wife. They looked like decomposed corpses with no eyes, only empty eye sockets, and were snarling at us.

Larry screamed.

"Holy shit!" I yelled.

Slowly they began to move down the stairs.

As quickly as we could we tried to get out the door.

"Shit, it's locked!" John yelled.

"Let's head back to the room!" I shouted. "Maybe we can break a window to get out."

We felt like we were trapped and being pursued by the dead.

John ran to the window and began to hit it with his flashlight. The first time he hit the glass nothing happened. John looked shocked. The glass was old and pretty thick. He struck it again and only managed a slight crack.

"Shit!' he yelled, as he began to get concerned.

"Oh, God!" I yelled as the spirits arrived in the room where we were.

What happened next was all a kind of a blur. I wasn't really watching as I tried to help John break the window. As the spirits tried to get Larry, he grabbed one of the lit candles they had brought and threw it at them. The candle went through the captain, hit the wall and drapes. The drapes began to burn.

The ghosts suddenly disappeared as soon the candle went through them and began to burn the drapes and the rest of the place started to burn.

It was then we began to hear a loud moaning and groaning throughout the Westcott Place.

"Damn!" Larry yelled as he headed over to try and put out the growing fire.

"Never mind that!" John ordered. "Help me break the windows so we can get the hell out of here!"

We immediately headed over and began to try and break the windows. We realized it was a race against time, because the fire was spreading rapidly. After several more attempts we managed to break the windows. We used our rucksacks and gear to brush away the broken glass and shards so we could climb out.

As quickly and carefully as possible I climbed out first. John helped Larry who was slightly injured through the window, before he himself climbed out.

Just outside the house we could hear the moans and groans and screams emanating from inside the Westcott Place as the fire spread.

As the fire began to grow in intensity, we stepped back we could see all of the spirits standing next to the windows. One of those spirits we noticed was that of Harry.

While I did not notice at first all three of us had tears running down our cheeks.

We moved further back and watched as the Westcott Place creaked, moaned, and groaned in its death throes as floors collapsed and it burned to the ground. The authorities and the fire department arrived as the top floor collapsed to the ground.

The fire department couldn't have done anything anyway since there were no hydrants nearby.

While we were being treated and attended to, we noticed that Larry's hair had turned completely white.

Afterwards, we were not charged with anything since our stories all corroborated and we had witnesses to say why we were there. I also believe we were not charged because of the fact that the Westcott Place was now gone. Somehow, we had done a kind of public service. Hell for a while we had people buy us drinks at the bar. We were almost like local heroes or celebrities.

They eventually found Harry's remains. Out of respect and to be courteous we both attended the funeral. It was the right thing to do.

"So what happened after that?" Mary asked. "What

happened to Larry?"

"Larry had heart trouble after that," David continued. "His hair turning white was part of that. I guess the fear and shock affected him physically. He was really never the same after that. He died while waiting for a heart transplant about ten years later. We both felt for him after that. He paid a dear price for that night in the Westcott Place."

"A short time later your dad met your mom, and I met my wife. I was offered an opportunity in Texas. My wife died when your dad was going through his first round of chemotherapy."

"Jeez no wonder Dad would never go to a horror movie," the younger David replied. "He lived through one."

"He tended to have nightmares too," Mary added.

"Yeah, me too," the elder David admitted. "At least his nightmares are over. Hopefully this closes the last chapter to all this."

ACQUITTED

He sat there at the kitchen table, staring into empty space, devoid of any real thought. Harry Leonard looked like somebody who had just been through hard times. He had four days' growth of razor stubble and his thinning gray hair was unkempt and uncombed. He took a deep breath as his mind wandered between limbo and oblivion.

Ever since he'd been acquitted for the murder of his wife, Aida, his life had been hell. No, not hell…but something close to it that seemed to be never-ending. As far as *he* was concerned, life in general had become much more difficult since his acquittal.

His family, his friends and even his neighbors had deserted him. Nobody wanted anything to do with him. They thought he'd gotten away with murder. All along, Harry had figured that if he was found innocent or even acquitted, nothing would have changed. He was very wrong. He had become a pariah, to say the least.

The worst of it all was, even his drinking buddies at the bar abandoned him.

"Piss on 'em," Harry had reacted. "Piss on all of them."

They had never found Aida's body. Harry had told the authorities that he hit Aida during a fight, she finally left him, and that he hadn't seen her since. He told the police that he'd been drinking that night and continued to do so, even after she left and that he had blacked out later that night.

Still, nobody believed him. *Especially* the police. They figured he disposed of the body, but could never find exactly *where.*

To them it was a slam dunk. He fit the profile and had all the tendencies and lack of alibi a prime suspect would have. Plus he had a history of abuse to throw into the mix.

Unfortunately, the wheels of justice do not always spin correctly and with a slick lawyer to grease the wheels, Harry was able to get off on lack of evidence coupled with technicalities. He would not do penance for the crime.

He, for all intents and purposes was a free man, but also a prisoner of isolation.

It didn't matter that he was acquitted. Harry was abusive and everyone knew it. Early in his marriage, he had gotten shit-faced and dunked Aida's head under water at a lake party, nearly drowning her. He'd also previously slapped, punched, kicked and knocked her down throughout the years

He also made threats ranging from stabbing, shooting and running over her with his car.

That didn't even include the *verbal* abuse.

He may have been acquitted, but those that knew him had already pronounced sentence on him. Harry avoided prison, yet the community had imposed solitary confinement on him.

But that wasn't the worst of it….

He closed his eyes and thought back to the acquittal night and the minor celebration afterwards. His lawyer advised against the celebrating. But Harry Leonard was going to do what he wanted. He always did. Damn the consequences. Bullheadedness wasn't a vice with Harry, it was his central most and best character trait.

At the bar, even his old drinking buddies moved away from him. It appeared even *they* had their own set of standards.

As he left the bar he walked outside, into the cool, crisp night air. He lit the second of his large celebration cigars and inhaled. Then he thought he heard a soft voice call his name.

"Haarrreee."

Harry turned and saw a darkened woman walking away. From what he could see, she resembled Aida from behind.

"Aida?" he said softly, a little shocked.

Harry started to follow the woman as she walked around the corner of another building. He quickened his pursuit. As he followed around the corner, he saw nothing but the parking lot, the road, another building.

Nobody around.

Harry stood under the light pole, shaking his head.

He figured he was either feeling guilty, or that he had a few too many and was just seeing things. It was just his imagination playing tricks on him.

He then went home, collapsed on his couch, and went into drunken slumber.

The next day, he went to his place of employment to see if he still had his job as a bulldozer operator for a construction company. Fortunately he did, but he was given the rest of the week off. The company he worked for was going to build a new subdivision in White Lake, and they needed every man they could get who was experienced with heavy earth-moving machinery.

Being home, for him, was the worst. The house where he spent the last fifteen years was giving him the creeps.

A creak here. A bump there. Everyday, it was something.

There were little noises that he could not explain away, no matter how hard he tried.

After returning home from work, he found the radio turned on. Not just on, but it was Aida's favorite station.

Two days later, the television was on again and tuned into to Oprah. Harry detested her and called her *that fat, rich uppity nigger-woman.* But Aida adored her and rarely ever missed a show.

Harry quickly began to check his house locks. They all appeared to be fine.

After two more days of coming home to find both the radio and television on, he finally broke down and called the police, saying that someone was breaking into his home and doing such.

They came out, but offered little help.

"You could set up a hidden camera. You know, to see who it is," offered an Officer Hunter.

Harry immediately dismissed that idea, due to the high cost.

"Thanks for nothing," he snapped. "I hope I doan hafta rely on you if my life depends on it."

After the officer left, Harry went to the party store and purchased a case of beer, and proceeded to polish most of it off while watching wrestling on the tube.

He eventually fell asleep, only to wake up the next morning to a headache and the channel now on that goddamn women's channel Aida watched. *Lifetime* or whatever.

He went to work like he always did. On his way home, he stopped off to his favorite watering hole to have a couple beers.

Harry wouldn't admit it, but he was afraid to go home.

Something about the things going on in his house didn't add up. He figured it was possible that he accidentally hit the remote when he fell asleep, or a power surge could have turned the radio on.

But more than once?

Was it possible?

And, if so, why was it always on *her* stations?

"*Cut it out,*" he muttered to himself. "*Yer friggin' losin' it. Git goin'. Fer Chrissakes, the old bat is dead an' there ain't nuthin' she can do tuh yuh now.*"

He drank down the last of his beer and headed for home, and on his way he picked up another six-pack.

When he arrived, the television was blaring from the living room.

As he set his beer down and entered, the television changed channels. Harry's heart skipped a beat. The television changed channels again. And then again.

He looked down at the end table next to his recliner. There was the remote control, and sitting on top of it was a small chair pillow that was half situated upon the armrest.

As soon as he moved the pillow, the television stayed on one channel.

Beads of sweat had built up on Harry's forehead.

He headed off to the bathroom. As soon as he left, the television began changing channels again.

While using the bathroom, Harry thought that he heard the hallway floor squeak from footsteps softly walking upon it.

Quickly, he finished his business in the bathroom and headed out into the hallway, then halted in dumbfounded thought. He knew what he'd heard. The floor *squeaked.* The only time that happened was when someone walked on it.

He went into his bedroom and opened his dresser drawer. He reached in and pulled out and old White Owl cigar box and from that a .38 revolver. He checked to make sure it was loaded.

"Okay, asshole, whoever yuh are," he whispered in a hoarse voice. "I got somethin' fer yuh. Whoever yuh are, yer dead."

He slowly began to check the other rooms as well as within their closets. After a short while, he lowered his gun and headed back into the hallway.

As he turned to head down the hallway, he was looking at a framed photographed portrait of Aida smiling at him.

"What in the hell are you smiling about?" he growled as he raised his pistol. "You old bitch."

Harry fired his .38 at the picture, leaving a bullet hole in her forehead.

Aida's smile morphed into an evil sneer of a grin. Then blood began to run from the bullet hole from Aida's forehead. Harry stepped back in horror as blood dripped down the surface of the portrait and then the wall.

He staggered back and turned to get out of there. As he reached the kitchen, he bumped into his older brother Burt.

"What the…." Harry exclaimed as he grabbed his own chest in heart attack manner.

"You all right?" Burt asked. "What's the matter?"

"Yuh scared the hell outta me!" Harry gasped.

Burt cast his gaze from Harry with his gun and then to Aida's picture with the cracked and broken glass and the bullet hole in it. "Nice shot, Harry." he said, shaking his head. "I see you're handling the acquittal nicely."

Harry turned again to look at Aida's picture and the blood was gone. He then looked at his brother handily, trying to figure out the tone of Burt's comments.

"Shuttup, Burt," he said. "She smiled at me….the picture…it…....it *smiled* at me real nasty….and it bled too. *I tell yuh it bled!*"

Burt looked at the picture and then at Harry.

"There's no blood Harry," Burt replied. Maybe it's the blood on your conscience, Harry. You know…. like Macbeth's wife. Are you all right? You look like you been under some stress."

"Things have been happening," Harry answered. "Really strange things. Lately little things have been happening. The TV's been on when I get home. The radio's been on. Little noises. Lot's of little things. I can't explain it."

"It sounds like your conscience is getting to you," Burt said.

"Who in the da fuck are you?" Harry asked, loudly. "Jiminy Fuckin' Cricket?"

"No, Harry," Burt said calmly. "But, you're the one who told us you didn't do it and we all knew your track record. You know you were an abusive husband. Even your old girlfriends called you Horrible Harry for slapping them around. So don't give me *I'm your brother* and *I've been acquitted* bullshit."

"Fuck you!" Harry yelled. "And fuck them too. They ain't nuthin' but a bunch of old whores anyways. So whattaya want? Why are you here?"

"I came by to see how you were doing," Burt replied. "In spite of everything, you are my brother."

"Yeah, Harry said. "Yeah, thanks for the friggin' support during the trial. Your testimony almost sunk me. Thanks a helluva lot."

"Now you listen and listen good, asshole," Burt snapped. "I am not going to lie for anybody. You, my wife, anybody. I only answered the questions the prosecution asked. I did not give them any information.

You beat Aida and you know damn well you did. What the hell was I supposed to say? That you were a pillar to the community and a great husband. That's bullshit and everybody knew it, and so do you."

Harry was irritated by what Burt said. "You coulda did more," he said a little defensively. "And not be so self-righteous. So why'd you really come here?"

"To see how you were doing,' Burt replied. "That's it."

"I'm fine," Harry replied. "You can go back to that whore wife of yours. I doan need you."

Burt swung and slapped Harry across the face. Harry was shocked and speechless. "That whore wife of mine was the one who said I should come over and see if you were okay," he said, seething with anger. "Personally, Harry you are an asshole. I'm leaving, but I will never come back. I hate to say this, Harry, but I've found I don't like you very much at all. You may be my brother, but I'm ashamed to admit it. I won't claim you. Why poor Aida married you I'll never know. Goodbye, Harry. Have a nice life. Because it's sure going to be a lonely one!"

Burt turned and left.

Harry stood dumbfounded as the back door closed.

"Yeah, I doan need you!" Harry yelled. "You goddamn Cain and Abel. Fuck you an' yer goddamn whore wife. And yer goddamn kids too."

He went back into the living room and sat into his recliner before the television. He was intensely bitter. He knew Burt would not return. Burt was just that way. He always did what he said he would do. He always had. He got up and went to the refrigerator. He ate bologna sandwiches and drank a six pack of beer for dinner that night.

He wasn't about to cook. That was a woman's job. *Hell*, Harry figured, *if women were a man's equal, then they could change their own goddamn flat tires and roof their own houses.* Otherwise, the bitches could cook the goddamn meals while a man would do the *real* work.

As far as Harry was concerned, a woman's job was to cook, clean and fuck.

And if they gave you lip, you simply put them in their place. If that took a few slaps or hits, so be it. It worked for his old man. That was until Burt got old enough to put a stop to that. Back then, Harry figured you could almost kill your old lady if she got too much out of line.

Like Aida.

Like he'd done with Aida for getting out of line.

At least, that's what others thought he did.

Besides, he reminded himself constantly that he was acquitted, and to Harry that meant the same as being innocent.

Harry got up to go to the bathroom and he walked past another picture of Aida.

"What are you lookin' at, you old whore?" he asked, feeling cocky once again and heading towards the bathroom.

As he turned his head to see where he was walking, he heard Aida's voice. "You, Harry Leonard."

Harry stopped cold.

All of the hairs on his body stood on end and he became pale.

Slowly he turned back to the picture. He heard it. He knew he did. He heard Aida. He heard her *voice.* He glared at the picture.

The picture began to bleed from the bullet hole that Harry made earlier. Aida's smile had changed to a sinister sneer-like grin once more.

Fear filled him to his very soul. He screamed and swung at the picture, knocking it to the floor.

Next he heard Aida giggle.

That irritating giggle that drove him crazy for all those years.

Terror again quickly filled Harry. He was breathing hard. He felt something warm saturating his crotch. He had pissed his pants. Harry quickly grasped the picture by the frame, took it to the garbage cans outside.

"Goddamn bitch," he muttered as he gawked towards his crotch. Damn bitch got me."

Harry took off his clothes and took a shower. Afterwards, he plopped down in his chair, turned on the tube, and started drinking beer. After an hour he fell asleep.

Sometime in the early morning hours, Harry woke up. He'd thought that he heard somebody call his name. He thought it had been Aida.

"Haarrreee."

Harry woke up.

The television was once again on the *Lifetime* channel. Harry then noticed that he was somehow wearing Aida's bathrobe. Quickly, he stood up. The house went cold. It was freezing. He checked the thermostat and it was set at seventy degrees. He was in disbelief. He did not remember putting on her bathrobe. He took off the robe, disgusted by its feel and presence. A chill ran through him.

He then turned on all of the lights in the house and returned to his recliner, where he tried in vain to get a little more sleep before work that morning.

After about an hour of trying to get a little more sleep, he gave up.

He went into the bathroom. After shaving, he jumped into a nice hot shower. After the shower, he wiped off the bathroom mirror mist to look at his reflection so he could brush his hair. Instead of looking at his own face, he beheld Aida's. He suddenly jumped back.

Then, her reflection disappeared, and the word *murderer* was there in its stead, scrawled as if somebody took their finger to the condensation and put it there.

Harry was terrified.

He quickly ran out of the bathroom, got dressed, grabbed his wallet and car keys and headed to work. He felt a chill throughout his whole body, and all day long he had trouble focusing on his work. So much so that his foreman even had to talk to him to see if he was all right. He said he was, and was finally able to regain his composure to do his job.

By the end of the day, he was starting to realize he had to go home.

Home, the one place he did not want to go to.

He went to the bar and ate his dinner as well as helped close it down.

Finally, after two a.m., he was on his way home.

Scared almost to the point of pissing his pants again, but on his way home.

Once at home, he entered the house.

Both the radio and the television were *not* on. Everything appeared pretty normal, for a change. Harry took a deep breath and let out a sigh of relief.

Whew.

Things were relatively back to normal for the next couple of weeks. Harry got into a routine of sorts. He would hit the bar for a couple of beers and a burger almost every night after work. For him, things were as normal as they could be under the circumstances.

In fact, in some ways they were even better.

Late one Saturday night, while he was at his usual spot at the bar, a mildly attractive middle-aged woman sat down next to him and ordered a drink. She asked him for a light and he obliged. Soon, the two were in a conversation. He found out she had been married three times and her name was Freda Kellner. She wasn't really looking for another man in her life, but that didn't mean she wasn't looking to get some.

Soon, both were back at Harry's place, inebriated and more than a little horny….

The next morning, Harry felt like a lot of stress had been lifted off his shoulders. While it wasn't the best sex he ever had, it was the best that he could get. As he began to stir, he felt her left arm lying across his side. The arm seemed familiar. There was a wedding ring on her finger. He was still drowsy, but he looked as best as he could at her hand. It was very familiar. The ring resembled the one he had given Aida. The hand had a scar on the fleshy part between the thumb and the index finger. Just like Aida's. Still, tired and still a little under the influence, he looked over at Freda. As the sleep slowly left his eyes, he began to realize that it wasn't Freda. It was Aida.

"Oh, my God," he thought, shocked. "*It's Aida. "How could that be*?"

His jaw stood agape and his heart almost skipped a beat. He recoiled in terror, almost falling out of bed. Freda then turned onto her side. As she did so, Aida's face was gone. He felt cold.

Harry got out of bed and went to the bathroom. He cupped his left hand in his face as he urinated. He then moved to the sink to wash his hands and face. As he looked in the mirror, there was Aida staring back at him. He let out a small shriek as he tried to contain himself.

Aida's face was gone. Was he losing it? He cupped his hands into his face. This was unreal, he thought.

He could also hear that the television was now on. He stood out in the hallway listening, when a cold hand touched his shoulder from behind. Harry jumped, startled. He whirled around ready to hit somebody or something only to see it was Freda, half-dressed.

"Sorry, I didn't mean to scare you," she said, frightened and apologetically.

Harry breathed a deep sigh of relief. "Sorry," he said. "But, yuh scared duh shit outta me."

"Is something wrong?" she asked, concerned.

"I juss thought I heard somethin'," he replied.

Freda let out a loud yawn. "Do you know what time it was?" she asked.

"I dunno, maybe eight or nine," he answered.

"I gotta use your bathroom," she said as she walked past Harry and closed the bathroom door behind her.

Harry checked the rest of the house while Freda used the bathroom. The radio was on in the kitchen as well. Freda emerged and headed back into the bedroom. She started to get dressed.

Harry entered the bedroom and watched, as if he expected to see Aida's face once again. He realized that the morning light showed the wear and tear of Freda's age and lifestyle. Last night at the bar, she had more make-up on, not to mention everybody looked a little better when you have been drinking and more than just a little desperate. He hadn't really noticed how she looked when she came up from behind him and surprised him. Now he did. He almost couldn't believe he brought that home and fucked it. He thought he had better taste than that.

"Well it was nice, Harry," Freda announced as she got dressed. "I gotta go. I'm supposed to go bowling with my girlfriends this morning."

Harry just nodded.

"Maybe we can hook up again," she said. "I stop in there a lot."

"Yeah, okay maybe next time," he blurted out half-heartedly, still not believing he brought that home with him.

Freda left. Soon, he was all alone in the house again. Not the place he exactly wanted to be, right now. At least, not by himself. The house hadn't bothered him in a while.

Now it did, again.

He realized that he had some yard work that needed to be done. He'd always taken care of the yard, until recently, with all that happened lately. He would at least be outside. Nothing happened outside.

After doing some raking and weed trimming, he began to mow. He cast a large shadow onto his backyard lawn and privacy fence from the western afternoon sun. He paid little attention to it as he went back and forth with his lawn mower. About halfway into the backyard, he glanced over to see his shadow pushing the mower, and a *second* shadow of a person standing in the yard a few feet away.

He turned to look and see who was there.

Nobody. There was nobody there. A sudden chill filled him. He stopped momentarily as he let the lawnmower continue to run. He looked around for about a minute and then decided to finish mowing.

When he finished mowing he put the mower in his shed and went into the house to retrieve a much needed and wanted ice cold beer. He sat down and relaxed on his porch while downing half of the beer. He felt a sense of accomplishment from a job well done. The work had at least taken his mind off of the strange things going on in his house.

At least for the time being.

He drained the last of the beer and went inside. It was getting near dinner time and he was getting hungry.

The house was quiet.

Almost too quiet.

There had been no television or radio on when he came in. He felt cautiously relieved. For dinner, Harry went down to the local 7/11 and picked up another six pack of beer and a frozen pizza that he could microwave. After eating, He fell asleep in his recliner. Snoring and dead to the world.

Sometime around three-thirty in the morning, he woke up to the sound of a woman calling his name. His head ached and his stomach rumbled from the cheap beer and pizza. Upon waking, he was in a partial daze and a little confused.

"Harrreeee…." The voice called out. "Harrreeee…."

Trying to wake up, he looked around frantically. Then he noticed that he somehow had Aida's bathrobe on again. He got up and quickly took it off in disgust. "What the fu…"

On the television there was a movie playing. It was called "*Acquitted*."

For Harry it was all too real.

Too real…because he was the star of this particular show.

The movie showed the events of the night of Aida's death and what exactly had transpired.

He watched in disbelief as the events unfolded on the tube before him, watched the portrayal of how he murdered and disposed of Aida. It then showed the trial and the sleazy, almost unethical tactics the defense attorney used in defending him. The movie took a turn to the surreal as it began to depict an undead Aida paying his attorney a visit, invoking a fatal heart attack brought on by fright when she appeared to him in the bathroom mirror.

Harry exploded in anger and kicked his foot into the television screen, sending an electric shock coursing through his body, causing him to howl in pain and finally pass out onto the living room floor. He awoke sprawled out on the floor. His body ached all over. His head throbbed and he felt stunned, unable to really move. His vision was blurred, but he thought that he had glimpsed Aida standing over him, grinning sadistically.

He finally brought his hands up to his face and rubbed his aching and throbbing head. After a few minutes he sat up and as he did so, he was still shaken from the shock. He looked at the TV and cursed. He would need to buy another one, not to mention clean up the mess.

It was almost seven a.m. He was late for work. *This is no way to start the day*, he thought.

When he arrived at work, it started to rain. His supervisor said he couldn't have Harry working a bulldozer in soft ground with the possibility of sink holes and especially near what the men called the Hell Pit. The Hell Pit was basically a real deep mud-filled swamp-like sinkhole. It was deep enough to where it would take several large double haulers full of dirt to fill in.

When the noon news came on the TV overlooking the bar afterwards at his favorite watering hole, he watched a report detailing how his lawyer, Marvin Lefler, was found dead of a suspected heart attack in his bathroom and a dead prostitute in his bed. Harry almost choked on his beer.

By evening he was very drunk. Drunk to the point of slurring his speech and little control over his own body. The bartender cut him off and called him a cab. Much to Harry's outrage, he called the bartender almost every swear word that he could still pronounce, but finally complied and was driven home.

After fumbling with his keys in the heavy rain, he finally let himself into his house. He stumbled through the doorway and into the kitchen. He made his way into the living room where he crashed on the couch and slept like a dead man.

The next morning, like clockwork, he awoke to a terrific hangover and the music blaring from the kitchen radio that was playing from Aida's favorite station.

He staggered to his feet and shut it off. He made his way towards the bathroom where he threw up and then ran some cool water on his face. He definitely felt like shit.

"Oh, God," he muttered as he looked into the mirror.

Looking back at him in the mirror was Aida. In her current decomposed and dirt covered state. She was reaching out towards him.

"Let's kiss and make-up, Harry," she said with a sinister grin, followed by a cold shrieking hysterical laughter. *"Kiss me Harry. Kiss me, honey. Please kiss me."*

He screamed "But, I was acquitted!!!" he screamed. "I was found innocent!!!" and stepped back as she continued to approach him. Harry picked up a glass ash tray that was in the bathroom and flung it at the mirror.

The mirror shattered and Aida disappeared. Harry was breathing hard and shaking.

"I was *acquitted*, you bitch!" he yelled at the mirror. "And there ain't a goddamn thing you kin do about it!"

As he finally changed his clothes and left for work, he had a sinking feeling it was going to be a long day. On his way to work, he realized it was his and Aida's wedding anniversary. Then he knew it was really going to be a very long day.

Harry and the rest of the crew were told by the foreman that the hard rain they had been receiving lately could still make some areas in the ground very soft, and the possibility of sink holes from the dirt erosion remained a real danger. They needed to be extra careful and walk the ground before using heavy machinery on it.

Harry went over to check his bulldozer and saw a set of petite bare footprints were around it. They came from the nearby swampy Hell Pit area.

Thinking little of it, he started up the large machine and commenced another day's work on the future site of the newest White Lake subdivision.

Just after lunch when he was working on leveling the ridge near the woods, he thought he saw Aida only a few feet from his bulldozer. He rubbed his eyes and stopped for a moment. She was gone. A chill ran through his body.

Then as he started to make another pass at the ridge, and he saw her again.

It was definitely Aida.

She was pointing directly at him, as if to accuse him, then she twisted the direction of the pointing upwards and into a middle finger. She had a wicked smile the whole time.

Fear quickly gave way to anger. An uncontrollable anger, resentment, and fury.

Then he thought, maybe she wasn't dead after all and was playing mind games with him. That had to be what it was. *No matter*, he thought, *this time he would make sure her sorry ass was really dead.* There would be no doubt in his mind, either. He knew they couldn't get him for it because he'd already been tried for it. There was no double jeopardy.

He drove his bulldozer forward at a faster speed. This time he was going to be sure to get her.

"I'll get you, you bitch," he snapped, as he drove the bulldozer at her. "I'll be sure this time. Try and take on a bulldozer, you old battleaxe."

He continued to drive at her with the large bulldozer blade down, and up the ridge.

Then, at the last second as he hit the top of the ridge, she faded and disappeared altogether. Harry cried out in panic as the large roaring bulldozer continued to the other side of the ridge, hit some unstable soft ground, and crashed downward into the pit.

"He didn't even stop," said co-worker, Frank Zurillo. "He just drove it over the ridge!"

"He musta lost it!" said the Foreman. "He musta went nuts!"

The other men shut off their vehicles and machines and ran to the top of the ridge. When they got there they saw the last of the bulldozer go under the muddy water, with no sign of Harry whatsoever.

A couple of men noticed a single pair of petit bare footprints leading from the pit, as the others stood there dumbfounded.

It took special divers one whole day to find the bulldozer in the pit and the better part of another to tow the bulldozer out of the mud, muck and water.

Harry's mud-covered dead body was still occupying the bulldozer seat with the look of shear horror frozen on his face. Clinging to Harry, as if hugging him lovingly, was Aida's year-old mud and slime-covered corpse.

The Trials and Tribulations of Marvin Lefler

For Marvin Lefler, life had not been the same since winning the Harry Leonard case. In fact, it had become strange to say the least. The strangeness wasn't just one incident or occurrence; it was a lot of little things adding up to build some kind of weird scenario for his defending the indefensible.

Instead of feeling like Perry Mason, or even Allen Dirshowitz at the very least, 'Marvelous' Marvin to his clients and 'Lousy' Lefler to everyone else felt uneasy. It did not feel like one of his glorious wins, where he wanted to champion the cause, the accused and most of all, himself.

He had no problem getting Harry Leonard off, even though he knew that he was guilty as sin. That part didn't matter. That's why his clients paid him. Besides, whether they were guilty or not, didn't matter. It was all about winning, that and making a name for himself.

It was the tactics that he'd used to get his client off that were beginning to make him uneasy. He had not only trashed the character of the missing, thought-to-be-deceased wife, but Leonard's own brother and sister-in-law, his neighbors and even the police. Everybody else was at fault for Harry Leonard's own personal behavior.

As he portrayed it, the man was a victim of other people's circumstances.

The real kicker was that he portrayed Aida Leonard as a needy, paranoid, jealous, mentally insecure woman that the accused had his hands full with and finally lost control. She merely disappeared after he finally had enough and hit her, trying to get control of her unpredictable emotions.

None of it was true, but as defense attorney, it was a legal strategy. Very questionable, bordering on unethical, but legal just the same. But, it wasn't about what was right, only what was legal when it came to Marvin.

Yes, he won the case by questionable tactics, but a win is a win. He threw enough doubt around to make the people wonder whether the Pope was Catholic. That was his m/o. He had defended everything from skinheads to pedophiles using this tactic. He zealously defended his clients while questioning the character, actions and motives of, not only the deceased, but their families, friends and the actual crime victims, not to mention a few witnesses. His defenses made the guilty innocent….and the innocent almost criminal.

Yet, even in victory, he felt different. A chill went up his spine immediately after the verdict as if a cold, icy hand from beyond had touched him. As if something tried to touch his soul. This unnerved him a bit and the uneasiness did not go away.

It was almost unsettling how he felt after the verdict.

This uneasiness continued to grow when Harry Leonard stubbornly decided to celebrate his acquittal in public. To Marvin, this seemed almost sacrilegious and inviting trouble. *Besides*, he figured, *why push your luck?* He had won, and not very many people liked the outcome of the verdict. He had defended worse, so it was a small matter to him.

For Marvin Lefler, the events after the trial were a little out of kilter after that. He had an initial series of interviews with local radio, newspaper and television reporters following the trial, where he lashed out at the prosecution, the police and anybody who was his adversary.

He was quick to learn that the trial did not bring him the fame he was seeking, but instead notoriety. He now felt more notorious than famous. More loathed than liked. More disdained than respected. Even at restaurants, the waiters and waitresses, while polite, and professional, were cool towards him. He could feel their disdain, but could not say anything because they were respectful.

This wasn't how he was supposed to feel. Even weasel-like shark lawyers like him who managed to get scumbags off on technicalities had some reason to feel vindication and adulation about their success. Still, happiness and contentment eluded him. The feeling of being a pariah had grown incrementally.

Like all good lawyers, he continued to do his job, defending his sometimes indefensible client. He filed briefs, made appeals and showed up for his court cases.

At least, the legal field was still his playground. Still, there was that uneasy feeling nagging at him.

Just over two weeks after the Leonard trial, he had all of his tires to his Porsche flattened.

He reported it to the police. "What do you intend to do about it?" he asked once they arrived.

"We will investigate it thoroughly," replied the officer, who arrived to take the report.

"It was probably one of you jackbooted thugs who did it," he commented snidely about the officer's response. "I know how well you guys love my defense of my clients…"

"Well, Mr. Lefler, if it was, I'm sure that you would defend their sorry rear-end," the officer snapped. "He's probably like all of the other misguided and misunderstood scumbags…oops, I mean youths…that you defend. Just the type of people you would invite home for dinner. Good day, Sir."

For the first time in his life, Lefler was speechless. He did not like it, that the officer in his honest response was so right in his assessment.

He also soon came to realize that, like Harry Leonard, he too was being ostracized. This put him on edge a little, because more than a few of his colleagues thought he was unethical and made it known how they felt.

Marvin was now having trouble sleeping. He was having dreams as if he were Harry Leonard committing the crime. He would be tired all day and then not be able to sleep at night.

Shortly after the flattened tires incident, he took his girlfriend, Diane Granger, out to dinner at the Fox and Hounds Restaurant. Once there, they ran into an old friend of hers, a ruggedly handsome businessman, Ryan Holcomb. As Diane and her old friend had some small talk, Marvin began to stew with jealousy. It was a kind of envy that it seemed all those around him were happy, enjoying life and other people. The longer she talked to him the worse it became. All kinds of sexual scenarios between the two ran through his head during their conversation. People, especially his girlfriend, shouldn't be enjoying a conversation that much with an old friend, when he didn't.

For the first time since they had gone out, Marvin Lefler was filled with rage and jealousy, and it showed. It was almost obvious that he was very jealous. Ryan could sense some of this and quickly said a polite goodbye to both of them. He had heard of Marvin's reputation for being a jerk at times.

When they got back to Diane's place, she knew something was wrong. "What's the matter?" she asked. "You weren't very friendly to Ryan…"

"Well, it was pretty goddamn obvious that you were flirting with him," he snapped. "You were practically all over him…"

"What?" she asked in disbelief. "I never gave any such impression!"

"I'm surprised you didn't ask to leave so you could bone him in the parking lot," he continued. "Hell, you almost looked like you wanted to suck his cock!"

"Are you nuts?!" she asked, protesting. "We are just friends. We've been friends since elementary school. We grew up together and I don't appreciate you talking to me like that! I want you to leave now!"

"I'll bet you do," he replied. "So you can call up Ryan or whatever the fuck his name was and fuck his brains out when I'm gone like some cheap whore! That's, if you ain't already nailing him."

"You jealous rotten bastard, sonofabitch!!!" she screamed as she slapped his face. "How dare you!"

After Diane slapped Marvin's face, he muttered "Bitch!" and backhanded her across the face, splitting her lips. Diane fell backwards onto the floor, hurt and in shock and disbelief.

Marvin realized what he had done and went to help her up. The hurt, angry look in her eyes made him stop. She slapped at his outstretched hand. "Get away from me," she seethed. He felt as if something had come over him, almost possessing him.

"I'm sorry, I lost my head," he explained. When he talked it sounded like it like it wasn't him speaking. Everything appeared so surreal. "I don't know what came over me. I was just angry and jealous. I'm sorry I lost control. I don't know what happened to me there…"

"Get away from me, now!" she said, teeth clenched, and filled with anger, as she got back up on her feet and held her split and bleeding lips. "Get out now, you bastard or I'm calling the police and pressing charges! We are done you motherfucking bastard!"

Marvin knew he had totally blown it with Diane. He had just destroyed their relationship with a single jealous rage. He didn't know what had happened, to himself, but it was strange.

"You seemed to have picked up some of your last clients more redeeming qualities," she said, as he headed towards the door. "Goodbye, Marvin. Don't bother calling or sending flowers. Maybe you should get your head examined."

Marvin left. In the course of just a couple of weeks he had his tires slashed and lost his girlfriend. He knew that she would probably not call the police but knew she was capable of doing other things that could be called getting even.

When he got home, he found all of the lights on in his house. He did not remember leaving them on. He then shut them off and went to bed. He slept hard. All night long he once again dreamed that he was committing a murder. He also dreamt that he heard somebody calling his name.

The next morning he woke up to his alarm clock. He reached over and turned it off. As he turned it off, he realized that the alarm clock wasn't the only thing blaring. The television, the radio, his CD player and every single light was on in the place.

What in the hell?" he asked as he got out of bed and proceeded to turn off all of the electronic devices.

He then showered, shaved and went into the office. Fortunately for him he had a pretty light caseload, which was perfectly all right with him. He was emotionally and mentally drained. The Leonard case had taken more out of him than he at first thought or cared to admit. It was the most draining case that he had ever taken part in.

He sat at his desk and cupped his hands over his face, thinking about all of the things that had taken place lately. He wished things would get back to some semblance of normality. But, knew that they would not.

The next few days were a menagerie of mistakes, miscues, conflicts, and more continued uneasiness.

As he returned home from work, he found that Diane had dropped off some of his belongings on his front lawn in the rain.

"Aw shit," he muttered, when he saw a couple of his five hundred dollar suits out on the lawn in the rain. He knew that was Diane's retaliation for hitting her. He scanned the clothes out on the lawn, and realized there must have been ten thousand dollars' worth of clothes there. As he began to pick up the clothes he knew that a few of the neighbors had to have witnessed the entire episode and were in all likelihood laughing at his misfortune. The last suit he came upon, had dog shit on it. Obviously the neighbors' dog did his business on it, with their glowing endorsement.

"The rotten fuckers," he muttered. "Rotten, no-good cocksuckers."

A police car, with two officers patrolling the area slowed down and stopped. The officer in the passenger side of the street asked if everything was all right.

"Yes," replied Marvin. "Everything is A-fucking okay. A real peachy fucking day. Can't you tell? Everything is fucking marvelous! Don't you have some niggers to beat up or something? I am fucking fine.

Can't you tell? I always stand out in the rain with my expensive suits all muddy like a homeless fucking person. Doesn't everybody?!!!"

"Okay," responded the officers with two wide, Cheshire Cat-like grins on their faces. "Glad to hear it. Have a nice day!" The officers were doing their best not to laugh as they drove away, but not being very successful at it.

When he finally got the clothes collected, he was totally drenched. As soon as he got inside of his house, he saw that somebody had walked across the floor and carpet in bare, mud-covered footprints. By just looking at them, he concluded that they were from a female.

"Goddammit, Diane!" he cursed. "Enough's enough already. I'm sorry I hit your ass, for Chrissake. But, enough is enough. You've gotten your goddamn pound of flesh." He followed the footprints through the house. He noticed that muddy handprints were also on the walls as well. Marvin continued to curse and swear at Diane. He was half-tempted to go and file a restraining order tomorrow morning against her, but he knew she could bring up his assault and that would not fare well for him. As for now, he would call the police and file a report.

After calling the police, he changed his wet clothes. When he left his bedroom he noticed that both the hand and footprints were gone. The police arrived just afterwards and he said that there had been somebody in his house. The police inspected everything, finding nothing. Marvin politely thanked the police for coming by and apologized for bothering them. Even if he didn't really mean it, it sounded at least diplomatic, for one of the few times in his life.

He sat down in his recliner and rubbed his eyes. He began to wonder if he was seeing things or just plain going crazy. He felt like he needed a drink. He decided to go out and have a drink or two to relax and unwind. Once at the bar, he was watching the local news. A prostitute named Angelique Periwinkle, who was suspected of murdering two of her Johns, was arrested and then paraded into a parked Oakland County Sheriff's Department car and hauled off to jail. Marvin saw something in her, and knew that he had another big case type of client. In spite of needing a little break from his work, he would go see her and offer his legal services.

The next morning, he went down to see her. She looked a little worse for wear in her orange prison jumpsuit, but other than that she wasn't too bad looking, he thought. She wasn't as nice looking as Diane, but not bad just the same. He thought she was doable as women went, and a much better looking than many hookers that he had encountered in his numerous courthouse appearances.

She was a little surprised to have his services offered to her at first. In fact, she was a little skeptical, but listened. Since she knew that she needed some legal help badly.

"I don't have much money," she responded. "I don't think I can afford you. I can pay you a little when I get back to work and give you a few freebies in the meantime."

"Not to worry," he replied. "It will all work out. We first need to post bail and get you into my custody. Then, we win your case. I think you were defending yourself from abusive Johns. That's the way I see it."

He got his client released and then bought her some clothes as he prepared her for the trial. He started to work on her defense. Though it was against some of his colleagues better judgment, he had her stay at his place in the guestroom because her apartment was a crime scene and to get her away from the prostitution element. She could stay there, watch television all day, sleep and basically just hideout while he worked on her defense. She didn't mind either, since she knew of his tenacious reputation and staying at his house was better than what she had been staying in.

Even as he flourished in legal element, at night his bad dreams continued.

A few weeks later, Marvin ran into Diane at a restaurant, where she was dining with Ryan. At first he didn't think much about it. Then as he thought more about it he became enraged. In his mind, he had been right to hit her for what he viewed as a betrayal. Throwing caution to the wind, he walked over to their table and confronted them.

"So, just friends, huh?" he said snidely, as he grabbed her arm. "For my suspicions I get thousands of dollars worth of clothes ruined because of you, bitch! Thanks a helluva lot! The clothes! The vandalism! Enough is enough, already. I knew you were lying when you said 'you were just friends'. I knew that you probably wanted to bone him. You cheap slut. I was right all along about you. You whore!"

"Let go of me, now," Diane said sternly. "You're clothes ended up on the lawn because you hit me and that's what you deserved! As for the rest I don't know what the hell you're talking about! Now let me go!"

"He hit you?" Ryan asked, as he looked at Diane's face and she nodded.

By now, a lot of the other diners were well aware of the verbal altercation between Marvin and Diane.

"You are a real tough man there Marvin," Ryan said sarcastically. "I'll bet you can beat any woman half her size. You're a real tough guy, aren't you?"

"Yeah, well, buddy I'm one that can sue the pants off of you, so cool your jets," Marvin said.

"Whoop-de-friggindo!" Ryan said. "That's supposed to scare me, you little prick? You might be a terror in the courtroom, but you ain't shit anywhere else, dickhead."

More people in the restaurant were now aware of the argument. A maitre d' came over to settle thing down. "Please Sir, please sit down."

"Shut up!" Marvin said loudly. "As for you Ryboy, I'll sue you into poverty, dickhead."

"You think that scares me?" Ryan asked. "You really think your threat intimidates me? God, you are delusional aren't you? You're a legend in your own mind. You're a real verbal tiger there. I bet you felt good hitting her, didn't you?"

"Yeah, I hit, her, so what, what do you intend to do about it?" Marvin asked, sarcastically. "I'll hit the bitch again, if she pisses me off and keeps doing shit to me."

"Let go of me," Diane said as she tried to pull away and he tightened his grip. "You're hurting me."

"Let her go, peckerhead," Ryan said firmly. "Or, I will do something about it that you will not like."

"Oooh, Mister Tough Guy is threatening me," Marvin said as he feigned fear. "Ooooh, I'm soooo scared…"

"You heard the lady," Ryan said. "Let her go. Now!"

"Yeah, what'll you do if I don't, asshole?" Marvin asked sarcastically as he squeezed her arm harder. "Hurt me, big boy? You ain't got the guts. I doubt you got the balls either. Besides, I'll sue the goddamn shit out of you! I'll sue you into poverty….I'll…"

Ryan stood up and threw a roundhouse right at Marvin's face, connecting with his jaw, and making a wicked crunch before he could even react. Marvin hit the ground with a dull thud, unconscious before he hit the ground, while a few people let out gasps and moans. Those that knew it was the infamous Marvin Lefler, thought it couldn't happen to a better guy. A couple of men who had more than a few drinks in them and no love loss for Marvin, walked up and checked out the unconscious barrister on the floor and laughed loudly. One counted to ten and then said "Yeah, he's out cold!"

"Winner by knock-out and new Champeen!" said the other one as he pointed to Ryan. They even offered to buy Ryan and Diane's meal and drinks for doing a great public service. The only criticism was that it took place in such a nice place.

"You think he's dead?" asked the first drunk.

"Hell, no, we ain't that lucky," responded his friend. "Besides, you don't throw assholes like this a funeral, you just slush them. I mean frush them. You flutch them. Never mind you put turds like him in the toilet and hit the handle."

The other drunk just nodded and laughed in agreement. "Nighty-night, dick."

Diane laughed at Marvin. "Such class, Marvin, such class. Why were we ever together, I'll never know. I've been trying to figure that one for a couple of weeks."

The manager, a maitre d' and a busboy helped get him up off the floor and called EMS and the police. The police did not press charges and Marvin was given a quick ride to William Beaumont Hospital in Royal Oak to see if he had a concussion. After a brief stay, he went home.

Once back home, he was welcomed by Angelique.

"What in the fuck happened to you?" she asked. "You looked like you ran into a wall, for Chrissake."

"I ran into my ex-girlfriend's new boyfriend," he replied. "I decided to use my head against his fist to prove a legal point. He's going to get a lawsuit he won't soon forget, either. I'll own him if it's the last thing I do."

"Well, you better sit down," she said. "Is there anything I can do?"

"I'll be alright," he said as he sat down. "I have been thinking about your case and what strategy to use. I think we can argue that you had a couple of customers that got violent with you and you acted in self-defense. Both men were known to have tempers."

"You going to be okay?" she asked once again, as she sat down on the floor in front of him. "Yeah, I'm more tired than anything," he responded. "I've been under a lot of stress lately and I haven't been sleeping well. My head hurts a little. I have a mild concussion."

"I know you haven't been sleeping," replied Angelique. "I've heard you, moan and talk in your sleep sometimes. I got up one night to go to the bathroom and you tossed and turned. You sound like you need a vacation or something."

"You think I could get one of those payments you offered me earlier?" Marvin asked. "I really need to relieve some stress. I could really use it right now."

Angelique nodded, knowing what he meant. She then proceeded to unzip his pants as she began to perform fellacio on him then and there, much to his pleasure and relief. He finally felt a little better about something. It was the first time in a while that had happened. Sometime, later they would make their way to the bedroom for more sex. It was exactly what he had needed. He slept for hours afterwards. Later in the night he had bad dreams that Aida Leonard was trying to get at him and he tried to ward her off. After a brief struggle he was able to get on top of her. He then grabbed her by the throat and squeezed, defending himself, until she finally disappeared.

When Marvin woke up, Angelique was in bed next to him on her stomach. She appeared to be sleeping soundly. He looked at his alarm clock. They had slept all the way through the night. He rubbed his face and then reached over to wake her up. As he touched her body. She felt cold. Very cold. He knew that she did not feel right. He called her name as he rolled her on her back. As she was turned over, he realized that it was not Angelique, but Aida Leonard.

He fell back in shock. He rubbed his eyes to make sure he wasn't seeing anything. When he re-focused, it was Angelique. Her eyes were open and staring blankly into nothingness. She had bruises around her neck. He knew that she was dead. Sometime during the night she had died. Worse yet, there were dark purple bruises on her neck as if she had been strangled. Then it occurred to him, that he must have grabbed her neck during or sometime after their second round of sex. He then realized that he must have strangled her as he plunged himself into her. He was in shock. It was too surreal. He thought it all had been a dream. That it all had been an unreal nightmare. Tears began to stream down his face because of what the ramifications would be. As a lawyer, he knew that he was done.

He climbed out of bed and entered the bathroom. After he used the toilet, he washed his face off and then looked into the full-length the mirror. Then he noticed that on the floor were mud-covered foot and hand prints. There on the mirror written in dirt was the word murderer. He stepped back in shock. He looked down again at the floor and there were a woman's muddy footprints. Then he caught a glimpse of something in the mirror. He looked up and there was Aida Leonard's rotting corpse looking back at him.

He screamed in horror. Aida was not only in the mirror, but was getting closer to him. She was coming towards him in the mirror. She was now out of the mirror coming closer. He screamed again as she fell onto him. He fell backwards into the bathtub and hit his head on the soap dispenser in the tub. Sometime between falling into the tub and hitting his head, Marvin Lefler's died, his heart stopping from fright.

He was found two days later when he was reported missing from work and after being a now-show in court, with strange mud, dirt and dead body matter on his naked body in the bathtub. He had a frozen death-mask of absolute horror across his face. Along with him, they found Angelique Periwinkle, his prostitute, client dead in his bed with his DNA and prints on her neck.

"Pretty weird isn't it?" asked a detective who was assisting on the investigation. 'Something doesn't add up. The only thing I can figure is he was boning her and then she must have attacked him and he strangled her. It just doesn't add up as to why, though."

"Yeah," responded the Lead Detective. "Regardless, it looks like the Devil is getting two for the price of one. Mr. Lefler sure gave us our trials and tribulations during his abbreviated legal career. Now he can defend his clients and himself in Hell. Then again, the rotten bastard might be right at home there. Let's wrap this up. It's pretty self-explanatory."

The Strange Case of Edmund Wainright

My name is John Brandon.

While I have been called a P.I. or a Private Dick, I am not your stereotypical private investigator who drinks hard liquor for breakfast, trouble for lunch and danger for dinner with a slew of dames in between.

My job is nothing like that and neither am I.

I am educated and received my training and skills during the war with the O.S.S. I can speak French, German and some Italian fluently. I am proficient in most firearms as well as explosives. I was also trained in judo, spying, espionage, surveillance and radio procedure. Unlike a lot of my colleagues, I parachuted into France a few months prior to the invasion and stayed until after the war's end.

After the war, I used my talents and skills set towards private and personal investigation. While I am not like the stereotypes in the movies, I will admit to having a penchant for the ladies and have been known to take sexual favors as partial payments from time to time. If that sounds bad, I am not one to turn down sex from an attractive lady. If it's offered I will indulge in it. I believe most men would.

Most of my cases involve surveillance and investigations of philandering spouses, background checks on mates and information on suspected blackmailers. Not very exciting, but they were cases where I did not have to use my piece.

I was grateful for that. Believe me, I had done more than my share of killing during the war. Most of it was regretfully necessary. Some were like that Nazi SS officer that murdered civilians, most of which were children….I took great pleasure in emptying my 'Grease Gun' magazine in that sonofabitch.

I even had a secretary, a middle-aged lady named Hazel Macready who was married to a police lieutenant, Henry Macready.

Like I said, most of my cases were pretty mundane and run-of-the mill and I was paid very well for them all, too. That is until the Edmund Wainright case. This was a case that was closed, but never really solved.

It all started with a call from my friend and former commanding officer Alex Wainright. He was concerned that his younger brother Edmund was coming back home with a Central European fiancé, Ilsa Draugr.

Edmund had been with the post-war occupation and part of the legal support staff that was prosecuting the Nazi War Criminals. He was all of twenty-one years-old.

I understood the family dilemma. The Wainrights were a wealthy and powerful family. They were headed up by Leonard Wainright, the family patriarch. He wanted to protect their own as well as the family fortune.

Alex said that he tried looking into her background, but admitted that he did not have the time or the resources to do so. That was why I was called. I still did. He said helping run the family business and its post-war expansion plans took up a lot of his time. On top of that, he was a newlywed himself, having married his high school sweetheart Mary once he got back from England.

Since I had been overseas to more than just jolly old England, I had more contacts and relationships with people there. So I still had a network of resources. I did not see Alex until after the war and we met up in Paris.

Alex said that I would be paid handsomely for my services and would be given ten thousand dollars to pay for any costs incurred during my investigation. I was told to make no mention of this to any other family members other than he or his father. I was also invited to an engagement party next Saturday at their Grosse Pointe Farms residence. They wanted me to meet the bride-to-be.

I knew that he wanted me to gauge her character and try to get a firsthand read on her as a person.

Once I was off the phone with Alex, I made some calls to my contacts at the State Department. After I made phone calls there, I checked the time and made calls to some of my wartime contacts overseas. I called German double agent and art dealer Eric Mueller. He knew a lot of the rich and powerful in Germany and Austria. He said that he would call me in one week. After that I called former allied agent and lover Heidi Enke, and artist and aristocrat Heinrich Weige. Both of these colleagues were well-connected and had a vast array of contacts and a way of networking with friends.

All three agreed to be my eyes and ears in Europe. If I needed to go there, I knew they would be a big help as well. We had done enough work together for them to know exactly what I needed.

By the time Saturday rolled around, I made sure that I arrived early enough to be one of the first ones there. I wanted to be able to observe her as much as possible.

After the usual greetings and the offers of hors d'oeuvres and drinks, I made my way through the place, mingling with guests and family. After about an hour of this, I was finally introduced to Ilsa.

Alex introduced me as his good friend and army

buddy to Edmund and Ilsa. I congratulated them and wished them the best. As I shook hands with the bride-to-be, I noticed how beautiful she really was. She was like a goddess with her long flowing blonde hair. Her eyes were mesmerizing. She was very nicely proportioned. The only critical thing I could say was that her complexion was a bit on the pale side.

When I touched her gloved hand after wishing her congratulations, I noticed it felt cold.

We talked a little. By her accent I could tell that she was from somewhere in Germany or Austria. By our brief conversation I could tell she was educated and cultured. I knew she had to be from old aristocracy or money of some kind.

I smiled, shook Edmund's hand and then moved on. After being given a glass of champagne, I was pulled aside and to a nearby study by Leonard and Alex Wainright to talk privately.

The old man told me in no uncertain terms that it was imperative I find out everything about her as I could as quickly as possible. He said if she checked out and proved to be 'acceptable' that he could live with his son marrying her. But he sensed something about her.

He admitted that even his mother Alice, their grandmother who lived with them, felt a kind of uneasiness about her character. Alex said his grandmother usually got along or liked almost everybody, sensed something wrong with her. While polite and friendly to her grandson's fiancé, she felt deep misgivings about her.

We soon left the study. I stayed at the party observing almost everything that I could. I did my best not to make eye contact with my target, as I pretending to be enjoying myself.

Eventually I was pulled aside by Leonard Wainright's

much younger and second wife, Shirley. She discretely led me to her private study where we proceeded to have sex. She called it her party favor. Either way, it helped me enjoy the party more.

I had heard rumors about the second Mrs. Wainright and her wandering eye, but not paid them much attention, until now. Supposedly, she was the reason the old man left the first Mrs. Wainright. After the sex, I could see why. I hadn't been laid like that since I was with a fraulein after Germany surrendered. Either way, I did not really care, because she wasn't my wife after all.

When we finished, we arrived back in time to hear them announce their plans to be married on July Fourth.

This gave me just a little over two months to find out what I could about the woman.

I caught Leonard Wainright looking at me. I could tell it was the look that told me to find out anything that could prevent this wedding and their pending nuptials.

After the announcement, I was approached by Alex and Edmund's younger sister Barbara, who had just finished college, to dance. So for much of the rest of the night; we danced and engaged in small talk. She admitted to knowing why I was there. She said that was her dad just being protective.

According to her, she liked the idea of Edmund getting married, but found his choice of women just a bit uncanny.

Sometime later I left the party and went back to my office. As I made a couple of late night calls, and read my mail, Barbara visited. Needless to say, we had sex on the couch in my office.

So, I basically nailed the step-mother and her step-daughter in one family in the same night. The only time I can recall doing something like that was when I was with two sisters in the red light district in Amsterdam. If that made me a cad, in some people's eyes, my defense is they were the initiators and very willing partners in our trysts.

By the end of the week, I received calls from my contacts at the State Department saying they weren't able to tell me much. It was as if she did not really exist because there were no records of her anywhere.

I hoped my three contacts in Europe had better luck finding out information.

This lack of information was not unusual. At least not considering some of the smaller countries and the way their royalty and aristocracy guarded their secrets and privacy. They were very careful about what they revealed.

I figured that the State Department was a dead end and would be of little or no help, except for maybe travel visas and diplomacy.

The next day Alex called me, saying that Ilsa would be staying in the guest house on the back of the property. He mentioned that she had a tendency to walk around the property at night. He asked my opinion on this.

I replied that it could be caused from the war. I asked him how many times he woke up at night after the war had ended. We both knew a lot of people that did not sleep well and had nightmares because of it. Hell, I even slept lightly at night because of it. It had become a habit.

Alex agreed, but had his doubts.

I kept digging for information, which was becoming an exercise in futility.

In between my investigative work was my ongoing affairs with Shirley Wainright and her equally amorous and slightly younger step-daughter Barbara. While potentially big trouble, at the time I viewed it as one of those fringe benefits of the job. At times, I felt like I was being paid to nail my client's women.

Like clockwork I received a long distance call from Eric Mueller. He said that he found some information on Ilsa Draugr. He said she was originally from an area in Northern Austria in Austria, or so she had claimed to those who Mueller had talked to. He said the town of Draugen was destroyed during the war and practically a ghost town. He said that he would look around for some information and if he did not find anything, that he might take a trip there if possible. I told him to hold off until we found out more.

It had been ten days since Edmund and Ilsa arrived back in the states. Since then some strange things were happening in and around the Wainright homestead.

Alice Wainright had suddenly taken ill, a short two days after Ilsa's arrival. From what Alex told me, she had become pale and weak to the point of being bedridden. The very best physicians and specialists were called in, but so far, to no avail.

Her condition was remaining constant, and even worsening.

Meanwhile the bodies of two people were found nearby. A teenage girl named Martha Waldecker was found face-down near Lake St. Clair. She did not live far from the Wainrights. The other body was that of Arthur Wilkins. He went out to fish one evening, as he was known to do in order to relax, and he never came back. He was found sitting on the dock with his pole still in his hand.

Neither body had any marks or signs of wrong-doing on them. Both appeared to have died under similar circumstances.

I did not think much of it at the time. In fact, it was little more than an afterthought to a couple of mysterious deaths.

Four days later, there were a couple of developments.

The first was, I received a call from Heinrich Weige. He said the town and area that Ilsa Draugr was thought to have come from was devastated during the war. He went on to say that the area was thought to have been bad or cursed prior to the war. He said that he was informed the town had more than its share of deaths. These deaths were not associated with the war.

Heinrich informed me that the people who had associated with her did not know much about her. She had no family to speak of and was thought to come from old, aristocratic money.

In closing, he said one acquaintance mentioned how strangely coincidental there were mysterious deaths in the area whenever and wherever she visited.

I thanked him for the information and hung up. I began to wonder about this coincidence.

No sooner had I hung up the phone and I received a call from Alex informing me his grandmother had died. It seemed she just became weaker and frailer to where she could not recover. It was as if her life just had just been drained from her in spite of the physician's best efforts.

He said the funeral would be in two days. I had Mrs. Macready send flowers and I of course paid my respects and attended the funeral. While at the gravesite, while the minister spoke, I kept wondering how Ilsa tied into this. My gut instinct told me she was somehow a prominent player in this.

I just needed to figure out how.

Whether it was from the shock of losing his grandmother and the hectic pace of planning a wedding, Edmund appeared to be out of it. It was like he was numb with shock, hardly talking or acknowledging people. Yet, it was more than that.

He was like a shell of himself.

During the wake, I watched Ilsa with great interest. She appeared distant and even aloof, without any sense of emotion. She said and did all of the right things, playing the helpful and caring fiancé, but there was something amiss. Something I could not put a finger on.

Where even Shirley Wainright was visibly shaken and stunned, Ilsa was not.

It was as if she expected it or knew it was going to happen.

At one point I was able to get her alone and talk to her. However she was not very forthcoming with any information at all. Talking to her, even briefly was an exercise in futility. One thing she did say that intrigued me was her comments on death.

As she walked away, I knew something was wrong. My O.S.S. training and surviving behind enemy lines had taught me to follow my instincts about situations and people. If something did not seem right, then chances are it was not. I was able to flush out German and double agents following my gut or instincts.

With Ilsa, I was beginning to get the feeling she was not what she appeared to be.

This reminded me of when I had to shoot a female German agent I had been close to. Well, not close to, but one I had been sleeping with. She was actually French, but was loyal to the Reich. I had waited until she had let her guard down to kill her. It was my job.

Ilsa reminded me of that agent in some way.

I talked to Alex privately about what I had so far and that I was waiting for more information. He seemed happy with my progress so far under the circumstances. It was then, Shirley Wainright suggested I go upstairs and talk to Leonard.

I suspected this was a ploy for a private rendezvous in another room. But knew I had to tell the old man the latest developments, whether it was or not.

Leonard had quickly retired to his bedroom because he was feeling faint and weak. I explained to him what I had just told Alex. He thanked me. Shirley then quickly ushered me out of the room so he could rest. This was one of those times. I did believe she really loved him. She just needed to get it more than she did.

From there, Shirley escorted me to her private study where I helped to console her sexually. About thirty minutes later we rejoined the others. A short time later, after giving my sincere condolences I left for my office.

I was tired and more than a little disillusioned with my progress on the case so far. I was running out of options on what to do next.

Once at my office I quickly went through the mail. After that I kept going over things in my head about the case. Finally, I called it a night and went home. I needed a good night's sleep in my own bed instead of the office couch. If not a good night's sleep at least a more comfortable one.

The rest of the week was one dead end after another.

It wasn't until my secretary, Hazel Macready mentioned that her husband told her about a little boy who was out playing in his yard at dusk and was found unconscious. Apparently he found to have been weak, pale and non-respondent to people. He was rushed to the hospital. She mentioned that her husband said he'd be alright.

She also mentioned that an elderly lady was found dead in her swing that was facing the lake. It was believed that she had a heart attack or something and just died.

There was one coincidence and that both cases were a short distance from the Wainright place.

The authorities did not make the connection or think much about it. For some reason both of these caught my attention. I felt as if these smaller almost unnoticed incidents were connected. My instincts told me they were somehow connected. I suspected they were connected to the Wainright case.

Proving it would be a different story.

I was getting more frustrated in the case. By the end of the week my frustration had grown to the point of being ready to take up drinking.

This frustration was broken up by the visit of an upset Barbara Wainright. Her father's condition was worsening and her brother Edmund was still not the same.

Barbara went on to explain how at her father's behest, had Alex take over and run the family business. She also told me how her step-mother, Shirley was at her father's side for the better part of the week.

I took Barbara out for a meal. Afterward, she wanted me to make love to her. So, I drove us to an out-of-the way place that would accommodate us. I might have been nailing her, but I did not want her to get a bad reputation.

Before we left the place, she said something that stuck with me. She wondered aloud if any of the Wainrights would be left if things kept going the way they were.

I know she was half-joking, but given she had just lost her grandmother, her father was now ailing and her brother was 'out-of-sorts,' that there was some seriousness to them.

She kissed me goodbye when I returned her to her

vehicle and thanked me for helping her to forget her problems for a while.

I desperately needed a break on this case.

By Sunday morning, Leonard Wainright's condition had stabilized and remained the same.

This was good.

At least he hadn't worsened. However, now Shirley and Edmund Wainright were now pale and weak. In the course of a few days two more family members appeared to be stricken with the same ailment. That meant four members of the same family were ill in the course of a couple of weeks.

Barbara Wainright had called and informed me that they decided to hire a couple of full-time private duty nurses to care of them.

As I read the Sunday paper an article jumped out at me. It told of a man named Roger Findley was found dead in his hammock yesterday morning. What stood out to me was that his property was adjacent to the Wainrights' Grosse Pointe Farms property.

This definitely raised my eyebrows.

I pondered the idea of doing surveillance on the property, but there were a lot of blind spots with the hedges and wooded areas and even some fences. I would need some help. I would also need the approval of the Wainright family and I needed my surveillance to be secret. I may have to do this another time.

Even if I just observed the guest house, the terrain was somewhat problematic for decent surveillance.

I seriously considered quitting the case, but I was too close to Alex Wainright to do that. In spite of the distractions of his sister and step-mother, he was my friend and I wanted to help him and his family.

As I weighed my options and tried to figure out what to do next, I received a surprise call from Eric

Mueller. I knew it had to be important being that it was either very late or very early morning in Germany.

The first thing he asked me was if I could fly there and how soon. He wanted to meet with me. It was important. He said he had information for me, but that I needed to see it first- hand.

While hesitant, Mueller had been a good and trusted friend and colleague. He had saved my life and kept me from getting captured during the war.

I told him that I would fly out early tomorrow morning.

He said that he would meet me at the Munich Airport when I landed.

After that, I called Alex and informed him of what I was doing. He hoped I found something there and fast. He also admitted that both his father and step-mother had taken a turn for the worse.

I told him that I would try and that I should be back in a few days.

After that I phoned my secretary, Hazel Macready, of what my plans were. I asked her that while I was away to keep track to see if there were any more deaths or illnesses happening in the area near Grosse Pointe Farms.

The last time I had flown the European mainland had been prior to D-Day. I had not really been in any hurry to return. For me, the war had made the continent like a very large graveyard.

I tried to sleep most of the way there, because I did not know how much I would get upon my arrival.

Several hours later and a couple of stopovers, I finally arrived in Germany. True to his word, I was met by Eric Mueller.

Upon seeing each other, we embraced like old war buddies would. He then quickly took me to an inn where we could get a good meal and a room to spend the night. Eric informed me that we would take a train to Northern Austria and the small town of Draugen.

On the train ride to Austria, we caught up with each other's lives and what we had been doing since the war had ended. We reminisced about those friends and colleagues we had lost.

It almost felt like we were trying to avoid talking about the reason for the trip.

As we entered Austria, Eric mentioned we would be meeting a man named Peter Bittrich who was an investigator of sorts with some very unique cases. He said that Bittrich had some information for me. From what Eric told me, Bittrich was a professor of history and anthropology. As a professor, he was well-respected at the university in Vienna.

After hearing this, I was even more intrigued, and yet also concerned.

We were met at the train station in Salzburg by Peter Bittrich. Bittrich was a tall, older gentleman in his early fifties, with thinning gray hair and was smoking a pipe.

I was introduced, we shook hands and then headed to his vehicle. Bittrich had us climb in his Kubelwagen, a leftover remnant from the war. Eric had me sit in the front passenger seat.

From there Bittrich drove us to Draugren.

As he drove us there, Bittrich explained that the town had pretty much been a ghost town prior to the war. He went on to say that the town had a bleakness to it. He said it was a kind of indescribable darkness. Nobody had visited it, except for different countries military units.

I sensed he was dancing around something, so he would not be laughed at or mocked in some way. My curiosity got the better of me and I decided to ask what exactly he was trying to say.

It was then that Eric spoke up and said my answers would lie in the town.

I knew then it was something they could not easily explain.

Finally, as we approached town, I could see it how desolate and decrepit the place looked. Much of it was in ruins. It was hardly a town at all, really. There were a few remnants of buildings, some of which had been burned out and destroyed. The few that were completely standing were gutted, abandoned shells of buildings with no doors or windows. Once in town, I could see what Bittrich was talking about.

I hadn't felt a chill like this go through since jumping into France prior to the invasion.

The town felt like it was a large cemetery and the buildings that were still standing were the headstones of the people who had resided there in the past.

It was then I noticed there was not a single living thing around. There were no stray cats or dogs. It was eerily quiet. Almost too quiet. I also noticed there were no birds chirping or any other animal noises. Only the occasional gust of wind causing the doors and bare tree branches to creak slightly.

The quiet was disturbing.

It was then that Peter Bittrich led us to a very old and very tiny cemetery in the middle of this little hamlet. In the center of the cemetery were the remains of a destroyed mausoleum.

The roof to the mausoleum or crypt had caved in and rotted, while one whole side wall had caved in. The door to it was open and only hanging on one hinge at the bottom.

Bittrich cautiously led us inside the damaged mausoleum. Once inside, he pointed to one of the vaults with a broken lid. There was a nameplate on the side that read Ilsa Draugr, Born 1046, Died 1066.

I was in shock and disbelief.

Before I could say or do anything Bittrich began to explain everything.

Bittrich explained to me that at the height of the Vikings' conquest and power they managed to control much of Europe and England. He said they even had settlements in Germany and Austria.

According to him, the name Draugr was an old Nordic or Old Germanic name for the undead or the undead that preyed on the living. He said the history of this town was plagued by such a creature and multiple times.

He went on to say that Ilsa Draugr was buried multiple times. He then led us to the cemetery and to a certain headstone. This headstone was faintly engraved, but still somewhat legible. It read Ilsa Draugr 1046 Died 1066 Died 1540.

He then led me to another headstone. This one also had the name Ilsa Draugr, Born 1046, Died, 1066, 1540, 1786.

When I commented this could not be right and that it had to be multiple people with that name, Bittrich added that there are other graves with her name on them and a few he was not quite sure of. He added that there was no body in any of the graves or the crypt itself.

He then handed me a large clasped envelope with a number of black and white photographs of the headstones, the disinterred graves and the empty crypt or vault.

I asked him what it all meant, and he explained that Edmund Wainright's fiancé, Ilsa Draugr, was an undead creature that fed on the living. He added that she had been around for a very long time. That was why she had no records.

He added that whether it was through happenstance, human actions or some kind of supernatural forces, she was somehow resurrected. Bittrich said that she would find a family and feed on them until they too succumbed, and would move on to another and another.

I mentioned how Wainright's grandmother had died and how now the father, step-mother and even possibly the fiancé were now ailing. I also mentioned how at least thee people were found dead nearby.

Bittrich looked at me in horror. He said that I needed to get back to them as quickly as possible. Before taking us back to the train station, he handed me a silver dagger for me to use against 'The Draugr.'

It was all so unbelievable and I could not believe what had been told. But it was also all that I had. As unbelievable as it was, nothing else made sense.

And that sense was tenuous at best.

On the train ride back to Munich, I asked Eric how he would handle this situation and what would he do under the circumstance. He admitted that he did not know. He said that he would probably tell a kind of limited truth, where the most unbelievable things were left unsaid or proven in front of my client.

I thanked him. It was probably the best piece of advice I could ask for. I also told him if he had told me any of this over the phone, that I would have thought him insane. Eric said he knew that and that was why he had me come and see it.

While it had been great to work with Eric again, it had been demanding too.

The flight home was both the longest and the shortest one I had ever experienced. Long in that it seemed to take forever to get home and short in that I was home before I could formulate any plans.

The only small comfort was the silver dagger in my possession.

I was dead tired by the time I landed at Detroit Metro Airport. I grabbed a cab and had them take me home. The jet lag had taken its toll and I slept long and hard into late the next day.

Upon waking up, I headed immediately into the office. There, Mrs. Macready informed me that Leonard Wainright's condition remained stable, but Shirley Wainright's had worsened. She also informed me that there had been a suspected suicide of an unwed mother named Margaret Banks. She was found face-down in Lake St. Clair, but drowning was not the cause of death.

I decided to call Alex to see if we could meet somewhere. He said we could meet tonight, at his office. He hoped I had something for him to use.

I hoped I did too.

That night I told him that I had information, but it was too unbelievable to totally share at this time. I told him that Eric Mueller was my contact on this, as well as an Austrian Professor Peter Bittrich. So I had their testimony and word.

I told him I had some photographs to show him but I was hesitant because the evidence I had was hard to believe, even for me.

Alex insisted on seeing the photos. I placed them out one by one, explaining them as I did so. All he could do was shake his head in disbelief.

I asked him if he ever had any doubts about my sanity in the past and whether he doubted my word as long as he had known me. I then added I had reliable sources, and that he knew one of them personally. They too had witnessed what I did. I admitted I had trouble believing this myself.

Alex then confessed that up until a couple of days

ago, he would not have believed any of this. But something happened that made him change his opinion and possibly question all that he knew was real.

He told me about how one of his neighbors, Mrs. Ellyse Kelly approached him and told him how her visiting grandson had witnessed something. He told me how she went on to say that her grandson woke up in the middle of the night and went to the bathroom. In the process of going, he happened to look outside from the upstairs window and saw a woman with glowing red eyes taking someone back to the guest house. He said she didn't really walk, but appeared to glide across the ground.

According to the woman's grandson, she looked around to see if anybody was watching and caught a glimpse of him. Or so he thought.

Alex said he was told that the woman was young and had a big tummy. She said he had a nightmare about it for days. She also informed him, this was not from a really young kid, but a ten-year-old.

He went to say that she asked if anybody was staying in the guest house and he replied, his brother was at times with his fiancé. She thanked him for his time and left, thinking it was a misunderstanding.

Alex went on to say he did not think any more of it until the authorities asked him if he had any idea who the pregnant woman was and if she possibly lived nearby.

He then admitted that a chill ran up his spine and what I had presented him only confirmed some of his suspicions.

He then pulled a bottle of VAT69 from the desk drawer with a couple of shot glasses. He said he thought that we both needed a drink.

Perhaps several.

I agreed. We stopped after six.

He then admitted that he had a kind of experience with a little girl at one of the concentration camps he had been to. She had told him where some graves were in the woods near the camp. When they discovered them, she had disappeared. They found the bodies, and one of them was hers. The guards had led them in the woods and shot them just before the camps were liberated.

Alex said that he never told anybody that story before and asked me not to tell anyone else.

So, he was not ready to rule anything out.

He suspected something was not right with Ilsa. He also admitted that there had never been so many people die at one time near the Wainright Estate. So, he knew this needed looking into.

I told him my plan was to keep surveillance on the place.

He agreed and offered to help. I knew he owned a firearm so we would both be packing heat.

From there we began to make plans for our next course of action. Since we had been drinking, we decided to start our surveillance tomorrow night. Nobody else would know and we would be hiding outside. We would give all of the hired help the night off and have Barbara stay in the room with her father and step-mother behind a locked door.

The next evening, darkness came quickly. Both of us were filled with apprehension and uncertainty of what we would find out. Barbara knew we were planning something when we had her stay in the room after dark. The only thing she asked for was a gun, since she knew there might be some danger. Alex gave her their dad's that he kept hidden in his nightstand.

The early summer night felt humid and clammy as

we stayed hidden in the wooded area towards the back of the property. Even armed, I knew we both felt nervous. As it became later our anticipation grew. I don't think either of us could recall a darker night except for maybe the ones we were out in during the war.

We waited patiently in the darkness.

Just after midnight our patience was rewarded. Ilsa Draugr emerged from the guest house. Just like the neighbor's grandson said, she appeared to glide across the grass. It was unnatural how she moved.

It was truly unsettling.

Slowly and methodically, she made her way towards the house. Every now and then she would look around to make sure she was not being watched. It was then that I saw her red, animalistic eyes.

Even being hidden as we were, those eyes sent chills through me that I will never forget.

Seeing nobody else around, she quietly entered the house.

We waited a few moments before giving pursuit. As quietly as possible, we followed her inside. We searched the main floor but found no signs of her. We knew then that she must have headed upstairs.

Just as we were starting to head up, we were surprised by Edmund Wainright. Somehow he followed us into the house. When he tried to prevent us from stopping her, Alex knocked him unconscious with his flashlight.

I was glad it was him and not me.

That was when we heard Barbara scream and some shots go off. We ran up the stairs. Once we reached the top, Barbara's scream stopped. When we arrived at the room, Ilsa was going after Barbara. Alex opened fire with his .38 emptying the handgun with little or no effect.

She turned around and looked at him with an evil smirk.

Before he could do anything else, she flung him against the wall as if he were a rag doll, dazing him.

She then glared at me with those horrific red eyes and evil grin. My heart sank as I began to fire my handgun with the same lack of effect as Alex's firearm. She had to have had a dozen shots in her, but there was no blood or anything.

Just as she grabbed a hold of me, Barbara hit her with a lamp she had grabbed. Ilsa then stopped her assault on me and backhanded Barbara, sending her across the room.

This distraction gave me the opportunity to grab the silver dagger from my belt, and as Ilsa turned her attention back towards me, I thrust the blade into the center of her chest. She let out a bloodcurdling, painful wail that seemed to reverberate through the house.

I watched as she staggered backwards, mortally wounded. Alex regained his senses and soon joined me.

As she staggered towards the stairs, Ilsa appeared to be rapidly aging. She was becoming more decrepit and haggard-looking. Even with her back to us, we could tell she was becoming more emaciated and skeletal.

Once she staggered down the stairs, she turned to face us. I could compare her to one of the corpses I saw from one of the concentration camps.

By the time she reached the backyard and after a few more steps, she collapsed on the ground in a heap.

We watched what had been Ilsa Draugr rapidly decay before our very eyes. After five minutes, all that remained was some dust and very old and tattered cloth.

A warm breeze came off the lake to help scatter the dust all over the yard.

Alex shook his head as I patted his shoulder. We had

won another battle together, this time as civilians.

After that, we checked on everybody in the house. Edmund was groggy and semi-conscious. He would have a bad headache for a day or two. Leonard and Shirley Wainright, along with Edmund, would be treated for a couple of months at a special clinic in Switzerland for unusual blood disorders or ailments. All would have a full recovery, though Edmund Wainright would not remember a thing about the whole affair or even Ilsa Draugr. I suppose that is a good thing considering the circumstances.

At least he would avoid the nightmares.

Because of her illness, Shirley Wainright suffered a miscarriage. Whether it was mine or not, we'll never know. It was best for both of us that it worked out that way.

Barbara Wainright admitted to me later that she too had been pregnant, but decided to have a medical procedure in Europe to end that. She said she was not ready to be a mother or wife. At least not yet, and definitely not with me.

I agreed. She had her standing and family to think of. We still remained friends after that, occasionally continuing the affair for a few years.

As for me, I received a pretty handsome payday for both the job that I did and to remain silent about the whole affair.

This case was not the last one that I worked on for the Wainright family. Eventually I did background checks on Edmund's new fiancé a year later, and even Barbara's eventual husband, who turned out to be a real nice guy.

When friends and family asked them whatever happened to Ilsa Draugr, their answer was she broke off the engagement and went back home and they haven't heard from her since.

But that was what happened in the Edmund Wainright case.

For me, the strangest case I ever had.

Into the Woods

The Michigan Firearms Deer Hunting Season was over a week old. Only the hunting die-hards were still trudging through the Northern Michigan woodlands in pursuit of that much sought after trophy buck.

By this point and for the most part, the less serious hunters were more interested in beer hunting and chasing the two-legged white-tailed does as opposed to their four-legged wild counterparts.

In the crisp autumn morning, an eerie hush fell upon many areas of the countryside. Only an occasional distant gunshot broke that silence.

Ron Bateman, Melvin "Pops" Simmons, Joe Wheaton and Norm Lyford had hunted the same area for years. It had been a pretty good area for them throughout the years, since they had managed to pull out a fair number of deer in that time.

But, like all good areas one discovers, others soon discover it too and it gets a little crowded and somewhat overpopulated with hunters.

They were now eyeing an adjacent area nearby. This new area was basically a couple of rye fields surrounded by wooded, forested hills and ridges with a stream to its immediate east.

After breakfast, they sat around discussing their plans for the rest of the day.

"I was thinking about scouting the area on the other side of the stream," Ron announced. "The area that kind of spooked Jon and Tom when they were scouting around the day before the season started."

"They didn't care for that area," Joe commented. "Something about it really bothered them. They wouldn't say exactly what it was, but they didn't like the area and made it quite clear they didn't."

"Didn't Jon say that he saw an old guy dressed in a brown hat and coat with a shotgun?" Norm asked. "He said the guy didn't seem right. Like he was out of time or something. He said he didn't look right and he didn't answer when he called out to him. He said he looked kind of gray and haggard."

"Aw bullshit," Pops muttered. "It was probably just some farmer or property owner patrolling what he thought was his area."

"I don't know," Joe replied. "Tom thought he saw a building or a structure in there too. He said he was walking and it was just there. He said he hadn't noticed it before all the other times that he had been through there. He said something about it did not seem right and he headed in the other direction."

"Those two are always imagining shit," Pops commented. "They both have an overactive imagination. Some years ago they thought they saw a glowing ball of light in a different area a couple of miles away."

"I don't know, Pops," Norm countered. "You don't go out near as much as they do or as far, so I have to cut them some slack."

"Shit, I might just go there anyway," Ron muttered. "It's near a great deer area so it has to be good. Besides if I see the old dude wearing brown, I'll turn his ass in. You're supposed to be wearing at least half blaze orange out there. The dumb bastard is lucky he hasn't been shot, for Chrissake."

"Yeah, it's against the law," Pops chimed in.

"Didn't Jon say the guy looked like a Jed Clampett only without the hound dog and the bubbling crude?"

Joe asked.

The others laughed.

"Yeah, he did," Norm laughed. "It's a shame they left yesterday, they could have showed us the area and where they went."

"So, who's doing what?" Pops asked.

"I'm going out in a few minutes," Ron answered.

"How about you?" Pops asked Norm. "Where are you going?"

"I'll go walk around for a bit," Norm replied. "Maybe I'll flush something out. After that I'm coming back here and drinking beer and watching fuck films."

"How about you, Pops?" Ron asked.

"Oh, I don't know." Pops admitted. "Probably sit around drinking beer and telling lies. I've been out enough. It's getting too cold for my arthritis. Besides, Bob, Don and Gary planned on stopping by today and somebody needs to be here when they arrive."

"Did they get anything?" Ron asked.

Pops gave Ron a look. "Those three, are you shitting?" he asked, sarcastically. "Shit, the closest those sonsofbitches get to hunting is when they step out of the cabin to go to the local bar and any two-legged does in there."

The others roared with laughter.

Ron lifted his one butt cheek and cracked off a very loud and smelly fart.

"Jesus Christ" Norm snapped. "Did you have to do that? Now, I'm ready to puke."

Ron just laughed.

"You fucker!" Joe muttered, after really smelling how bad it was. "You better scrape after that."

"No wonder you never see any deer," Pops commented. "They can smell your ass ten miles away. The army should use you as a poison gas weapon."

"I'm heading out," Ron announced.

"Yeah, thanks for leaving us with that," Joe said.

"You're welcome," Ron laughed.

"We'll be out in a few," Norm said, grabbing a Penthouse magazine as he started to head to the bathroom. "I've gotta take a shit first."

"Let us know how everything comes out," Ron said. "See you out there."

By the time Norm got out of the bathroom, Ron had a fifteen minute head start on them.

"Well, are you ready," he asked Joe.

"Yeah, as soon as I can go in there," Joe replied. "We didn't know whether you fell in or decided to take up residence there."

"Well, when you gotta go, you gotta go," Norm explained.

"Did you at least open a window or spray some Glade?" Pops asked.

"Nope," Norm replied. "I thought I'd leave you my calling card."

"Calling card my ass!" Pops exclaimed, as both men laughed. "Open the goddamn window!"

Out in the woods, Ron climbed out of his truck. He always liked the second week of hunting best. The crowds were a lot smaller and there were a lot fewer hunters out in the woods. This was the time for the true hunting die-hards.

He zipped up his coat, put on his hat, and pulled out his gun case. He then pulled his 30.30 out of the case and began to load it. Once he did that, he put the case in the back seat and closed the trucks doors. He was not going to lock it, because there was nobody else out there and he expected Norm and Joe to be out there soon.

He slowly and methodically made his way towards the area that the others said bothered Jon and Tom. As he made his way through the nearby rye field, he felt like he was being watched. This was not unusual for him, he always felt like that. Ron figured the deer were always nearby watching for him when he began to trek through the woods.

Unlike the first week of hunting, it was terribly quiet. There were no gunshots whatsoever, not even distant ones. There was no breeze rustling through the trees or anything.

Just dead silence.

As he made his way into the area that had bothered Jon and Tom, he suddenly was gripped by a strange fear and paranoia. It made him shudder a bit. After standing there scanning the area for a moment, he brushed it off as just being the power of suggestion.

There was nothing to fear out here. Not when he had a fully loaded 30.30, extra ammunition, and a big hunting knife.

Ron looked around anticipating seeing something or someone nearby, but didn't see anything at all.

Finally after he just shook his head and muttered "Stupid." In frustration at himself for working himself into being fearful. He knew better than that. There was nothing out here, other than him and some very well-hidden deer.

Ron continued for a while. The only signs of deer that he saw were tracks and droppings. He did manage to scare up a couple of partridges that broke the silence of the entire area. He decided to continue walking for a while in the hope that he would scare something up. After a while he stopped and decided to rest. Finally, he sat on a large fallen tree trunk contemplating what to do next.

He decided to press on. He took a leak and then approached a brook that branched off from a larger creek. He had to check it out since all animals tended to go to water at one time or another. Ron knelt down to take a look for deer tracks, finding a fair number of fresh ones. he looked to see if they headed in any particular direction.

He followed a few that headed back to where he came from, while others headed in the other direction. It was a tough choice.

"Which ones do I follow?" he asked himself. *"Decision, decisions."*

As he scanned the area for the best possible way to go, he caught the sight of somebody a short distance away. It looked like it was an older gentleman in a brown jacket and hat carrying a shotgun.

"Hey!" Ron yelled. "Hey, buddy! Over here! Hey man! You need to be wearing blaze orange! Hey asshole! Are you listening?!

The old man just kept walking, as if ignoring or not able to hear Ron calling to him. He watched as the old man headed into the thicker brush. Ron decided to follow the man somewhat concerned about his condition.

After following as best he could for a few hundred yards, he lost sight of him. There was no sign of him or anybody else. He decided to continue onward for a bit. Finally he stopped again, about fifty yards in front of him, surrounded by thick overgrown trees and brush was an old decrepit and dilapidated cabin.

"What in the hell?" Ron muttered in disbelief.

He eyed the place warily before moving towards the cabin. The closer he became, the older it looked. The door was half rotted away from age, the windows were no longer in it and there were a few visible holes in the roof.

As he moved closer, a chill ran up his spine and felt

goose bumps on his arms in spite of wearing an outdoor hunting coat. Run pushed the door open with the barrel of his rifle to see inside.

In spite of no windows and holes in the roof, the inside was dimly lit.

He suddenly had the idea of using the old cabin as an oversized deer blind.

With some hesitation he pressed on, entering the cabin. Upon entering the cabin, the door suddenly closed behind him. He then came face to face with what had been the old man that he had seen earlier. The old man had no eyes and looked like a corpse. Ron's screams of terror and anguish were muffled by the trees and the landscape.

Only a few nearby deer took brief notice of a distance muffled scream from some human that had been nearby earlier.

After parking next to Ron's vehicle, Joe and Norm began to scout the area, with them ending up near the stream where he had last been.

"He's been here," Norm announced. "There's his tracks. He must be following them."

After they passed by where Ron saw the cabin they looked around cautiously.

"I can see why Tom and Jon said they didn't like this area," Joe said. "I don't care for it either. I get a bad vibe from here."

"It is a bit spooky," Norm admitted as they passed by where the cabin had been. "Let's get out of here."

In vain, Ron screamed from inside the cabin for his friends, but they did not see or hear him. As they walked away, he broke down sobbing, knowing that he was doomed to spend eternity there.

"You hear something?" Joe asked.

Norm listened intently. "No," he replied.

"Enough of this shit," Joe said. "Let's get some beer. Ron can catch up. He's a big boy and can join us later."

"Sounds like a plan," Norm agreed as they both headed back to their vehicle, oblivious to what had happened to their friend.

After Ron did not return, the authorities made an extensive search and other than his abandoned vehicle never found a thing. His disappearance was a complete and utter mystery. They figured he became lost and was a victim to the elements, animals, or even foul play. It was left an open case that was never solved.

***

"Hey look at that guy," local hunter Steve Blake exclaimed. "He ain't wearing any orange."

"Yeah, he isn't," agreed his friend Peter Barnes. "Isn't this that area where that guy disappeared last year? You know the guy who went into the woods and never came back."

"Yeah," Steve agreed. "Why do you ask?"

"Because he looks like him, only different somehow," Peter said.

"What was that guy's name?" Steve asked aloud.

"I think it was Bateman," Peter replied. "Bateman. Ron Bateman I believe."

"Think we should report it?" Steve asked.

"No," Peter said, suddenly pale. "He's gone. I don't know where he went. It's like he just disappeared."

"Let's get out of here," Steve suggested. "I've heard a lot of people don't like this area."

"I can see why," Peter said. "Let's go."

The Walking Doll

Dorothy Frederickson's Purchase

It may not have been love at first sight for Dorothy Frederickson, but it was damn close. It was definitely more like a strong want or desire. It had been a while since an inanimate object had grabbed her in such a way, but it had nonetheless.

As she eyed the plastic female cherub in the brightly-colored package of cardboard and cellophane, she just knew that she had to have it for herself.

At just over three feet tall, Walking Wanda, the Walking Doll, would be a wonderful addition and playmate for those who wanted her, and she was to be enjoyed by the young and the young at heart.

Dorothy thought it was fortuitous for her that she stopped by the CVS to pick up her heart medicine, or she would have otherwise never have found her. So she plunked down another twenty dollars for the doll and headed home.

"Welcome to your new home," Dorothy said as she carried the doll, a few groceries and her prescription into her small White Lake Tudor-style cottage.

After putting her prescription and her few groceries away, Dorothy began to study Walking Wanda's box. She then began to carefully open the box so as to not damage the doll or the box itself.

Finally, she pulled Walking Wanda out and beheld her. After a few moments, Dorothy placed the doll on the floor in a standing position. For a fraction of a second Dorothy thought doll's facial expression changed, but chocked it up to the loneliness of being an old widow with no pets.

Dorothy looked at the back of the box, where the instructions told her how to get Wanda to actually walk.

"Just raise the arm up, then back down and she'll walk," Dorothy read the instructions out loud. "Okay then."

Dorothy raised the arm then lowered it, and watched as Walking Wanda began to trek across the floor—a whole five feet.

"Oh, very good Wanda," Dorothy laughed. "You'll be excellent company I see. Well, try and be a good girl while I make dinner for us."

Once she finished making dinner, Dorothy sat down in her chair with her food. She noticed that Walking Wanda was not in the place she had left her in. Dorothy just shook her head and thought. "*You're going to be like a child who has learned to walk and just won't stop.*"

After the usual evening fare of the news, *Wheel of Fortune*, *Jeopardy* and flipping through the stations until she found something reasonably entertaining, she fell asleep like she always did, waking up an hour later.

When she woke up, she was surprised to find Wanda next to her. "Now you quit that Wanda," Dorothy snapped. "It's time for bed."

Dorothy headed off, exhausted from running her errands during the day. Even though she did not talk back, she at least had Wanda as company and that was better than nothing.

As Dorothy slept, she dreamt that she heard a soft little girl-like voice calling her name.

"Dorothy," the voice cooed softly. "Dorothy."

While the voice sounded soothing and pleasant, the dream was not. She tossed and turned, moaning and groaning from the unpleasantness of her dreams and bad sleep.

By the time the beams of the morning sunlight stretched across Dorothy's aged face, she had been awake, just lying there debating on getting out of bed. As she turned to get out, she was greeted by the permanently happy expression of Walking Wanda's face as the doll was standing next to the bed.

"Oh," Dorothy said recoiling in shock, thinking it was a person at first.

Being startled by the doll's close-up presence, Dorothy lashed out defensively, striking the doll and knocking her down. Dorothy stared at the doll a few moments, before realizing it was Walking Wanda. Finally she climbed out of bed.

Once out of bed she picked up Walking Wanda. "Sorry, but you really startled me, Wanda," she said, carrying the doll out to the living room.

Dorothy went about making her usual breakfast of tea and toast while she watched the *Today Show.*

"Well, I need to straighten up a piece, Wanda," Dorothy announced. "It's been over a week since I checked upstairs."

Dorothy then slowly headed upstairs. "*Damn,*" she thought. "*It's getting harder to do these stairs.*"

The first few steps were not too bad for her, but the middle section of stairs was incredibly difficult and almost torturous for her. After finally reaching the top, she stopped to catch her breath. After a couple of minutes she was able to finally move to the other rooms. Fortunately for her, the rooms were still pretty neat from the last time she had cleaned, and only had to do some minor dusting and straightening.

While she did not want to admit it, she was going to have to hire a cleaning lady for the upstairs. If not once a week, then maybe once a month.

After a few minutes of minor housekeeping and making sure everything was alright, she slowly made her way down the stairs. When she reached the bottom of the stairs, Dorothy was once again out of breath and tired. She knew that she had to sit down.

Dorothy headed into the living room and collapsed into her chair, where she quickly fell asleep.

A couple of hours later, she woke up to find Walking Wanda standing next to her. While somewhat shocked and surprised she found it somewhat comforting in an odd way.

Dorothy took her heart medicine and ate lunch. She did not know what was worse about getting old, the loneliness of losing people you loved and enjoyed or the physical infirmities and not being able to do what you once could do. Both were bad and at different times one seemed worse than the other. She found neither enjoyable.

With the exception of a couple of different TV shows, Dorothy's routine was pretty much unchanged.

Even though she did not talk, at least she had Walking Wanda to keep her company.

When Dorothy went to bed for the night, she placed Wanda in a chair across from the bed.

Once again, after sleep had overtaken her, Dorothy dreamt that someone was calling her name. Just as before the voice sounded like a soft, little girl voice.

"Dorothy," the voiced cooed. "Dorothy. Dorothy."

While soft and friendly, something about it was disturbing to her.

Disturbing and frightening.

Once again, her sleep, while deep and hard, was not a restful one.

Sometime during the night she heard a loud thump. Somehow, Dorothy was able to work it into her dreams and ignored it.

Once again, she heard her name being called in the soft, little girl voice. This time it sounded much closer.

"Dorothy," the voice softly cooed. "Dorothy."

Finally after hearing her voice called, she began to awaken. Groggy and half-asleep, Dorothy began to open her eyes. As she opened them and began to focus, much to her shock and horror stood Walking Wanda right next to the side of her bed. The doll's face was less than two feet from her own.

It was then that the doll's smile grew, and her right eye winked at Dorothy.

Dorothy's shock and horror were overwhelming. Try as she did to scream, she could only muster a panicked gulp as a sudden growing pain filled her chest.

Dorothy tried to climb out of bed and reach her heart medicine. But as she struggled with the blankets, her infirmities and rapidly-increasing chest pains, it became more and more in vain. Eventually, the pain became so intense that Dorothy passed out from the pain.

Overwhelmed by fear and terror, Dorothy Frederickson's heart stopped beating.

Before her body was even cold, Walking Wanda, with her permanent smile on her face, placed her tiny plastic hand in Dorothy's.

Walking Wanda had finally found a home.

Davey Brundage's Delivery

Davey Brundage never really cared for Dorothy Brundage's house. To him it was always kind of dark and creepy. There was nothing specific in general that bothered him, he just wasn't fond of it.

Dorothy Frederickson, on the other hand, was one

sweet nice old lady that, as far as he could remember, had always been kind and friendly.

He liked her, and that was why he was taking some food over like his mother had requested. He quickly walked up to the front door.

He peered through some of the individual glass panes that were in the door. He could see the house was dimly lit inside and not much more. Davey knocked on the door.

There was no answer.

He repeatedly knocked on it again and again.

Still, no answer.

Davey decided to look in the front window from the porch to see if anybody was home. Because of how dimly lit the house was, he still could not see anything.

As he headed back to the door, some movement of the inside door curtains caught his attention. Davey looked down and was startled to see a three-foot-tall doll peering back at him.

"Holy shit!" Davey exclaimed as he staggered backwards in shock.

Instinctively, he ran back to his home.

"Mom, I think there's something wrong at Mrs. Frederickson's house!" he yelled, running into the house.

Before his mother could say anything, she suddenly realized that she hadn't seen or heard from her in a week. Marie Brundage then called 911.

Lester and Barry's Ill-Fated Burglary

"The old lady's been dead for a week," Lester Quarrells said in a hushed tone to his friend Barry Parker, as they approached Dorothy Frederickson's house in the middle of the night. "That old battleaxe had some pricey antiques and jewelry in there the last time I worked on her house. Real high quality, expensive shit. I'm telling you."

"Okay," Barry muttered. "We split it fifty/fifty. Right?"

"Correctomundo," Lester agreed. "Just follow me. I know the layout."

"Will do," Barry agreed.

Slowly they headed to the backyard. They were careful to not be seen or heard in the night. As they reached the backdoor, Lester produced a small crowbar. As quietly and stealthily as possible, he pried open the door.

They made their way through kitchen.

"Silverware?" Barry asked, softly.

"Yeah, on our way out," Lester said. "Let's look for money and jewelry first. Don't make this any harder than it needs to be."

"Right," Barry agreed.

As the men entered the living room, they came across Walking Wanda.

"Hahaha, look at that," Barry said, pointing out the doll to Lester. "Who'd have thought an old lady would have that?"

"Shut up and keep looking," Lester replied, as he started looking around.

Lester headed for what had been Dorothy's bedroom. He quietly entered and began to look around in the darkness with his flashlight, while Barry began to look around in the living room.

As Barry searched around, he caught some movement out of the corner of his eye. He noticed the doll was in a different place than when they first saw it. He shook his head and went back to what he was doing. One again, as he was searching the premises, he caught movement out of the corner of his eye. Barry turned and then he saw it. The doll was actually *walking* towards him.

He gasped in horror and staggered backwards.

"Holy shit!" he yelled. "This place is haunted! I'm outta here!"

Barry then took off for the back door, quickly exited the residence, and ran the rest of the way home

"What the hell?" Lester asked as he emerged from the bedroom to see Barry leave in a panic. "Shit."

Lester looked around to see the doll over near a telephone that was off of its charger. He figured that he'd better hurry and find some valuables before somebody noticed he was in there.

"Shit," he muttered in disgust and frustration at being unable to find anything.

As Lester looked out the front window from inside the house, he noticed a police car drive down the street and thought it was better to leave and possibly come back later. He then hurried out the back door and started to make his way to the driveway, only to be confronted by the White Lake Police with their guns drawn on him.

"Freeze!" they said, and he put his hands in the air and was arrested.

One patrol car with two officers waited for the locksmith to come and fix the back door.

"Does anybody live there?" an officer in another police car asked his partner.

"No, I don't think so, why?" the other officer responded.

"Well, the strange thing is, dispatch said the call came from someone inside the house," the first officer continued.

Kathy Taylor's Estate Sale

It had been over a month since Dorothy Frederickson's funeral, and almost all of the legal papers and procedures had been completed. As her niece and closest living relative, the burden of handling the estate had fallen on Kathy Taylor.

Fortunately for her and her family, they lived relatively close in Ortonville to make the trip there less arduous and costly, than had they lived out of state or even up north. After a three-day weekend of going through her aunt's belongings, she had managed to get all of valuables, including silverware and china, her personal and legal papers, and other small items of both sentiment and value.

Now all that remained was the furniture.

The furniture and that doll.

Walking Wanda.

Her daughter, Caitlyn, found it to be a new friend and companion to help her deal with the boredom of having to be there while her mother tried to get things ready for an estate sale.

Kathy did not care for Walking Wanda. She found the doll somewhat disturbing, especially after she witnessed it follow her daughter from one room to another.

Caitlyn was in tears over not being allowed to bring home the doll right away.

Now as Kathy was doing inventory on the furniture and other items, Caitlyn was playing with Walking Wanda. Deep down, she wished her husband John was there and with their son Jimmy who was at his baseball practice.

At one point, she thought she heard not only

Caitlyn's voice but another one. When she went to check, Caitlyn explained it was her pretending with her friend Wanda. Kathy decided to let it go.

"*Let's see,*" Kathy thought. "*We have the silverware, the china, the jewelry, the valuables and all of the papers. Check, check, check, check and check. We donated Aunt Dorothy's clothes to Sunset Living Home. Check. The appliances, furniture, the estate sale. Check.*"

After a while, Kathy noticed that it had grown quiet in the living room where Caitlyn had been. She decided to go in and check on her. She found Caitlyn on the couch and Wanda standing nearby as if on guard duty.

Suddenly a chill ran up her spine.

Kathy knew she had a bit of a problem on her hands. She knew that Caitlyn loved the doll while the rest of them thought it was a bit creepy.

Kathy went back to doing the inventory. After checking off what was on her list, she turned around to see Walking Wanda standing in the doorway.

"Jesus!" Kathy exclaimed loudly, startled by the doll's sudden appearance.

Kathy screamed as the doll began walking towards her. Her blood ran cold from sheer terror at the sight of it. Wanda stopped a few feet short of reaching her.

"Wanda wants to play with you," Caitlyn giggled, having woke up from her nap. "Don't be scared."

Kathy was both speechless and in shock.

"Come on Wanda, let's go play," Caitlyn said as she turned the doll around, and it followed her back into the living room.

Kathy just watched in horror as the doll followed her. She knew there was something wrong with Walking Wanda. *No doll should act that way*, she thought.

Kathy quickly finished her inventory and decided to leave. She got Caitlyn ready to go home.

"What about Wanda?" Cailtyn asked, almost pleading.

"Maybe tomorrow," she replied, knowing full well it was a lie.

"But what if someone wants to buy her at the mistake sale tomorrow," Caitlyn asked butchering the word *estate*.

"I'll put her away tomorrow so nobody can buy her," Kathy replied.

"Goodie," Caitlyn exclaimed.

Both left for the day.

When Kathy returned the next morning, she put Walking Wanda back in the box her aunt had carefully saved, and placed her in the attic.

Fortunately for her, they were able to sell all of the furniture, appliances and belongings left in the house. While Caitlyn was initially upset by her mom 'forgetting' about Walking Wanda, she eventually moved on to other things.

About two months later the house was sold.

The New Home and Doll Owner

Gwen Jackson had finally found her dream home. As an artist, the place was perfectly laid out to her liking. As her family helped her move the furniture into place, she decided to put some of the items she hardly used in the attic.

She pulled down the stairs from the ceiling and climbed up with her milk crate in hand. She then turned on the light and nearly fell when she jumped back, surprised by a three-foot tall doll in a box.

"Goddamn!" she exclaimed, and then laughed at herself for being afraid, and then placed her milk crate across from the doll.

"Walking Wanda," she said while reading the box. "How nice…and still in its original box."

Gwen grabbed the doll's box and brought it down out of the attic.

"Hey everybody, look what I found up in the attic," Gwen announced. "It's a doll called Walking Wanda."

About the Author

Tom Sawyer is a Michigan writer. Since starting out as a 17 year-old, with a weekly newspaper, he has authored the novels *The Lighthouse, Fire Sale, The Sisigwad Papers, the Last Big Hit*, the *Dracula* sequel *Shadows in the Dark* and the acclaimed collection *Dark Harbors*. He has also written a number of short stories that have been featured in various publications. A lifelong Waterford resident, he and his wife Colleen have three children.

Look for us wherever books are sold.

If you thought *this book* was cool, check out these other titles from the #1 source for the best in independent horror fiction, **BLACK BED SHEET**

The first official publisher's anthology showcasing the exemplary talents of the authors of Black Bed Sheet Books

READ US OR DIE!

Our first ANTHOLOGY!

edited by Jason Gehlert

978-0-9886590-6-3

www.downwarden.com/blackbedsheetstore

He's been waiting for this. So have you. Wherever books are sold.

The only authorized biography directly from the master himself

Buy it today!

foreward by Peter Cushing

The Price of Fear

by Joel Eisner with Vincent Price

www.downwarden.com/blackbedsheetstore

ISBN: 978-0-9886590-2-5

www.downwarden.com/blackbedsheet

www.downwarden.com/blackbedsheet

www.downwarden.com/blackbedsheet

Extreme Science Fiction
Read the sensational debut novel!
GENESIS
Book One of the Kingdom Come Series
WADE GARRET
BLACK BED SHEET
www.downwarden.com/blackbedsheetstore
GENESIS
WADE GARRET

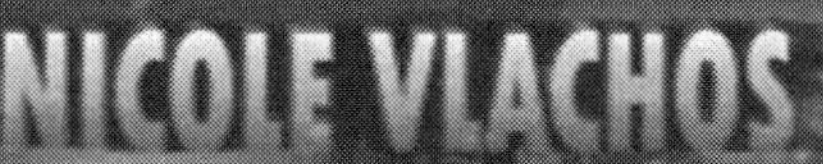
NICOLE VLACHOS

Bone Sai

__Wherewolf by Franchisca Weatherman. 978-0-9833773-7-5__

When a pack of werewolves hits a small southern town, the local Sheriff realizes this is one case he can not solve alone. He calls in the F.B.I. to help him take down the killers that are taking the lives of the local teens. When the wolves abandon the town for the streets of New Orleans during Mardi-Gras celebrations, the hunters become the hunted in an all-out war where no one may survive....

www.downwarden.com/blackbedsheet

Morningstars by Nick Kisella

While at his dying wife's bedside, Detective Louis Darque is offered a chance to save her by his biological father, the demon B'lial, but at what price?

Whispers in the Cries

by Matthew Ewald

978-0-9833773-6-8

Hunted by the shadowed entity of his grandfather's past and its brethren of demonic beasts, Randy Conroy must survive the nightmare his grandfather could not. A thrilling ghost tale of the Queen Mary and haunted souls.

Meat City & Other Stories by Jason M. Tucker 978-0-9842136-9-6

Take a trip along the arterial highway, and make a left at the last exit to enter Meat City, where all manner of nasty things are clamoring to greet you. Granger knows what it's like to kill a man. When the corpse of Granger's latest victim staggers to his feet though, all bets are off. These and other slices of horror await you on the raw and bloodied streets. Enjoy your visit . . . .

Nevermore by Nik Kerry

. When Raven's world comes crashing down around her and her thoughts turn to suicide, this is exactly what she does. As she swings the last swing of her life, she jumps off, sprouts wings, and flies away to another world where she finds a group of teenagers just her age who accept her into their lives.

What would you do if you woke up in hell
and couldn't remember a thing?
An unforgettable science fiction journey
Stygian Rift
Jayra Almanzor
Winner, the 2013 English Academic Award, St. Justin Martyr, C.S.
www.downwarden.com/blackbedsheetstore
Short tales of terror from the authors of
CHOPHOUSE and Halloween IV
When NIGHT DARKENS the STREETS
HORNS
*
John Grover
and special guest
Nicholas Grabowsky
illustrations by
Gary A. Gabbard
www.downwarden.com/blackbedsheetstore

STATION HOUSE
"Reading Horns makes me want to grab a camera and shoot the creepiest film ever made!"
HORNS
author of Chophouse
Horns
"Chophouse makes me SCREAM!"
—Linnea Quigely, Return of the Living Dead
CHOPHOUSE
A NOVEL BY
HORNS

www.downwarden.com/blackbedsheet

www.downwarden.com/blackbedsheet

www.downwarden.com/blackbedsheet

HALLOWEEN IV

The Ultimate Edition

WITH ADDITIONAL MATERIAL INCLUDING THE
NEVER-BEFORE-PUBLISHED ORIGINAL EPILOGUE

Nicholas Grabowsky

Sponsored by Black Bed Sheet

Watch BLACK HAMSTER TV on Veetle.com

Listen to Francy & Friends radio show

www.downwarden.com/blackbedsheet

We employ and recommend:

Foreign Translations

Cinta García de la Rosa
(Spanish Translation)
Writer, Editor, Proofreader, Translator
cintagarciadelarosa@gmail.com
http://www.cintagarciadelarosa.com
http://cintascorner.com

Bianca Johnson
(Italian Translation)
Writer, Editor, Proofreader, Translator
http://facebook.com/bianca.cicciarelli

EDITOR STAFF

Felicia Aman
http://www.abttoday.com
http://facebook.com/felicia.aman

Kelly J. Koch
http://dressingyourbook.com

Tyson Mauermann
http://speculativebookreview.blogspot.com

Kareema S. Griest
http://facebook.com/kareema.griest

Mary Genevieve Fortier
https://www.facebook.com/MaryGenevieveFortierWriter
http://www.stayingscared.com/Nighty%20Nightmare.html

Shawna Platt
www.angelshadowauthor.webs.com/

Adrienne Dellwo
http://facebook.com/adriennedellwo
http://chronicfatique.about.com/

William Cook
http://lnkd.in/bnC-yMd
http://www.amazon.com/Blood-Related

and HORNS

Made in the USA
Columbia, SC
19 June 2024

37017632R00207